MELTDOWN

JAY FORDE

MELTDOWN
Jay Forde

Published by Peewit
Cover design by Peewit

ANTARCTICA

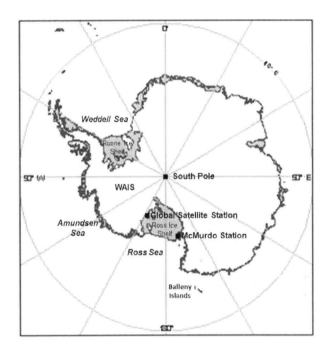

Saturday 1st September
Antarctica

Charlie Fallon, known as 'Chuck' to his close friends and working colleagues, was going about his routine duties on the Western Antarctic Ice Sheet (WAIS). As a senior scientific analyst, he had been on assignment down in this frozen hell-hole for approaching five months, enduring the permanent night of the Antarctic winter. Now, as summer approached, he was working alone in the frozen wilderness, collecting scientific data from the satellite research stations belonging to Global Energy plc., his British based employers.

Global Energy, one of the largest international oil companies in the world and founded back in the fifties when oil strikes were plentiful, had worked long and hard to obtain the licence to have the sole drilling rights for oil extraction in this harsh environment. Beating off all the competition, they had already invested vast sums of money to guarantee their future and keep their shareholders happy.

The WAIS accounts for only about ten percent of the Antarctic Ice Sheet and is an inhospitable place. Bounded by the Ross Ice Shelf to the north-east, and the Ronne Ice Shelf to the north-west, it is difficult to imagine a bleaker, yet more unspoilt and pristine wilderness. Glistening in the summer months a brilliant blinding white with all the ice particles suspended in the frozen air, it is plunged into darkness during the long winter months when temperatures rarely rise above -50°C.

Chuck was one of the few people who worked in this remote part of the planet. His primary base location was the McMurdo research station located on the southern tip of Ross Island, on the eastern fringes of the Ross Ice Shelf. Home to more than a thousand brave and hardy souls during the summer, employed in scientific research and the associated support activities, the numbers drop to a mere two hundred in the dark winter months.

Chuck routinely had to head out to Global Energy's much smaller remote station, some four hundred miles away across the Ross Ice Shelf. He would spend a few days at a time there to check on the installations. This remote station comprised a small research base housing the recording and monitoring equipment and an even smaller accommodation pod where up to three scientists could live in close confines for a few days at a time. Sitting on the WAIS itself, close to the boundary with the Ross Ice Shelf, it was kept well-stocked with tinned food and fuel for cooking and heating, but it was basic - a desolate place with no real home comforts.

Chuck had been dropped off by the McMurdo station helicopter two days earlier to complete a three-day cycle of data collection, maintenance and resetting of machines and equipment. He was alone in the remote station on this visit, his first since the period of perpetual winter darkness had begun to recede. In the steadily intensifying daylight the expanse of the icy wilderness surrounding him was daunting and he felt uncharacteristically lonely.

He had left the accommodation hut earlier that morning and had been out on the skidoo, performing his maintenance visits to the remote outlying recording units north and west of him on WAIS, using the snow bike to get around quickly and easily. Chuck was dressed in the latest hi-tech thermal gear with only his piercing blue eyes visible through his goggles. He should have been insulated from the freezing temperatures but, being out in those sub-zero conditions for the length of time he had that day, the extreme cold had managed to get through the clothing to his extremities. Inside his mittens, his fingers felt clumsy as he fumbled to open the external door of the main scientific measurement station on his return.

Once inside it was relatively warm by comparison, being maintained at a steady temperature to prevent the equipment from freezing. Chuck removed his outer layers of clothing while he made himself a warming drink of hot chocolate. He wrapped his hands around the hot mug and winced as the heat began to permeate through to his fingers. He experienced the tell-tale, painful throb of the blood flowing back to his cold digits as his circulation gradually returned.

After a while the pain in his hands subsided, and wiggling his fingers, he settled down to work at his workstation. Before him a bank of computers and instruments monitored all seismic activity, ice thickness and meteorological conditions, receiving the data from transmissions sent by the outlying recording units he'd checked earlier. There hadn't been anything significant to report from the data received in quite some time, the odd unexplained spike or two on the seismic read outs in recent days, but nothing to cause him any real concern.

Just before he had flown out to the remote station Chuck had stopped by to speak to his boss, Graham Platt, and had found Graham's office empty with the door open and papers strewn all over his desk. Deciding to leave him a message, Chuck grabbed a pen and notebook from his pocket and leant on a file on the corner of Graham's untidy desk to compose his note.

As he had bent over the desk to write, he couldn't help but notice the name printed on the file he was resting on: 'PROJECT UNDERMINE: CONFIDENTIAL'. Unable to resist taking a look, Chuck had flicked through the content, his heart beating quickly fearing Graham's return at any moment to catch him snooping through confidential reports. One page had really caught his attention: A timetable for deep core drilling activity on WAIS, something he was unaware was happening. "Strange," he mused, "I wonder what that's all about?"

Chuck had heard "canteen whispers" in recent weeks that the company had been doing some new, off-piste exploratory work a few hundred miles north-west of the remote station on WAIS. It really looked like these whispers had now been accidentally confirmed and that Global Energy *were* indeed carrying out some secret exploration. Memorising the schedule to the best of his ability and scrapping the note he had planned to leave, he had managed to put the file and everything it contained back exactly as it was before leaving to catch his flight.

Now, two days later, Chuck noticed that the readings were much more extreme than usual, and the seismograph was far more active than he would usually expect - even allowing for any secret drilling Global Energy were up to. Additional spikes were showing up and they were occurring with increased frequency and force. He needed to investigate these new readings in greater detail and report the outcome of his analysis to Graham.

Chuck saved the daily log file as usual and then also dropped an extra copy of the recorded history onto his laptop so that he could begin to analyse the data in his own leisure time that evening. There wasn't a lot to distract him in his moments of free time: He had exhausted the accommodation hut's supply of DVDs some time since. He liked to investigate any unexplained activity to try and work out a pattern of events and better understand this unstable environment. Having reset the equipment and graphs for the next twenty-four hours recording, he made a mental note to check the recorded data on an hourly basis that day in case of any further activity.

It was just then that he felt the first real rumble below his feet. The measurement station shuddered visibly, rattling the equipment on the shelves above the workstation. Being made of steel, like the containers used on ocean tankers, the recording station wasn't a structure that was easily moved yet it was rocking on its base. Chuck glanced at the newly reset seismograph, noticing that the needle was going wild as the intensity of the vibration increased.

"Jesus!" he said to himself, "that was no small shift." It felt serious. "I'd better call the base and try to get out of here."

He picked up the satellite phone and punched in the fast dial number for the main McMurdo base communications centre.

"Chuckster!" came the reply. "What's up my man, are you freezing your ass off out there at the recording station?"

"Hi Greg, yeah, it's as cold as ever and I'm always three parts frozen, but listen, I'm not happy - something's happening underground out here that's weird. Has anyone there seen or said anything?"

"Yep, someone over here has noticed some increased activity from the readings on our equipment over the last couple of days. They're saying that they're not aware of anything that might be causing it, so they kind of discounted it. The techies in the lab said they doubt it's anything to worry about, but they'd keep an eye on it from here just in case."

"They think there's nothing to worry about do they? Screw that!" Chuck retorted, blue eyes flashing. "I just experienced a real shaker a few moments ago which really rocked the station out here. 'Quake intensity and frequency is increasing Greg, and I think it's serious. I need to get off the sheet and report back to McMurdo base immediately. This needs more investigation and I can't do it here when the building is rocking and rolling around me."

"OK, OK, keep calm, we'll send out the chopper to get you. I hope you're not pulling a fast one here my friend; the boss will chew your balls off if you're using this as an excuse to get back into the warm! Stand by for more information on the transport." Greg put a call into the transportation office and told them that Chuck Fallon was in trouble out on the sheet and needed evacuating from the remote recording station as soon as possible.

Minutes later, the helicopter lifted off from the helipad at McMurdo, hovered for a few moments, then turned, dipped its nose and climbed steadily as it headed out across the Ross Ice Shelf to collect Chuck. Even with the heater turned fully up, it wasn't that much warmer on board than it was outside, but at least Bill Bond, the pilot, was saved from the bitter biting wind. Tall, slim and wiry with grey-flecked dark hair,

Bill was a seasoned pilot and knew his aircraft inside out. With a top speed of 200mph, he knew it would take him over two hours to reach Chuck, and even with the extra fuel tanks fitted to his Eurocopter145 he would have to conserve his aviation diesel if he was going to have enough to complete the return journey.

As Chuck waited for his transport back to McMurdo, he decided to start putting his thermal base layers back on ready to evacuate at a moment's notice. He kept himself busy by studying the data being reported on the various instruments before him. The deep tremor he had felt earlier had not abated as he would have hoped, but instead was developing into an almost continuous rumble emanating from deep underground.

"What the hell is going on here? What can it be?" he asked himself rhetorically.

Suddenly, the vibration intensified, causing him to fall off his chair. "Christ!" he exclaimed as things started falling from shelves all around him, and the whole research station started to tremble. "Where's that fucking chopper?" he shouted out loud, getting more concerned for his safety.

Fearing he was in the middle of an earthquake, Chuck decided he would be safer outside the research station. Grabbing his laptop, he stuffed it into the top of the survival rucksack that was lying on the floor against the wall near the door. He pulled on a balaclava, covering his fair hair and short boxed beard, zipped up his red Parka and pulled up the hood, then put on his thermal mittens. Picking up the SatPhone and the rucksack, he headed out into the bitter cold once more.

As soon as he was outside he punched the quick dial number for McMurdo again, wanting an update on what was happening.

"Chuck, the chopper is on its way to you," was the answering message from Greg. "We're watching what's going on down there and you were right to be concerned – we all are here too. Just hang on mate, Bill is a great pilot, and if anyone can get you back safely to base, he can."

"Just make sure he gets here as quickly as he can Greg, it's not good out here," said Chuck, ringing off. He paced around nervously as he waited for some sign of his rescuer coming over the shelf. He knew that they would be doing everything to get him back to McMurdo, but he had an increasing level of anxiety about the whole situation and wanted out of there as soon as possible before things got any worse.

---- 2 ----

Saturday 1st September
Antarctica

Flying over the Ross Ice Shelf, Bill Bond noticed some unusual dark markings in the surface of the ice shelf that hadn't been obvious two days ago when he'd delivered Chuck to WAIS. The more he looked, the more pronounced the shadows became. From the height he was flying, it looked as though the surface of the ice shelf was crazing like a piece of antique pottery. What the hell was going on down there?

Increasing his speed to the maximum he could safely fly at to conserve fuel, he hoped he would be able to rendezvous with Chuck in time. He needed somewhere safe and solid to land, and with the crazing of the surface, he was beginning to think that might not be easily achievable: A fragile surface is no use to a helicopter. If the worst came to the worst, he would need to hover above the ice, and hope that Chuck was fit enough to be able to get aboard under difficult conditions. This would not be an easy task even for someone from the special services forces, let alone a middle-aged scientist who had probably only done enough exercise recently to scrape a pass at his annual medical assessment.

Apart from the difficulty of getting Chuck aboard, just being able to hover the chopper for any length of time in the katabatic winds of the Antarctic was going to tax the most experienced pilot. Was he up to it? There was only one way to find out, and it wasn't going to be pleasant. Still, that's what he was paid to do, and do it he would. He hadn't let anyone down so far in his service career, and he wasn't about to start now.

Bill glanced at his watch, did some quick mental calculations, and concluded that it would be another fifteen or twenty minutes before he got to Chuck. Switching on the VHF radio, he tried calling him at the research station.

"McMurdo 1 to station B, can you read me Chuck?"

No answer. Maybe he was too far away for the relatively short range of the VHF radio signal, although at the height he was flying, he thought there was a good chance that the line of sight signal would reach the research station. He tried again a couple of minutes later, but still there was no reply. Where the hell was Chuck? Bill was certain that the signal would reach from this point, he had called from this distance several times before and been received. Maybe something was really wrong. "Hell, I hope he's OK," he thought, "I really like the guy."

Down on the ground, Chuck was scanning the skyline, desperate to see the any sign of the chopper coming to get him. The rumblings below the ice had continued unabated: The ground shook beneath his feet every few seconds with increasing ferocity. "Come on, come on Bill. What's taking you so long? I need to get off this ice, and soon."

Just then, with a thunderous crack, a split three feet wide appeared in the ice sheet between Chuck and the research station, stretching away towards the Ross Ice Shelf in the distance and knocking him off balance. Jarring his elbow on the ice, the SatPhone flew out of his hand and tumbled over the edge into the crevasse. "Damn, that's all communication lost," he lamented. He shuffled over to the crack to have a closer look, lay on his stomach and inched towards the edge. Peering cautiously over, not certain the ice would hold his weight, he noted the crevasse went straight down as far as he could see.

Not knowing what to do, he slid back a couple of yards from the edge to gather his thoughts, then he got up and stood motionless as the growling noise beneath his feet continued to grow and the crack started to widen before his eyes. Within minutes the split in the ice had opened to five feet and appeared to be getting wider by the second. He had to decide before it was too late to choose: Which side of the crack should he be on? Within moments, the gap would be too wide for him to jump, and if he failed to reach the other side, he would fall into the crevasse and would be a goner. The crack went far too deep for him to be able to survive the fall, and ice was notorious for closing again after a while. He would be deep frozen within minutes, and would remain there for a long, long time. It could be hundreds or even thousands of years before his body would be rejected by the ice and subsequently found by humans or eaten by fish.

He thought about skirting around the edge of the crack, but it ran on as far as the eye could see in both directions, and probably much further. There was no way he would be able to get to the end of the split before it would open another tranche, if it didn't go the length of the sheet already.

He made up his mind. He would have to leap the gap before it was too late. He took several paces backwards then gathered his thoughts. He would only have one try at this, so it had to be right. As he was getting ready to start his run up to make the leap from the part of the sheet that was falling away, he thought back to his lack of prowess at athletics at school. He had never been a great sportsman, maybe average at best, so how far could he possibly long jump now at his age?

Except for his emergency pack and the clothes he was wearing, all the survival gear he would need was inside the station, and if there was any chance he would have to spend the night outside, he would need every single piece of kit there was. He also knew that the chopper would be looking for the station, and not a lone person out on the ice. He *had* to get across the gap and get to the survival gear. He took a deep breath, thought to himself "here goes," and started to run towards the chasm.

He had only taken three paces when there was another deafening crack, exploding through the frosty air. The research station instantly sank into the ice, disappearing into the chasm. Panicking, Chuck dropped to the floor once more and slowly crawled his way forwards towards the edge for a second time. Peering over the lip of the crevasse again, he looked down into the depths: Somewhere down there was the research station. He thought he could see some grey shape wedged between the walls of ice, about a hundred feet down, but he wasn't sure. Thank God he hadn't made the jump, otherwise he would have been down there with the station, and probably dead due to the fall. He said a little prayer of thanks: Someone up there was watching over him, but he still had to get himself out of this hell hole.

With the station gone, he was truly alone on the ice sheet, part of which appeared to be receding, or at worst slipping into the Ross Sea. He realised that his only chance of survival now rested in the hands of Bill Bond and the chopper that was coming to collect him.

He looked around him, trying to keep calm and assess the weather. Dark clouds were gathering in the distance, and that meant trouble. Storms kicked up in the Antarctic within minutes, and any snow falls would make him invisible to the pilot. He wondered whether Bill would be able to find him anyway with the research station gone. The station would have been his normal navigation point from quite a distance, as it easily stood out against the stark white surroundings. Would Bill assume he had perished with it? Would he fly around and search the area or not? His red Parka would only be of use in clear conditions to help Bill spot him, so if the storm hit before the chopper arrived, he would simply disappear into the white-out. It would be no use overnight either, the temperatures dropped too low for him to survive. His own mortality flashed into his mind. He was only forty-two, no age to consider dying; he had too much living still to do.

The prospect of having to spend a night on the ice sheet with full exposure to the elements was looking more and more probable as the minutes ticked by. Hypothermia would set in very quickly, and the body's vital organs would simply shut down. He started to scrape at the snow and ice to dig himself an ice cave using the ice pick and shovel from his survival pack. Part of his survival training had taught him that he needed to get out of the wind in a small enclosed space to try to retain his body heat. People had been known to ride out storms in the Alps, and any form of shelter would be better than being totally exposed to the elements.

Looking down at the ice and trying to locate the research station, Bill Bond re-checked his GPS co-ordinates to confirm its location. Yes, he was on the right course, but there was no station in sight. "What the Hell?" he exclaimed. All he could see from his height of 300 feet above the frozen wilderness was a fragmented ice field; giant slabs of ice with dark fissures snaking between them. If he didn't know better, he'd have thought he was off course, flying over an ice-floe.

As he circled around the area where the research station should have been, he saw a giant crevasse had appeared in the ice. As he flew over the crack, he thought he could just make out something way down deep inside the chasm that might have been the station. "Shit!" he thought, "that's not possible."

Hovering above the site of the research station, he had just begun to radio his findings back to McMurdo when he noticed a movement of red out of the corner of his eye. Chuck had come up out of the ice-hole that he was digging and was on the ground waving frantically at him. He had obviously got out of the station and clear of it before it was swallowed up.

"Thank God for that," Bill said to himself. "He got out and made it OK!" He continued his call to McMurdo reporting the news and then moved the chopper across towards Chuck.

"Hallelujah, I might get out of here alive yet," Chuck thought, seeing the chopper approach.

Bill gingerly lowered the chopper towards the part of the ice sheet closest to Chuck, looking to touch down on the craft's skids. As he got lower, the ice just behind Chuck split, and another chasm opened: He was effectively on an ice island now. It was clearly too risky to attempt a landing on such a fragile surface, there was no way of telling how long the island would last before it also disappeared down like the research station. He would have to find an alternative way to get Chuck aboard, and fast.

Chuck had heard the ice split behind him, and as he turned to see another chasm open, his heart sank. He didn't think the island would sustain its own weight for long with nothing around it to support it. This could be it, so near to being rescued, and yet so far. He knew that there was no way the ice island would be able to support the weight of the helicopter. It was no use: He was as good as dead.

Bill Bond hovered twenty feet off the ground above and to one side of Chuck, assessing the situation and weighing up the alternatives. The downdraft from the rotors was making it impossible for Chuck to see anything clearly, so signalling his intentions wouldn't serve any purpose: Chuck wouldn't know what he was trying to do. There was a safety ladder aboard but to let it down he would have to release the controls. Not a good idea. There was only one real choice: He had to hover motionless just three or four feet above the ice shelf and allow Chuck to climb aboard, and then he would have to hang on while they moved away to more solid ground where the helicopter could touch down. Could Chuck manage that? He would have to.

Bill looked all around the helicopter and then focused on the sky. He didn't like the look of the clouds that were forming above, it looked as though a storm was about to close in. Whatever he decided to do, he would have to be quick. He came in closer on his approach, hoping that Chuck would understand what he was trying to do.

Chuck could see that Bill was bringing the chopper in low and slow to let him get aboard, but he worried that the rotors might dip and catch the surface of the ice sheet and decapitate him. Still, what other option was there? He had to go for it if he was ever going to get off this bloody ice. It might be time to seriously re-think his career if he got out of this scrape.

Shielding his face from the ice crystals that were being blasted at him in the downdraft, Chuck crawled his way towards the hovering helicopter. It was hard work making any progress, and twice he was forced flat on the ice by the downward pressure from the rotor blades, but eventually he made it to a point where the chopper was directly above him. He managed to get onto his knees and reached above him, but the helicopter's skids were just beyond his fingertips. Somehow, he needed to stand up. Forcing himself into a crouching position, he took a moment to steady himself. The chopper was still hovering right above him; Bill was doing a great job of holding his position even in the rapidly deteriorating weather. Chuck pushed himself upright and grabbed one of the skids. He miraculously managed to hook his arm over the top and linked his hands together. That was the easy part, now he had to climb aboard.

He tried to hook his leg over the skid, but failed once, then twice. On his third attempt he finally slung his leg over successfully and hooked the skid behind his knee. The moment he achieved this, Bill lifted higher a few feet, turned the chopper and headed across the chasm to where the research station had once stood.

Having thought that he would climb aboard before moving away, Chuck was hanging on for dear life, terrified that he might lose his grip. He gritted his teeth and forced himself to hang on as he crossed the open void of the crevasse, unable to stop himself from looking down into the depths as he passed. He knew that if he let go now, he was certainly going to die. The question was, how long was he expected to hang on for?

Reaching the other side of the chasm and an area of uncracked ice, Bill hovered once more a couple of feet in the air. Chuck dropped to the ground and rolled away while Bill touched the chopper down, minimising the weight on the ice by maintaining lift through the rotors. Waving frantically to Chuck to climb aboard he waited until the door had opened and Chuck climbed in. A second later, before Chuck had even closed the door behind him, Bill lifted the chopper off again, hovering a few feet above the ice while Chuck strapped himself into his seat, then they set off back to McMurdo.

"That was fucking close," said Bill. "You were really lucky not to end up at the bottom of that chasm inside the station. What the hell is happening?" he fired at his shaken passenger.

"I've absolutely no idea Bill. I honestly didn't think I would make it out of there. Thanks for coming to get me, and thanks for being such a damn good pilot. I owe you big time."

Peeling away from the WAIS, back across the Ross Ice Shelf on the way back to McMurdo, Chuck sat in silence, reflecting on his narrow escape. He hadn't really taken it all in and didn't want to talk about it; he preferred to retreat into his own world for a while. Bill recognised this, and focused on flying the helicopter back to base, leaving Chuck in peace. There would be plenty of time to chat later if he wanted to.

In his dazed state, Chuck looked down on the sheet that had very nearly claimed his life. He wasn't going to be in any hurry to get back on it soon. The surface around the lost research station was now covered with deep fissures running in myriad directions. Flying over the crazed surface, he thought, no, he was sure he could see reddish threads running at the bottom of one of the crevasses that had opened. Something looked like it was glowing hot, deep down in the ice. He shook his head in disbelief. No, it couldn't be. He was probably imagining it, he must be in shock.

Without really thinking about what he was doing, Chuck took his mobile phone out from his jacket pocket. Leaning over towards the helicopter door he shook the phone twice to activate the camera. He put the lens against the plexiglass and took several photos. He would have a look at them later when he had recovered from his ordeal. Slipping the phone back into his pocket he withdrew back into his protective mental state while Bill Bond raced back to McMurdo ahead of the gathering storm.

---- 3 ----

Sunday 2nd September
London

In the boardroom at Global Energy, the company directors had convened at very short notice to address the crisis. It was a Sunday morning and they would have approximately twelve hours in which to come up with a credible story before they imagined the news would break and the shit really hit the fan.

Ray Bergman, the CEO of Global Energy, had received an urgent message late the evening before from the Antarctic Exploration Station at McMurdo. The message had said that there had been a massive fracture in the WAIS and neighbouring Ross Ice Shelf, and that the Global Energy remote scientific research station had disappeared into an ice crevasse. The main problem was that the fault in the ice sheet was close to the sites of their secret drilling experiments. If it was discovered that Global Energy had triggered the problem they would be in deep shit. They had to cover things up quickly.

Ray had immediately summoned the board to an emergency meeting the following morning. Their situation was desperate, the company's lucrative Antarctic drilling and exploration licence was at risk, and the board members realised that they were all in survival mode. All family and other commitments were cancelled until further notice, food and drinks had been ordered in, and the meeting was effectively 'in camera' until they had a working solution that would be acceptable. The shareholders would go ballistic if they ever found out the truth, share prices were bound to go into freefall and every member of the board would be lucky to escape with their job intact at the end of it.

As soon as they had all assembled in the boardroom, Ray called the meeting to order. There was no preamble, no flowery introduction, he just hit them with the facts, his piercing brown-eyed gaze making direct eye contact with each director in turn. There had been an unfortunate side-effect of the experimental deep core drilling that Global Energy had carried out in the developing oilfields in Antarctica. This process had used a revolutionary form of sonic blasting to try to release some of the massive reserve of methane hydrates that had been trapped in the ice and this had been done without the knowledge or approval of the various treaty countries laying claim to the Antarctica territories. All the board members already knew that this unofficial drilling had taken place surreptitiously alongside the official extraction of some of the huge potential reserves of oil that they were licensed to drill for, and knew it would, if successful, make a fortune for the company. It was imperative that their secret be kept.

"I want us to look as though we are above board here people," said Ray. "Give me a press release that will let the world know that there is an issue in Antarctica, but that exonerates us entirely. You have two hours to come up with the first draft. I'll be in my office, let me know when you have pulled something together. Jeff, with me," he said to Jeff Ramsey, his number two in the company. The two leaders left the conference room as the other board members looked at each other in disbelief and bewilderment. It was time for them to earn their huge salaries.

Ray Bergman was pacing the floor of his office while Jeff Ramsey sat quietly cleaning his spectacles in the visitor's chair watching Ray's movements intently. Ray might be diminutive in stature, but he had a big presence and was feared by most of the board. Eventually Ray spoke.

"Jeff, can you guarantee that no-one knows that Global Energy are behind the problems in Antarctica?"

"I'm pretty sure that's the case, Ray," he replied, "unless you count the people in the team down at McMurdo who might have put two and two together."

"We can't afford any leak whatsoever that it was our 'research' activity that was behind this glitch Jeff: We signed the Antarctic Treaty after all. We must do whatever it takes to cover this up completely. We can't be held to account for the error, however minor it is; it would mean we would be totally excluded from any drilling and extraction down there. Period. That would be curtains for Global Energy's Antarctic activity and put a mammoth hole in our profit forecasts."

Jeff knew that the Antarctic Treaty was in place to protect the sub-continent, the last true pristine wilderness in the world and owned by no-one. The repercussions of ignoring the terms of the treaty by undertaking unapproved exploration would bring the weight of the whole developed world down on Global Energy's shoulders in anger. They would be ostracised both morally and ethically, which would also mean financial ruin. As all the board members no doubt realised, this would be the end of the road for the company as a major player in the energy market.

"I could make some discreet enquiries down at McMurdo Ray to get the state of play. Graham Platt is a good company man and has his ear to the ground."

"Great, get on to him right now and brief him," ordered Ray. "I want a total clampdown on gossip, and I want to know everything that is being said down there, without exception across the board, everyone down to the cleaning staff. If anyone expresses any opinion I want it squashed immediately even if heads have to roll, and I want to know about it straight away."

Jeff was back in Ray's office within the hour. "The news from McMurdo isn't great, Ray," he announced. "One of the employees, Chuck Fallon, he's the scientist who was actually out at the remote research station when the tremors started, has already been voicing his opinions about the likelihood of some local exploratory drilling as being the cause of the problem. Right now, he's just venting his spleen and it's being treated as idle speculation, but apparently one or two people are starting to listen to him. These guys aren't stupid, and they will soon start looking into the seismic logs, asking questions and forming their own opinions from the answers, especially those who know that the research station disappeared into a crevasse on the ice sheet, and that the ice shelf itself has now got a bloody great crack running across it."

"Damn! I was worried this might be the case. Right, we need to move fast: First, put a communications block in place, no contact from McMurdo with anyone from the outside world. Channel it all through head office instead. Make something up to justify the situation; say that the tremors have broken the communication channels down or something similar. Next: get yourself down to McMurdo straight away Jeff. I'll get Jayne to arrange for the Lear Jet to be on the runway within the hour. I need you to iron out any creases, smooth any ruffled feathers, and get all the staff singing from the same song sheet, so to speak. As for Chuck Fallon – leave him to me. I'll handle him myself."

Jeff turned and left the office. Ray picked up the phone and called Jayne Grey, his PA. "Yes Mr Bergman?"

"Yeah, Jayne. I need the Lear jet prepped and ready with a flight plan for a trip to McMurdo within the hour for Jeff. Can you get onto it right away please?"

"Yes sir, right away." Jayne had worked for Ray for many years and was used to his abrupt manner. Efficient and quiet, she was the perfect foil for her fiery boss.

Ray gathered his thoughts, then picked up the phone and called McMurdo base, asking to speak to Chuck. He was connected without delay.

"Hi Chuck, it's Ray Bergman here. I gather you have had a lucky escape when the research station slipped below the ice. I hear it was a very close thing and I'm really pleased you weren't still inside at the time. Good job you had the sense to get outside. I also hear you experienced the ice tremors first-hand. Can you tell me what happened and what you think might have caused them?"

Chuck was immediately on the back foot. He'd never spoken to anyone from the Executive floor of Global Energy before for any reason, let alone the CEO. Why would he be calling now? Something major must be happening here for him to get a personal call from Ray Bergman. He needed to be careful what he said.

"It was like nothing I've ever experienced before, Mr Bergman. The whole ice sheet was shuddering, and giant crevasses like the one that swallowed the research station opened up all around me, crazing the surface of the sheet. The chopper couldn't land and Bill Bond the pilot flew brilliantly to get me off the ice alive. I owe him my life."

"It must have been terrifying," soothed Ray, "and thank goodness we managed to get you out of there alive. I hear that there was a storm approaching too, and that if it had hit before you were rescued, things could have been much worse."

"Yes, fortunately we got away literally minutes before the weather closed in on us, otherwise I doubt I would be talking to you now sir." He paused for a moment to gather his thoughts, before asking tentatively, "Do you think it could have been anything to do with Global Energy's activities sir?"

"I'm absolutely certain it wasn't," came Ray's swift reply. "This definitely has nothing to do with Global Energy."

Chuck remained silent. He knew only too well from the confidential report he had seen, and the data he had collected and had subsequently been examining, that an exploratory programme was underway. Why on earth would Ray Bergman be denying it? Before he had a chance to pose the question, Ray jumped back in.

"Listen, I think it would be a good idea to get you up here to head office as soon as possible for you to come and debrief the board first hand – we need to know what has happened straight from the horse's mouth as it were. I'll send down the company jet to collect you so be ready to leave tomorrow morning at short notice. You deserve some R&R after your ordeal and a bit of time to yourself at home will probably do you a power of good."

"Thank you, sir, that's very kind of you, I'll get my gear packed and be ready to leave as soon as the plane arrives," said Chuck.

"Good man Chuck. I'll see you very soon, enjoy the flight home and make the most of all the facilities on offer aboard."

The phone went dead with a click. Chuck sat back in his chair, breathed deeply, and reflected for a moment. Things were happening all too quickly for him to understand the true significance of events. His initial euphoria at being able to ride in the Executive Jet was soon dampened by doubts about his future. What the Hell was happening? A one-on-one phone call from the CEO; and the need for a personal debrief to the board? He had never operated in these circles before and it was all very daunting.

Monday 3rd September
Antarctica

The Global Energy executive jet touched down at McMurdo less than twenty hours after Chuck had been speaking to Ray Bergman. It had given Chuck some time to think about what had happened, reflect on his discussion with Ray, and to have had another look at the photos he had taken from the helicopter, and the data on his laptop. All the evidence appeared to point to the fact that the natural disaster on the ice sheet *had* been caused by Global Energy's unsanctioned exploration activities, although he knew that would be the last thing Ray Bergman and the rest of the board would want to hear him say. It would mean disaster for the company if this got out and he was sure that this was definitely not what Global Energy would want.

Concerned for his future within the company, he had decided that it would be best if he kept his opinions to himself for the time being, and played his cards close to his chest until he was able to get a feel for how events were developing. In the absence of further data, he was in the dark about the latest situation. Maybe the tremors had already stopped, and the ice sheet stabilised again. He would look at the recordings he had copied some more when he got the chance but now wasn't the time, and on board the company jet certainly wasn't the place.

He made up his mind that he needed to keep a private copy of the data he had gathered somewhere safe, just in case, as insurance, and so he dropped everything onto a memory stick and put it in his wallet.

Within a few hours of landing at the base, Jeff Ramsey was concluding his discrete enquiries and had Chuck settled safely aboard the jet. He'd collected all hard and soft copies of the data pertaining to the incident, and he had questioned Greg the radio operator who had launched the rescue, and other scientific staff at some length. Graham Platt had confirmed that only a few rumours had started to circulate about the incident but that no-one really seemed to know what had happened, neither the extent of it nor the cause. The general focus seemed to be the heroism of Bill Bond and the dramatic rescue of Chuck Fallon. "A perfect distraction," thought Jeff.

With this thought fresh in his mind and having briefed Graham on how to keep things on an even keel, Jeff re-boarded the jet, and in no time at all it was back in the air heading homeward.

The journey back to the UK required several refuelling stops and a change of pilot, but Chuck was well looked after by the hostess, while Jeff seemingly worked non-stop and left him in peace. Despite the obvious luxury that he was enjoying, Chuck was still looking forward to getting home again after his several months away. In the meantime, he decided to relax, and nestled back in his plush leather upholstered seat enjoying the once-in-a-lifetime experience and attention of a luxury flight. "Me, on a private jet!" he wondered. "Whatever next? I must be in demand!" Little did he know how much he would rue those words in the days and weeks to come.

---- **5** ----

Tuesday morning 4th September
London

The Global Energy board convened the next morning, several hours before the jet carrying Jeff and Chuck had landed back into the UK.

"I don't need to stress to you all the importance of distancing ourselves from everything that has happened down in Antarctica," opened Ray, pacing around the boardroom. "The company simply cannot afford any scandal, or the repercussions from such, on this scale. We must take every measure, whatever that might be, to present Global Energy as an innocent party."

He paused for a moment to let this sink in then sat down at the head of the table.

"You have all been in meetings since Sunday, and so far, nothing at all about the incident has appeared in the press, let alone indicated that anything has been attributed to Global Energy. We need to keep it that way." He looked around the room at the other directors. They visibly withered under his stare as he focused on each one in turn. "Right, what contingency story lines have we got?"

Terry Smart, the Director for Marketing, rose from his seat and made his way to the front of the room to show the board his proposal. Younger than his fellow directors and stylishly dressed as always, he felt on the back foot: What he had to offer wasn't nicely put together, there hadn't been time for that. The proposal was strictly for the directors' eyes only until the strategy had been agreed. Then, and only then, would he let Alison Duster and her publicity team massage it into appropriate material for a press release. At this stage, the ideas were his and his alone. The question was, would the board like what he had to say? He cleared his throat which had suddenly gone dry. Necks were on the line here, and the other board members were looking to him to take the lead on this – after all, it's what he was hired to do. Giving the right message was invaluable, giving the wrong one was suicide. He had to get this one right.

Walking over to the flipchart, he took the marker pen and wrote two words - 'PLAUSIBLE DENIABILITY' - then he turned to face the board. "What does anyone know about our activities down on the WAIS? What records exist that could point towards

Global Energy as the cause of the problem? How will anything get into the public domain? You all know full well how the press twist and manipulate stories to suit their own political aims and agenda. So, who outside this room knows that 'PROJECT UNDERMINE' even exists, and if so, what it is all about?"

Henry 'Digger' James, Director of Research Operations, chipped in. "Outside of this room, only the guys down on the WAIS in the exploration team know about it." One of the elder statesmen of the Global Energy board, Digger had achieved his position through results and hard work, not charisma, and he commanded the respect of his colleagues on development matters. "I have already set up an investigation by Graham Platt, my McMurdo manager, to find out exactly what went wrong down there. At this moment in time we don't know what effect the sonic blasting has had on the sheet itself, but it appears that the eastern extremity of the ice sheet and the neighbouring shelf seem to be breaking up."

Digger continued, "We have obviously declared our official exploration activities so there should be no comeback there, but this side-line probing for the methane hydrates has all been done under the radar. As far as I can tell, there are no documented reports from the site of these deep core drills."

"Can the epicentre or whatever you call it be pinpointed?" asked Ray.

"Not exactly," said Digger, "but if it could, we have several logged flight plans that show we *have* had teams down there lately. That in its self might spark an investigation that we would be hard pressed to avoid. Questions will be asked as to why we were there at all."

"What is our response then?"

"The official line will have to be that we have been placing more recording devices, set deep into the ice cap so that we have accurate readings at various depths to be able to truly assess any seismic activity. And of course, these would have to be placed into a drilled core to be effective."

"Can we take people out to these spots to show them if needs be?"

"Yes, we can, we put them there as a contingency; a 'belt and braces' approach as it were. We have made everything look above board with these redundant recorders. I thought it would be best."

"Good. Smart move Digger," said Ray, "let's run with that for now."

---- 6 ----

Tuesday afternoon 4th September
London

The Lear Jet touched down at London City airport and taxied over to the terminal. Being a private plane, Chuck assumed he wouldn't need to go through the usual customs and immigration procedure and was soon proved correct when a smartly dressed official escorted him through a priority channel. Once landside he was impressed to see a uniformed chauffeur standing in the arrivals hall holding a sign with his name on it. "Wow, they're really pulling out all the stops for me," wondered Chuck. "Why am I suddenly so important?" There was no sign of Jeff Ramsey. The guy had kept to himself on the flight back, either sleeping or working, but that hadn't bothered Chuck. Quite the opposite: He hadn't fancied making polite conversation with the rather taciturn right-hand man of the CEO.

The Mercedes S-class saloon he was ushered into swept him quietly through the afternoon traffic into the heart of London. Global Energy had had their headquarters on Victoria Street for over twenty years alongside some of the world's other major oil companies. In fact, Victoria Street had become a real 'oil alley' in many ways with high-class restaurants and bars lining the ground floor of many of the impressive skyscrapers. Chuck had of course been to HQ a few times before, usually for national research meetings, but he'd never been up to the executive floors. He noticed that a private elevator manned by another uniformed employee served these floors and wondered if he would have been granted admittance if it hadn't been for the current situation.

The elevator doors opened on the seventh floor into a large plush lobby with original works of art lining the walls and antique furniture grouped attractively in intimate clusters for visitors to relax in. The reception desk was straight ahead, staffed by two well-groomed and attractive women: The importance of good first impressions flashed through Chuck's mind. He approached the reception desk to announce his presence but the older of the two women pre-empted him, welcoming him warmly to Global Energy and asking him to wait for Ray Bergman's executive assistant who would be along to collect him shortly. All this attention was in danger of turning his head, but

Chuck couldn't shake off the nagging doubt that something wasn't quite right.

Five minutes later, Jayne Grey approached him and asked him to follow her along to the CEO's office. The deep carpet muffled any sound as they progressed along a wide corridor towards double doors at the far end. "Well here goes," thought Chuck as Jayne opened them and stood to one side allowing him to pass through, and he entered the CEO's lair.

Ray rose from his plush chair, came out from behind his massive desk and strode across the floor to greet him, with his hand extended. Chuck took the offered hand and was rewarded with a firm gripping handshake. "Good to see you Chuck, how was the flight?" was Bergman's opening remark. Chuck stood there almost dumbstruck, but Ray swiftly moved on, inviting him to sit down. Chuck sank into possibly the most comfortable leather sofa he had ever sat on. The level of pure opulence and comfort between this office and the furniture in the accommodation unit he'd just returned from made him smile somewhat ironically.

"The flight was just fine, thanks, although I am feeling somewhat tired after the trip," Chuck responded.

"Well we won't keep you long, Chuck. I just wanted you to give an initial commentary to the board about the series of events you witnessed. And then we've booked you into *The Dorchester* hotel, so you can head over there and get a good night's sleep. Tomorrow is soon enough for a detailed report."

"That's very good of you, sir. I am sure my mind will be more focused and together in the morning."

Ray took Chuck through a private door in the rear of his office which opened into the Executive Conference Room. Around the boardroom conference table, all twelve members of the board awaited him, looking somewhat dishevelled and weary Chuck thought. He was surprised to see Jeff Ramsey sitting amongst the group. "Christ, how did he manage to get here so quickly?" he wondered.

"Everyone, this is Charles Fallon, Chuck, our research analyst from the Western Antarctic Ice Sheet who was unfortunate enough to be right there in the remote station on the Ross Ice Shelf when this whole situation kicked off. Chuck, in front of you are the members of Global Energy's board. You probably recognise Henry James, your Director of Research and Development, and that chap over there is Terry Smart, our Director of Marketing and Public Relations, who I know is keen to understand what exactly happened." Ray continued around the table naming the directors and their roles in the company. Chuck had seen photographs of some of the board in the company information bulletins, but there were a couple that he didn't know. He tried to remember their names and faces so that he could answer them personally if they asked him any questions.

Ray continued by addressing the board. "In recognition that Chuck has just survived a somewhat traumatic experience followed by a long flight back to the UK, I have asked him to just give us a brief overview of his experience of the events in Antarctica today, and to come back tomorrow to give us all a detailed report. Chuck, over to you."

"Thank you, sir. Good afternoon everybody. As Mr Bergman has alluded to, I am a little jet-lagged now, but I will do my best to outline the series of events and answer any initial questions you might have," said Chuck. He paused for a moment to gather his thoughts. All the board members waited silently for him to begin his story. He took a breath and started his tale.

"I had just completed my routine maintenance checks of the research equipment, setting new recording sheets into seismographs and other recording instruments, and final collation of recent data transmissions from the remote outposts, when I became aware of a shuddering from beneath my feet. It felt to me as though it was coming from deep below the ice sheet, and it was accompanied by a distant rumble. My first thought was that it was an earthquake but there was something about it that didn't ring true with the usual seismic activity down there. Anyway, I decided to call through to the base at McMurdo to see if they had felt or heard anything, but before I had a chance to do so, the intensity of the phenomenon suddenly escalated and so I called and asked the station controller to send transportation urgently to get me off the sheet as soon as possible and back to base. A helicopter was despatched straight away to collect me, but I knew it would take over two hours to arrive and the shuddering of the ice below the remote station and associated noise were getting stronger and stronger. Equipment was being shaken off the racks and desks. I decided at that point that I needed to be outside the station in the open, and so I put on my survival gear and exited the research station as quickly as possible to look for the helicopter. It seems this decision saved my life."

Chuck choked up during this last sentence and had to stop talking for a few seconds to regain his composure before continuing. He had visibly blanched when remembering the series of events that came next and how close he had come to death. The board members sat there patiently while he took a sip of water from a glass that was offered to him, then regained his composure and continued with his story.

"Literally seconds after I exited the research station a great chasm opened in the ice right below it, and the whole remote station simply tumbled into it and disappeared. If I hadn't left when I did, I would have been stuck inside it and been a goner there and then. As it was, I had a lucky escape from the station, but with more fissures opening all around me, I still didn't think I had a cat in hell's chance of getting out of the situation alive," he recounted. "To add to this, I could see storm clouds were building on the horizon and I was convinced at the time that there was a chance that the rescue mission would be aborted until the morning. Obviously, the helicopter pilot and the crew at McMurdo didn't know that the research station had disappeared and that I would have perished from hypothermia, even with the latest technology survival gear the company provides."

"We would never abandon any of our employees unless it was impossible to help them," soothed Barbara Seeder, the Director of HR. She was the only woman on the board Chuck noted, and she was a colourful presence in the otherwise sea of grey suits. Something of a power dresser in her designer Chanel suit, coiffured hair and immaculate make-up, Barbara was by no means a shrinking violet.

"That's good to know, ma'am, and I'm pleased to say that the pilot, Bill Bond, did not abort the mission to rescue me despite the impending storm and the fact that the ice sheet had fractured like crazy paving around me. Thanks to Bill's amazing flying skills, he was able to get to me in time, and, recognising the precarious state of the ice, he managed to hover a couple of feet above it so that I could hold onto the skids, while he lifted me across the chasm to safety before setting down the helicopter very gently on more stable ice to enable me to board properly. We only just got out of there in time and away before the storm caught up with us. The strange thing was, that I'm sure I could see a faint red glow from deep within some of the fissures as we flew over them on the way back to McMurdo."

Just before he announced to the meeting that he had taken some photos of the fissures, Chuck noticed the quick look that passed between Ray and Jeff Ramsey, his number two, and he quickly back-tracked on his plan, simply saying, "But I think I probably imagined it in all the stress of the situation. All I can say is I am glad to have got out of the situation alive."

"It sounds like you were damned lucky to get out alive Chuck, thank God. And thanks also to the skill of this pilot Bill Bond: The guy deserves a commendation and a fat bonus payment for his courageous action. Would you see to it please Barbara?" said Ray. Barbara Seeder nodded her assent and made a note in her planner to action.

"Now Chuck has given us a flavour of what happened, I propose we let him head off and get some rest before facing the barrage of questions I am sure you will all have. So, Chuck, thank you for your time, sleep well and we look forward to seeing you at nine o'clock in the morning," said Ray concluding the meeting.

Jayne Grey had stopped taking notes. She put down her notepad and stepped forward to escort Chuck from the conference room, leaving him at the elevator saying, "The same chauffeur that picked you up from the airport will meet you downstairs and take you along to your hotel." "Thank you," said Chuck wearily.

---- 7 ----

Tuesday evening 4th September
London

Chuck couldn't believe his eyes when the chauffeur-driven Mercedes pulled up in front of *The Dorchester*, and a liveried doorman in green top-hat and tails opened the door for him. "I wish the family could see me now," he thought. It was hard not to let the opulence of the surroundings make him forget everything that had happened to him, but he still had the deep-set sense of unease in his gut that had been with him since Ray Bergman's initial call. "Oh well, nothing much can happen to me tonight, so I may as well enjoy myself," he concluded.

The receptionist allocated him a superior room on the 8th floor with stunning views over Hyde Park. He swept back the curtains and visually feasted on the open green space facing him. After several months of nothing but white on the ice sheet, it was a wonderful sight to him. Despite being very tired, hunger was his over-riding feeling just at that moment. "Should I have room service, or dine properly in the Dorchester Grill?" Chuck pondered. "Damn it, I'll shower and change and hit the restaurant ... it's probably the only time I'll ever have the opportunity."

Fifteen minutes later, with his beard trimmed and with his fair hair combed neatly, Chuck was ushered into the gilded and ornate dining room, the lynch pin of *The Dorchester*'s culinary experience. While somewhat traditional in its style and the food it served, the quality screamed from every small detail. "Fillet steak, medium rare," Chuck decided. "I'll have all the trimmings and a decent bottle of claret to wash it all down." He was on company expenses after all!

By 9pm, replete and slightly tipsy after finishing the whole bottle, Chuck made his way upstairs to his room. He set an alarm on the clock to wake him in the morning and collapsed onto the enormous feather bed. "Heaven," was his last waking thought before he fell into a deep sleep.

Back at Global Energy HQ, Chuck's earlier departure had opened a floodgate of questions from the directors, all calling out at once. "Do you think he knows anything?" "Does he suspect our deep core drilling activities?" "What do you think he meant by a faint red glow?" "Is this the beginning of the end for Global Energy?" And still the questions kept coming.

"Quiet!" shouted Ray over the cacophony that was his board of directors. "We need to remain calm and think rationally, not scream out and behave like a bunch of hyenas. For God's sake, you're all professionals! Pull yourselves together!" he snarled.

The noise rapidly abated until all the directors were shamefaced, looking down at their hands. "That's better," said Ray. "At least I can hear myself think now."

"What we need to do is focus on damage limitation and getting our version of events out there before the press come hounding us. Obviously, the location of the incident is in the area where Global Energy have sole drilling rights so as soon as news of the situation leaks we'll be their first port of call. And in my book, attack is the best form of defence, so we need to be upfront about the existence of this "natural" disaster and notify the press of its occurrence as soon as possible. Terry, which of the major dailies on both sides of the pond are most pro-Global and will present things in a favourable light?"

Despite their concerns for the company, the directors admired the calm and authoritative way that Ray had taken charge: He wasn't their CEO for nothing.

"I suggest we place it with the *Independent* and *New York Times* to start with," replied Terry. "I have a good contact at both publications and can pull them onside as soon as we're ready."

"Excellent," commented Ray. "What we need to do now is draft a press release. Digger, can you work with Terry on this to add the technical input? And if the pair of you can have a first draft circulated by end of play today we will all be able to review it before Chuck Fallon returns in the morning. Any other questions or comments?"

"Do we need to take any steps with regards to Mr Fallon?" queried Barbara Seeder. "An official and documented de-briefing for his personnel record? Maybe some compassionate leave and counselling to help him recover from the trauma of nearly losing his life? I would advise we play things by the book in this regard – we need him working with us and not against us," she emphasised.

"Until we have a chance to see what he has to say tomorrow morning, then I think it's a little premature to make any definite plans Barbara. What we do know is that we have to keep this little misadventure firmly on a need to know basis, and deal with any leaks firmly and effectively," responded Ray.

"And on that note, I think we should call it a day for today. Thank you all for your time and let's reconvene tomorrow morning at 7am to review the draft press release and formulate questions for our Mr Fallon."

As the directors began to depart, Ray called out to his number two as he went back through to his office. "Jeff, a word please." As soon as Jeff had followed him through, and with the office door firmly closed, Ray fired out, "So what do you think Jeff? Did that research nobody have any clue about our secret activities do you think? You do realise we will have to close him down if he starts to spout anything but the company line on this Jeff."

Used to Ray's outbursts, Jeff took time to consider his response – he knew Ray valued his measured input. "I think it's too early to tell, Ray. Right now, Fallon is still fixated on the horror of what just happened to him, and apart from the one throw away comment about the faint glow in the fissures, which if you noticed he didn't mention again, he gave no indication that he thought there had been anything untoward. I immediately picked up his laptop with the seismic data readings on it when I was down there in McMurdo quoting standard policy in such events, and so he has no hard evidence to link Global Energy activities with any spikes in the seismic readings. What harm can he do us without real evidence?"

"Fair point," said Ray. "I guess we just need to stop him spouting theories to friends and family, and the press too should they contact him. But Terry should be able to manage that angle. Okay, let's assume for tonight that Fallon is still a good company employee getting a good night's rest at our expense."

---- 8 ----

Wednesday 5th September
London

Chuck woke to the sound of the alarm next morning with a slight headache. He was feeling rested but initially wondered where the hell he was. The sheer size and comfort of the bed and the sumptuous decor of his surroundings in the hotel suite were so far removed from his normal existence that it took him a moment or two to remember what had been happening. Glancing at his watch he realised he had set the alarm for the wrong time in his tipsy state the previous evening and was in danger of running late for his 9am meeting: There would be no cooked breakfast for him this morning.

As usual Ray Bergman had made sure he had his cooked breakfast. Being American this didn't comprise the eggs and bacon beloved of so many Brits, but instead a short stack of pancakes with maple syrup and a side of crispy bacon, his favourite, the maple-kind. On alternate days he varied this with blueberry pancakes but today, he felt he deserved the full works. His metabolism was working overtime as the pressure of the current situation caused adrenaline to course through his body. He needed the extra calories.

Replete, he arrived in the office at 6.45am in readiness for the 7am roll call with his board of directors. He was feeling confident and upbeat that things would go his way. He'd reviewed the draft press release the previous evening and was happy with the general gist of it: No blame should ever be associated with Global Energy.

The chauffeur was waiting in the hotel lobby as Chuck exited the elevator. "My God, how did he know when I'd appear," thought Chuck. "If ever Big Brother was in existence, this is it." Chuck nodded to him as he walked over to the reception desk to check out and settle his account. "Good morning, Mr Fallon, we trust you slept well," opened the receptionist.

"Very well, thank you. Could I settle the account for room 807 please?"

"That has already been taken care of for you sir. Your company has an account with our hotel and your bill has been charged to it."

"Oh my God, I hope they don't think I was excessive," thought Chuck, remembering the expensive meal from the night before. But everything in *The*

Dorchester was expensive to him – his Global Energy salary simply didn't run to this type of place.

With a nod to the chauffeur, Chuck walked outside to the waiting Mercedes and slipped into the rear seat. The traffic on Park Lane was heavy: Rush hour was in progress, so he settled in for a slow drive.

Twenty minutes later, at 8.45am, the car pulled up outside Global Energy's head office, and for the second time, Chuck approached the private elevator to the executive floors. "Here we go," he thought, a faint headache still niggling its way across his forehead. "I hope I can answer all their questions."

Jayne Grey was there to meet him in the reception area as he entered the executive lobby and indicated for him to follow her. She showed him into the conference room where, once again, the board all sat waiting for him. All their eyes followed him into the room as he took the only vacant seat – the one that was next to Ray Bergman.

"Good morning, Chuck," welcomed Ray. "We all hope you had a good night's sleep and are ready to get down to brass tacks this morning." The rest of the board nodded to him.

"Yes, I did, thank you, sir, and yes, I am," replied Chuck.

"Okay, well let's get started. You gave us a good overview of the course of events yesterday Chuck, so we don't need you to repeat yourself on that. What we do have are various questions we'd like to throw at you to get a better insight on several areas. Don't worry if there is anything you don't feel able to answer."

Turning to Henry James, Ray said, "Would you like to kick off Digger?"

"No problem Ray. Good morning Chuck. As Ray said, I hope you're feeling well rested." Chuck nodded in response. Digger moved straight into his dialogue. "I'd like to open the session by asking you about the research data you observed in the days running up to the incident. Can you describe to us exactly what you were seeing in the data recordings out at the remote station please?"

Chuck thought for a moment before replying, "From what I can remember, everything seemed pretty normal for the routine drilling schedule that had been made available to all the McMurdo staff, sir. We were seeing spikes in seismic recordings corresponding with the timing of the drilling and occasional blasting, but in between, levels were as expected."

"Good, good," commented Digger somewhat absentmindedly. "So, everything was normal and Global Energy's routine drilling activities weren't causing any identifiable problems," he reinforced. "And on the day in question, Chuck, had there been any drilling and blasting scheduled?"

"Well that's the perplexing thing Mr James. No drilling or blasting was scheduled for that day and so when I heard the deep rumble and looked at the output on the seismograph, the appearance of increasingly erratic spiking completely threw me. As I said yesterday my first thought was that it was an earthquake, but I know the pattern I would expect to see for that and this bore no resemblance."

"Interesting," commented Digger. "As you say, normal earthquake activity does have a typical pattern. Right, I'd like to go over some of the output data with you in more detail. Do you have a copy of it?"

Chuck hesitated for a fraction of a second before replying, "No sir. The only copy of the data was on my laptop, and I handed that over to Mr Ramsey down at McMurdo." All eyes around the table switched to Jeff Ramsey, who nodded his agreement to the statement.

At this stage in the proceedings, Chuck didn't feel comfortable in admitting to the copy he had taken of the data, securely secreted in his wallet on a USB memory stick. Something in his subconscious was telling him to keep quiet about it. "But I'd be happy to look at the output with you if Mr Ramsey has the laptop to hand?" he offered.

"That would be no problem," Jeff Ramsey said. "It's in my office. Digger, I suggest you come along after the meeting has ended and I'll give you the laptop so that you can review the data."

"A good plan," commented Ray. "Thank you, Digger. Barbara, I believe you had a couple of questions for Chuck also?"

"Yes, I do Ray. Good morning Chuck. First, I'd just like to reiterate how pleased we all are that no harm came to you down on the Ice Sheet. It must have been a terrifying experience for you."

"It was ma'am. On several occasions, as crevasses were opening around me, when the research station disappeared, and with nowhere for the rescue helicopter to land, I truly thought I was done for. I will forever be in Bill Bond's debt for his perseverance in trying to rescue me. The whole thing is like a horrible nightmare that I can't seem to get out of my head."

"I'm sure it is, Chuck. And to help you overcome the trauma, I am going to propose that you take a month's paid leave to start immediately. What I'd also like to propose is that you have a chat with the company's grief and trauma counsellor. I think it would help you come to terms with your experience and allow you to put it behind you," she continued.

Chuck felt rocked back on his heels. A month's paid leave? Trauma counselling? Whatever would they suggest next? Was this what all responsible employers would do, or was there another agenda going on here? The thought of the USB stick in his wallet was burning a hole in his brain. "I really want to take the opportunity to study that data at length," he mused, but in response to Barbara's comments he replied, "That is very generous of the company, but I don't feel it is necessary. A few days rest and I'll be ready to resume my duties."

"We wouldn't hear of it," interjected Ray. "It's the least we can do after everything you have been through. Consider yourself on leave from later this morning when we conclude this meeting. And just let either Barbara or Jeff know if there is anything you need during that time," he wrapped up.

"Okay everyone, does anyone have any more questions for this poor guy before we cut him free?" Nothing was forthcoming, so Ray turned to Chuck saying, "Thank you for your time this morning Chuck. My secretary Jayne will see you out and the chauffeur take you to wherever you want to go. Use the time off to recuperate and catch up with family and friends, and please do give some consideration to Barbara's suggestion of speaking to our trauma counsellor. I can personally recommend it," he concluded, liking his finishing touch. He'd never actually even spoken to the counsellor in Barbara's department, but the thought of someone subtly prying into Chuck's mind appealed to him. "Belt and braces," he thought.

As soon as Chuck left the room, Ray waited a few moments for him to get out of earshot, even though the doors were several inches thick and effectively soundproof, then he turned to the board saying, "Okay, let's formalise our plan of action. Nicely handled Barbara, Digger. I feel you showed both our caring side and underlined that there were no abnormal activities down in the Antarctic very well. Hopefully that will be positioned firmly in Fallon's mind and he will be a good boy and go off and enjoy a month of being paid to do nothing."

"So, first things first: The draft press release. I trust you have all had the opportunity to review it? Comments please?"

Being the only one who felt comfortable in challenging Ray publicly and knowing that Ray would already have reviewed and amended the article to his liking, Jeff Ramsey took the floor to put forward his thoughts. "Generally, I think the release is very good, strongly worded and absolving Global Energy of any responsibility. My concerns are two-fold: One, around the timing of its publication and the other, wondering if we're being a little too assertive in the tone of the article. The lady doth protest too much, springs to my mind," he closed.

"Hmm. I wanted to discuss the timing in open forum this morning," responded Ray. "With regards to the wording, I thought we had all agreed we needed to be forthright in our approach ... attack is the best form of defence etcetera, etcetera."

"Yes Ray, I know we agreed on that yesterday, but pondering on it overnight, I did wonder if we would be better offering an unbiased commentary on the events, almost being the one bringing it to the public's attention while subtly getting our position across, along the lines of Global Energy being in the best position to comment on what might or might not have happened down on the ice sheet, being the ones who have closely monitored all seismic activity over the last three years," offered Jeff.

"I concur with that," said Ray after considering Jeff's input. "A more subtle approach, looking like we're horrified at the ecological impact of what has happened; how our expert data analysis gave no indication that anything untoward was brewing; that we suffered great losses in terms of the remote recording station and all the equipment inside it; and that we very nearly lost one of our key scientists if it hadn't been for the heroic flying of our McMurdo base pilot. Yes! This is good! Global Energy will come out looking like the victim, the compassionate eco-warrior and the hero rolled into one. Excellent. Well done Jeff ... you just earned yourself a bonus. Terry: Rewrite the press release along these lines. Keep in some of Digger's technical stuff to demonstrate we are the experts down there but soften up on the aggression. We want to be seen as being the good guys, sharing the news with the world and offering our expert opinions to help in understanding the situation. In other words, Subtext: Global Energy are great guys."

Ray was delighted with this approach. While he would never admit it to anyone, he knew his manner could be somewhat rash and abrasive, but this is what had got him to the top of one of the world's most successful corporations. He'd learned at an early age that the key to success is to surround yourself with people who could plug your deficiencies without realising they were doing so, but who would not challenge your authority and position. In this regard, Jeff Ramsey was almost the perfect number two: Quiet and considered, a giant of a man in comparison to him, and probably the closest thing Ray had to a friend. Again, not something that he would admit to: Barriers always needed to be upheld, if he was to maintain control.

"And that just leaves the timing of the press release. Terry what's your view?" he asked the Director of Marketing, "bearing in mind it is the 21st century and modern communications being what they are it's hard to keep anything under the radar for long. We need to be the ones leading with this story and controlling any fall-out."

"Well we know things are pretty well locked down at McMurdo – the communications black-out seems to have done the trick on that front - and that to the best of our knowledge the activity was contained to the WAIS and neighbouring Ross Ice Shelf where we had sole access. Nothing has appeared in the press to date and as such I can only conclude that any leaks are plugged and so we can choose our timing within reason," commented Terry. "That said, I propose we look to get it into this weekend's editions. That gives us up to forty-eight hours of down time before the markets re-open on Monday for any impact to have become yesterday's news."

"I like your thinking Terry," said Ray. "So, are we all in agreement?" he queried.

"What about Mr Fallon leaking anything to the press?" asked Barbara.

"You leave Fallon to me. I'll tie him up with responding to sufficient follow-up questions for the next day or two that he won't have time to think about contacting the press before our article hits," concluded Ray. "Meeting closed folks," he said curtly as he headed out of the conference room and back to his office.

---- 9 ----

Thursday 6th September
Dorset

Chuck was delighted to back in his own home in Corton Denham, and to be reunited with his parents who lived in nearby Sherborne. They had hosted a small home-coming party for him the previous evening. It was a small intimate family affair held in recognition of the life-threatening situation he had just gone through, allowing for his jet-lag of course. Over the dinner table he had given them a brief overview of what had happened, playing down the threat to his life so that his parents wouldn't fret quite so much, focussing instead on the view of the crazed surface from the helicopter when he'd been collected. He didn't want them to worry unduly should he have to return to McMurdo. "Less is more," was his conclusion.

The only family members missing from the gathering were his sister Dominique and her husband Skip, who were in New York preparing their boat to cross the Atlantic on the return leg of their three-year sailing adventure. They'd had an amazing time exploring many new islands, and they had made some great new friends from around the world, but despite their obvious sailing expertise, Chuck could see the shadow of concern for them in his mother's face. No matter how often Dom or Skip explained to her that they were competent sailors and that they didn't take any unnecessary risks, he could tell that she never quite believed them and lived on her nerves when they were away from safe havens making long passages.

He looked forward to seeing them again too. He and Dom, being close in age, had always been confidants and he wanted to be able to discuss the happenings on the ice sheet with her. Indeed, she was the only person he felt comfortable sharing his thoughts and opinions with, and he knew that she would give him a no-nonsense view on his suspicions. But that would have to wait until she returned, giving him plenty of time to fully analyse the data he had brought home and get his thoughts straight.

He had lost his laptop when Jeff Ramsey took it from him as they were leaving McMurdo to return to the UK and so he would now have to dig deep into his own pockets and buy himself another one that he could keep private from Global Energy. Even though they were infinitely more expensive than a PC, he decided that he was going to splash out the extra money and get himself a new Macbook Air. He wanted the extra resolution of the screen display to be able to really study the photos he had taken with his mobile phone camera, and the recorded seismograph readings, and because the Mac was solid state, it would withstand a lot rougher handling than the equivalent PC.

With the thought of one month's paid leave stretching out in front of him when he woke that morning, Chuck pondered how he was going to use the time constructively. He was very quickly bored and would need something to occupy his mind. He wasn't the sort of person to go and sit on a beach somewhere basking in the sun reading a book. He needed to keep himself busy. Yes, he wanted to analyse the data that he'd brought back with him but that wouldn't take him four weeks. He supposed he could visit friends, maybe catch up on some gardening, but even so, the time off loomed in front of him: He'd have to get himself organised.

Three hours later, having dressed, breakfasted, shopped for provisions, and opened his mail, he decided to phone his oldest friend, PJ, at work and suggest meeting for lunch.

"PJ, old mate, it's Chuck, I'm just back from the frozen south. How're you doing? And are you free for lunch?" he opened.

"Hey, great to hear from you Chuck, I was only wondering how you were getting on down there just the other day: You must have some incredible stories to tell of abominable snowmen and such like," jested PJ. "And yes, lunch today would be great. Where do you fancy?"

"I wondered about The Horse if that's okay for you? I can book a table if it is."

"The Horse would be perfect – I always enjoy their pizzas. Shall we say 1pm and I'll meet you there?"

"Looking forward to it, mate. See you later," replied Chuck.

The prospect of something to do lifted Chuck's spirits and he happily strode off an hour later to meet his best friend. It was over three months since they'd last spoken and so there would be plenty of news to catch up on from both sides.

Two hours later, with a Diavolo pizza and most of a bottle of Pinot Grigio inside him (PJ had stuck to one glass seeing as he had to return to work after his extended lunch break) Chuck was just explaining about his month of paid leave.

"Why don't you go on holiday mate?" suggested PJ. "You know, somewhere warm and sunny, a complete contrast to Antarctica. How about a cycling trip in France? Trekking in the Alps? What about a sailing holiday in Croatia or Greece seeing as you love it so much? In fact, why don't you offer to crew for Dom and Skip on their trip back from the USA if they haven't left already? That will use all of your month up quite nicely," he said.

The idea of an Atlantic voyage really appealed to Chuck – he'd not had any days off during his time down at McMurdo as there was nowhere to go and nothing to do anyway, so he and the other employees just worked all day every day – and the thought of even some sun on his bones after months of snow, ice and sub-zero temperatures was incredibly attractive. But he did want to undertake the data analysis and so would need some peace and quiet to do this. Maybe PJ's idea of crewing for Skip and Dom wasn't such a bad one: Three to four weeks with no interruptions, at one with nature, and spending quality time with two of his favourite people on the planet. It was a no brainer.

"That, my friend, is a great idea! I'll give them a call as soon as I get home, I'm sure they won't mind me being aboard for the crossing," Chuck announced.

"Yes! The more I think about it the better it is. In fact, it's a perfect opportunity. Atlantic here I come!"

Thursday 6th September
Manhattan, New York

Skip stood on the pontoon of the marina and loaded the last slab of twenty-four cans of beer onto *Aztec*, his and Dom's 47-foot Bermudan sloop. *Aztec* had been their home for the last three years as they had travelled various parts of the globe. "There, that's everything of importance on board now, we should have enough to get us all the way back to England!" he grinned. Dom rolled her eyes in exasperation: She knew just what he was like, and there was no chance of breaking his long-standing custom of having a nightly sun-downer wherever he was, whatever the conditions and the weather, but only one.

They had sailed away from England three years earlier, leaving their former jobs behind them, to cruise the Mediterranean fully before heading across the Atlantic to the Caribbean. Now, after extensively exploring all the islands, and surviving two hurricane seasons tucked safely away in well protected anchorages, they had made their way northwards from Fajardo in Puerto Rico, through the Turks and Caicos, and Bahamas, and along the eastern seaboard of America to the North Cove Marina in New York. Now they were ready to head back home to catch up with friends and family.

They'd been studying the weather forecasts almost constantly for the last few days, looking at the various sailing weather websites for a good weather window in which to start their passage, but the winds were consistently being reported as coming from the wrong direction.

"For God's sake!" exclaimed Skip. "Why can't the damn winds swing round to coming from the south-west to help us on our way?"

Usually the trade winds were settled from the south-west by September but because of the position of both the Azores High and the Jet Stream, the winds were still from the east, just the direction they wanted to travel. And because no yacht can sail directly into the wind, both Skip and Dom knew it would be slow progress, having to tack back and forth across the wind until the trades finally decided to shift back to where they should be.

When they'd crossed over to the Caribbean two years ago they'd had friends on board with them, someone to share the watch shifts with, so that lack of sleep hadn't been a problem. This time, the prospect of sailing "two up" would, they knew, lead to serious sleep deprivation for both, something Skip coped with better than Dom. But after a few days at sea, usually the first three being the worst, they knew a routine would be established and it would get easier. The biggest downside to sailing two up was the lack of company: Typically, when one person was on watch, the other was asleep and vice versa. "The stereotypical ships that pass in the night," thought Dom.

"So, what are the weather patterns suggesting to us?" queried Dom. "Is there a good time to leave showing up on any of the websites? And remember, we can't leave on a Friday because it's bad luck!" she teased.

"There's no change at all in the bloody forecast," replied Skip angrily. "Do you think we should say 'sod it' and just set sail and get on with it? Let's face it, we both know that when we are sailing for up to a month or so at sea, we're bound to experience every type of weather condition known to man."

"Well if there's no change in the next couple of days, I think we should go," said Dom. "I want to get home in time to enjoy some of the British autumn, maybe even an Indian summer such as it is, and have an opportunity to show off my tan before winter clothing layers are needed!"

Later that afternoon their SatPhone rang. It wasn't a phone they used with any regularity but was always switched on for emergency use, especially when on passage, and for picking up emails and weather forecasts along the way. This wasn't a scheduled call, so something must be wrong.

Dom grabbed up the phone, and pressed the green button to accept the call, fully expecting to hear bad news, only to hear her brother's cheery voice.

"Hi Sis, how're you doing?"

"Chuck? What's the matter? Is everything okay? Are Mum & Dad well?" she instantly asked.

"Everything is fine Dom. Can't a big brother call his little sister to wish her bon voyage these days?"

Dom exhaled slowly and pulled herself together before replying, "Of course you can! It's great to hear from you Bro. Where are you calling from? Are you still down in the frozen wilderness?"

"Interesting you should ask that Dom. I'm actually back home in the UK … and have been given a month's paid leave."

"What have you done wrong Chuck? No-one gets a month's paid holiday for nothing. Oh my God, you're not injured, are you?"

Chuck smiled to himself. His sister was always protective of her big brother. "No, I'm fine sis. There was a little incident down on the ice sheet that I got involved in and had to be rescued from and, as a result, the company directors feel I deserve a month to recuperate from the trauma, that's all."

"What on earth happened to you? Are you sure you're okay?" she asked.

"Yep, I am truly fine. There was an unexplained earthquake or tremor of some sort that opened great fissures in the ice that swallowed the remote recording station I was occupying. Fortunately, I had the good sense to get out onto the ice before it was swallowed up, and I was rescued by helicopter. It was touch and go at one point when I was somewhat isolated in the middle of two crevasses, but don't tell Mum that when you speak to her: She thinks it was just a routine pick-up."

"Christ, Chuck. So, what are Global Energy saying? Are they blaming you in any way for what happened?"

"No, not at all. In fact, they couldn't have been nicer. It seems I am something of a hero in their eyes and they're almost falling over themselves to be kind to me. They laid on the private company jet to get me back to London and put me up overnight in a suite in *The Dorchester* with a sumptuous dinner. Then, they offered me counselling, and gave me a month's paid holiday. A more suspicious man would wonder what it was all for."

"And are you suspicious something is afoot?" queried Dom getting straight to the nub of it.

"Hmmm. I'm not sure Dom. To be honest, I did inadvertently walk into my boss' office and happened to see a report lying on his desk that was talking about a programme of undisclosed exploratory drilling and blasting which I knew nothing about. And in the days before the incident there were some unusual readings on the seismograph. Ray Bergman, the CEO of Global Energy, is adamant the earthquake is nothing to do with the company. They're currently studying the data from my laptop that had been recorded up to and including the time of the tremor."

"What? They've impounded your laptop? They must think you did something or know something," challenged Dom.

"I see you are straight to the heart of the matter as always, sis. Yes, I handed it over to the number two guy who flew down to escort me back to London, and he has held onto it ever since. The thing is, unbeknown to them, I backed up a copy of the data to a USB stick that I have right here in my wallet. I'm hoping to analyse it myself properly over the next day or two and would like to chat things through with you when you get back," Chuck said.

"It all smells a bit fishy to me," responded Dom, "and by the way, we're not going to be back for about four weeks, but once we are back in the UK, I'd be happy to discuss it with you then."

"Well..." said Chuck, "that was another reason for my call. I know it's a tough crossing for two handed sailing, so I was wondering, how do you and Skip fancy an extra crew member for your voyage back? I could get a flight out to JFK tomorrow and be ready to sail straight away. The weeks at sea would give me plenty of time to analyse all the data I've secreted away, and I can discuss it with you as I go. What do you think sis?" he asked.

Without hesitating, Dom answered with a resounding "Yes!" An extra watch person would mean more sleep for all of them on board, and three sets of hands were infinitely better than two. Also, to spend four weeks with her brother after a three-year absence, and given their usual busy lives, would be a real treat. Plus, their telephone conversation had worried her on some level, so it would be nice to know he was away from harm's way in the middle of the Atlantic. As ironic as that might sound to a non-sailor, being out at sea is one of the safest places in the world. Having

Chuck aboard *Aztec* would be a real win-win situation for all of them.

Chuck was thrilled too. He was really looking forward to the extended sailing trip, and he booked his flight straight away. Within an hour of ringing off from his call with Dom, his seat was confirmed, his taxi was booked to take him to the airport, and his collapsible holdall was packed for the trip.

---- 11 ----

Thursday 6th September
London

Back at Global Energy HQ, Digger James had fired up Chuck's laptop, and was engrossed in poring over the collected scientific data stored on the hard drive. After a while examining the findings, he shut the laptop down, stowed it away in the credenza in his office and locked the cupboard. He needed to keep it secure and away from any inquisitive employees' eyes. He knew that people were curious at the best of times and this was very sensitive information that couldn't be leaked at any cost. He closed the door behind him, and made his way up to Ray Bergman's office, knocked once and entered before waiting for an invitation to enter. This was important information that couldn't wait.

Ray looked up from his desk and raised an eyebrow. He had worked with Digger for many years and knew the signs when Digger was stressed. He stopped reading the document in his hands and waited for

Digger to impart his news. He could see from the look on Digger's face that it wasn't going to be good. Digger took a breath and launched straight in. Better to get it over with. "Having looked at Fallon's laptop and the seismic recordings, I just don't know what else can have caused this tremor Ray, other than our exploratory deep core drilling. There are no other readings to suggest anything other than a man-made trigger for the event," he concluded.

"That's not what I wanted to hear," growled Ray, his brown eyes flashing annoyance. "Can anyone else draw the same conclusions?"

"Well, no. Not unless by some chance they manage to access our company data. And we know that by impounding Fallon's laptop we have that securely nailed down. However, with any noticeable earth movements, the various seismic recording stations around the world will have picked up on the readings and will be forming their own interpretations, but without our drilling and blasting schedule they'll have nothing to tie it to Global Energy, and so they'll have no choice other than to assume it is a natural phenomenon," said Digger.

"Hmm," commented Ray, unconvinced. "The sooner we get this press article out, the better." He picked up the phone and pressed the intercom button.

"Jayne, get Terry Smith in here would you? I want him to give me an update on where we are with getting the press article into print."

Terry Smith joined them within five minutes. He was feeling rather pleased with himself, having achieved a front-page article in both of the chosen publications.

"Hello Ray, Digger. Great news! I've just come off the phone with the *New York Times* and we're set to hit the front cover in the early edition the day after tomorrow. Same with the *Independent*, so we're all set," he reported.

"Good work Terry," commented Ray. "We need to get our interpretation of the event out there as soon as possible without it looking as though we are desperate. I'll leave it with you. Keep me posted on progress from here on in." "Sure Ray, of course I will," said Terry, as he headed back towards his office. Digger nodded to Ray, then returned to his office to resume his analysis and dig even deeper into the recorded data.

Ray had been trying to get hold of Chuck on and off throughout the day to ensure he was still a company man. The inability to contact him at his home had him wondering where the hell Fallon was, and he undertook to try once more.

"Jayne, get Fallon on the line for me. I need to know where he is and what he's up to."

"Certainly Mr Bergman." Jayne rang off and within a minute was back on the phone. "I managed to get him on his mobile sir," she said before putting the call through.

"Thanks Jayne." He paused, waiting for the tell-tale click to know the call had been connected. "Chuck, hello, this is Ray Bergman. I just thought I'd touch base with you before the close of play to make sure you have everything you want, and to see if you'd given any thought to Barbara's idea about speaking to a counsellor?" Ray queried.

"All's well at my end sir," Chuck reassured, "I had an enjoyable day catching up with family and friends yesterday and thinking about how I'm going to spend my month off. In fact, I've just agreed to crew for my sister and brother-in-law on their passage back to the UK from New York on their sailing yacht. They're returning home after three years away and it will give me four weeks to focus on the sailing, to clear my head and get over the trauma of what happened. I trust that is okay with the company sir?"

"I think that's an excellent idea," retorted Ray, instantly liking the thought of Chuck, the only possible loose end, being away from any contact with the press for such a long period. If there *was* a furore over the incident, by the time anyone could reach the individual at the centre of it all, it would be old news and the focus would be on the latest event instead of this one. "And don't worry if your trip runs over the month we've talked about, Chuck. We're not going to quibble over an extra day or two's absence after what you've been through."

"That's very kind of you sir," thanked Chuck. "I'll be leaving for New York tomorrow morning and unfortunately that means I will be out of touch from that point until I get back to the UK. Is there anything else you need to ask me or for me to do before I leave?"

"No, you just head off and enjoy the trip," concluded Ray, "and we'll speak on your return."

For very differing reasons both Chuck and Ray Bergman were very satisfied with the outcome of their conversation.

---- 12 ----

Friday 7th September

Chuck was at Heathrow Airport in good time for his flight to JFK International Airport in New York, and he bought himself a new Mac computer in the duty-free electronics store. He would be able to start looking at the data on the memory stick as soon as he was able to upload it. Thankfully, there would be a power supply available in his airplane seat, so he could keep his batteries charged and be able to work throughout the Virgin Atlantic flight.

His flight took off at 9.30am. Having paid for the flight himself he was sitting in the premium economy section. It was not quite the same as the luxury of his last flight on the corporate jet, in fact, the two flights were like chalk and cheese. Still, he was sitting comfortably in his favoured window seat, luckily with an empty place beside him. He would be able to work on the data uninterrupted, and besides that, he was excited about seeing his sister again and the forthcoming month afloat. Even though neither he nor

Dom had sailed as children, their parents having no love of the water, the two of them had both gravitated to the waves while at university, Dom as a proficient dinghy sailor and Chuck as a wind-surfer. It was only when Dom got together with Skip that she applied her sailing skills to bigger yachts and was now as enthusiastic about sailing and the sailing lifestyle as her husband.

His flight touched down at JFK International Airport seven hours later and Chuck stepped through the airplane's open doorway and walked out onto the skybridge and into the terminal to go through customs and immigration. Despite having a US visa, he had to join the lengthy queue with the visa waiver programme travellers to be processed. "What's the point of spending all that money when it doesn't actually do anything for you?" he thought to himself. Eventually he collected his holdall and stepped out of the terminal into the warmth and sunshine of New York. "Wonderful," he thought as he strolled across the tarmac to the pickup point where there was an Über taxi waiting for him. He knew from Dom that *Aztec* was berthed in the North Cove Marina next to Battery Park on the south-western tip of Manhattan Island, so he settled back in his seat to take in the sights of one of the world's greatest capital cities. The taxi crossed

Brooklyn Bridge into downtown, passing the One World Trade Center, and he saw the Statue of Liberty out on Ellis Island on his way to the marina. "If only I had more time," he thought, "I'd really like to have a good look around."

On arrival at the marina, Chuck thanked the taxi driver who handed him his holdall out of the trunk. He stood still for a moment while the car drove away and reflected that he couldn't believe he was so far removed from the frozen wastelands of Antarctica as he took in the splendour of the Manhattan waterfront skyline. His joy was greatly enhanced when he caught sight of his sister and brother-in-law running down the pontoon to greet him. They both looked fit and well, tanned and lean after their extended trip. Dom's dark hair was cut short and had lightened in the sunshine, while Skip had more salt then pepper in his hair Chuck noticed with a wry smile.

"Chuck, Chuck. Welcome!" Dom shouted, leaping into his arms and planting a big sisterly kiss on his lips. Skip strode along behind her, weathered and bearded after his lengthy time afloat, but beaming a great big smile, obviously equally as pleased to see his brother-in-law.

"Great to see you, mate," he grinned, gathering both Dom and Chuck together in a big bear-hug and lifting them off the ground. "Steady on Skip, I've been through the wringer a bit lately!" said Chuck grinning fondly at his brother-in-law. "Sorry Chuck, I guess I got a bit carried away," replied Skip as he threw his arm round Chuck's shoulders and steered him down the pontoon towards *Aztec*.

Two hours later, Chuck's gear was safely stowed in one of the aft cabins and *Aztec's* newly formed Atlantic crew were enjoying a gin and tonic or two in the cockpit as the sun slipped down behind the trees to disappear below the Statue of Liberty just across the bay. "This is amazing," he thought to himself as he sipped his sundowner. "I can't believe only a few days ago I was looking at the bottom of a crevasse in Antarctica, and now I'm here in Manhattan."

"Just think, this time tomorrow we'll be on our way," announced Skip. "No contact with the real world for about a month. Heaven."

After a good night's sleep, they all awoke refreshed the next morning and rushed around making the final preparations for their departure. Dom managed to get extra provisions to cater for the additional hungry crewmember, the water tanks were filled to the brim, and the last-minute fresh produce they had ordered was delivered and stowed in the fridge and freezer, both now filled to the brim. *Aztec* was re-fuelled, and the jerry cans were filled and stowed. The outboard engine was removed from the dinghy and fixed to its travelling bracket, and the dinghy had its cover fitted before it was lifted out of the water onto the davits. As the final tasks, Skip paid the marina bill, then went along to the Customs and Immigration office to do the necessary official paperwork to clear them all out of America. Shortly afterwards, Skip fired up *Aztec's* engine, then they slipped their dock lines and headed out into the Hudson River.

Later that day, as the coastline of New Jersey dropped lower and lower on the horizon, Skip and Dom started to settle into their familiar sailing routine while Chuck became familiar with the boat and how to operate her.

Later still, the outlying shallow waters off Long Island had been left behind, and the depths they were sailing in were steadily increasing. They knew that they were now on the long haul back to the UK with only themselves to rely on, having to be totally independent and self-sufficient, irrespective of whatever Mother Nature decided to throw at them. From now on, it would be three hours on watch, six hours off watch including sleep time, every day for the next month and more until they reached their destination.

Even with three of them aboard, it would still be a demanding trip, with no physical points of reference whatsoever until Land's End came into view on the horizon. Any contact with the outside world would be restricted to calls on the VHF radio to passing freighters or cruise liners, or emergency phone calls via the SatPhone - something they hoped they wouldn't need to do.

They knew the Atlantic was a vast ocean, and the likelihood of them sighting another vessel along the way was slim, but to Skip and Dom, it was a familiar passage-making experience, and they knew that they could rely on each other come what may. Having Chuck on board as well was a real bonus.

---- 13 ----

Saturday 8th September
London

"Major incident in Antarctica!" screamed the
headlines. *"Global Energy reports the discovery of
unexplained seismic activity close to the Ross Ice Shelf."* The
detailed article, was almost word for word the press
release written by Terry Smart and approved by the
Global Energy board, and went on to explain that, *"An
earthquake-like event had caused major fissures to appear in
the Western Antarctic Ice Sheet and Ross Ice Shelf, several
miles long and hundreds of feet deep, and that one of Global
Energy's scientists had been dramatically rescued after the
remote research station he was working in only moments
before had tumbled into one of the crevasses and was lost."*

The phone lines were going crazy as shareholders,
the press, TV channels from around the world, and
various science organisations tried to glean more
information on the event. Global Energy had clearly
positioned themselves as the discoverers, and expert
commentators, on the hitherto unreported event and

Ray Bergman, Jeff Ramsey, Terry Smith and Digger James fielded calls throughout the morning as the news broke. Of course, the press was also asking to interview the unfortunate employee who was involved but were succinctly told that he was unavailable for comment and was taking an extended leave of absence. All questions would be addressed by the board.

About the same time that *Aztec* and her crew had finally cast off their dock lines and sailed away from New York, back in London Ray Bergman magnanimously congratulated himself on a potentially disastrous situation made good. The early feedback from the business press, which would critically influence the financial markets when they re-opened on Monday, was very positive and appeared to exonerate Global Energy from any blame. Indeed, the company was receiving praise for bringing the matter to the public's attention and attempting to explain what might or might not have happened.

Turning to his fellow directors, Ray said smugly, "Well Barbara and gentlemen, I think we can safely say that our announcement strategy couldn't have gone better. With the communications lockdown in McMurdo and now with Fallon out of the picture and unreachable on the high seas for the next few weeks, we should be in the clear. If we stick to our story, no-one will have any reason to doubt us, and by the time he gets back to the UK, the news will be stone cold."

"Should we lift the communication lock-down now then Ray?" queried Jeff.

"After the markets open on Monday, and assuming our stock hasn't crashed by then, I see no reason why not."

"The thing I still don't understand," said Digger, "was why no other seismic monitoring station has reported anything. We know that tremors can be picked up from around the world and something of this magnitude must surely have flagged up somewhere."

"I don't understand it either," commented Ray, "but I'm not going to look a gift horse in the mouth, so to speak. It rather suits our purposes that we were the first to bring it to the world's attention."

"Well I just hope it doesn't come back and bite us on the ass," interjected Jeff. "As we have now temporarily suspended the exploratory drilling, there hopefully won't be a repeat event, so things will die down and become yesterday's news."

"Yes, we'll give it a couple of weeks for everything to settle down and then think about recommencing the programme," closed Ray.

Little did the directors realise that similar data *had* been recorded elsewhere, and was being exchanged and analysed already, albeit within the scientific exploration community. It might not have made it into the popular press from these sources yet, but that didn't mean that the best minds in the world weren't analysing and deliberating the situation and trying to understand the cause.

The International Volcanology & Seismology Organisation (IVSO) had already contacted the Chairman of the Antarctic Treaty Organisation some days earlier to apprise him of the seismic readings associated with the event. While they had not reached any conclusions as to the cause of the tremor so far, Global Energy's headline grabbing article had certainly come to their attention and raised one or two eyebrows. Global Energy's attempt to highlight the situation and provide a somewhat simplistic theory on its cause had already ruffled a few feathers within the corridors of the IVSO. Indeed, it was unequivocally felt that the IVSO needed to correct the Global Energy viewpoint as soon as possible.

---- 14 ---

Monday 10th September
The Atlantic

Aztec was 300 miles east of New York. Skip, Chuck and Dom were just settling down to their evening meal. "Mmmm," murmured Chuck sniffing at the food on his plate. He loved his food, particularly fresh fish, and he had been looking forward to tucking into his dinner. Dom smiled at the compliment he had just unwittingly paid her.

They had had a bit of luck that day: Skip had been trolling a fishing line off the back of the boat and had managed to catch a decent sized Atlantic Pollock on a simple squid lure. Once the fish was landed on the deck, a drop of cheap gin in the gills saw its speedy and painless departure from the land of the living, and, more importantly, prevented the need to wash the decks down of the blood that was normally associated with killing a catch. Blood in the teak decking was a bugger to remove, and Dom didn't like to watch the process anyway.

"Great!" commented Skip when the fish was landed, "this will keep us going for a few days." He and Chuck had immediately set about gutting and portioning it up for cooking. Dom had dusted the fish in seasoned flour ready to pan fry it and served it with a green salad and some sautéed baby potatoes. It wouldn't be long before they exhausted their fresh food supplies and would be living on canned foods, so they would make the most of still having some fresh produce available.

They had become quite inventive with preparing meals on just three gas rings and an oven. Dom often wondered how quickly she would adjust to a five-burner, double oven on their return home. Living on board for the last three years had taught them a great deal about energy conservation, economy and scant use of water, power, food and fuel. When things are in short supply their value increases, and on a boat in the middle of an ocean, *everything* is in short supply.

Having the bonus of fresh fish was truly an unexpected feast. Countless attempts at fishing had proven fruitless in the past, maybe it was Chuck's lucky presence on board, or perhaps Skip was getting the hang of it at last! "Still, I must never look a gift-horse in the mouth," she thought to herself as she took another forkful of the tender white flesh.

So far, their trans-Atlantic crossing was running very slowly because of a lack of wind coming from the wrong direction. They were having to repeatedly tack across the wind, covering many miles but not actually making much way in terms of reducing the distance to their destination. With only enough fuel on board to recharge the batteries every day, their progress was really at the mercy of the weather, and the weather patterns were not typical of the season. By rights they should have been enjoying south-westerlies all the way home, but instead the breezes were still coming from the east.

Being out in the Atlantic with only a VHF radio and SatPhone, the crew of *Aztec* had no idea about the events that were happening around them in the wider world. Chuck had brought them up to speed about the happenings down in Antarctica over a couple of stiff gin cocktails on the night he arrived in New York, but since being at sea, the real world had withdrawn. What to eat, the weather patterns, the daily progress of the voyage, and the sighting of marine life had become the only real topics of conversation. Chuck had been going over the photos he took after the quake, and the captured data on his laptop, and the more he analysed it, the more he had withdrawn into his shell. He was obviously in a deeply reflective mood. Dom was itching to discuss what had happened with Chuck at more length, but she recognised he needed a few days or more to switch off and come to terms with life after his harrowing near-death experience.

"He'll talk to us when he's ready," Skip said to her as they were changing over watch in the evening. "Just give him time, Dom. I know patience is not your strong point, but on this occasion, you will just have to wait until he is ready to talk."

"I know," she replied, "but I am really worried about him. He's usually more open but he won't say what he is thinking about. He keeps looking at his laptop and muttering to himself, but when I ask him what he is looking at, he just closes it down and says that I wouldn't understand it."

"He's probably right," said Skip, "all those graphs and charts look alien to me, give me a nautical chart any day."

---- 15 ----

Tuesday 11th September

Global Energy's price on the stock market had held its own when the markets re-opened after the weekend, and everyone on the board of directors had breathed a sigh of relief. Full communication with McMurdo was back on stream again, and everything seemed to be back to normal. It was business as usual. No-one from Global had given any thought to what the state of play was out on the ice sheet itself, nor even contemplated sending a helicopter to fly out over it to have a look.

While the Global Energy directors had all but forgotten the incident in their scramble to avoid being blamed, the IVSO scientists certainly had not, and were continuing to monitor developments using satellite photography. It was considered too dangerous to send anyone out onto the ice sheet itself, after all, Global Energy had very nearly lost one of their valued scientists. The myriad crevasses now gave it the appearance of crazy-paving, so they weren't willing to risk lives. Even though there were no longer any new seismic readings to report, there was certainly some lateral movement in the adjacent giant Ross Ice Shelf.

What even the IVSO didn't realise was the full extent of what was happening on WAIS hidden from sight at great depths. Global Energy's sonic blasting programme had set up a perfect resonance within the earth's crust underneath the ice sheet, one that had amplified itself through the rock formation and had triggered a rupturing of the mantle. They had no idea about the magma escaping the earth's crust, melting the underside of the ice sheet and forming a honeycomb of ever-growing caverns as the ice melted away; nor of the sheer scale of the enormous volumes of meltwater escaping from under the ice sheet. This meltwater was flowing under the glaciers and acting as a lubricant, accelerating the flow of the ice sheet, and pushing away the adjacent ice shelf as the end of the glaciers calved and fell away.

Slowly at first, but steadily gaining speed, a huge portion of the Ross Ice shelf was beginning to break away from the landmass.

---- 16 ----

Wednesday 12th September
600 miles from New York

Chuck awoke refreshed after just under six hours of sleep and was feeling more like his old self. He had taken the midnight to 3am watch, and he had used the time effectively. He had thought long and hard about what had happened to him and had decided on a plan of action, and he was itching to discuss it with Skip and Dom when he joined them in the cockpit for breakfast.

Their progress aboard *Aztec* was still slow going. The winds were still much lighter than they had hoped for, and still from the wrong direction, but they were all happy to be counting the miles down to their return to the UK with whatever progress they were making.

"So, are you looking forward to getting back home then Dom?" asked Skip. "Do you think you'll settle back down to real life again without too much trouble?"

This was something they had discussed on and off on several occasions during their three years away from home. Would it be possible to go back to their former lives once more and be content with a localised existence after their adventures? They had been in some interesting situations along the way, enough to test the strongest relationships, and they had come through them all relatively unscathed. Most people couldn't even dream of experiencing some of the things that they had.

"To be honest," said Dom, "yes. I'm ready for a change. That's not to say I want to sell *Aztec* though, but the thought of all that extra space and the chance of a bath when I want one is heavenly!" she laughed.

Skip was inwardly very relieved to hear that Dom wanted to keep *Aztec* and not sell her to the highest bidder like an unwanted chattel, she was his pride and joy, much more than a mobile floating home, she was a living extension of his personality. She could sail like a bitch some days, but on other occasions when the winds were favourable, she simply lifted her skirts and flew through the water with consummate ease. Sadly, that hadn't happened so far on this trip and their progress home was excruciatingly slow.

"Good morning world!" Chuck announced as he poked his head above the companion way. "Someone's in a great mood," muttered Skip, tired after his recent watch duty and in need of some sleep. "Ignore him,"

Dom counselled Chuck. "He's always grouchy when he's tired. Grab some breakfast and come and join me in the cockpit."

Chuck went below into the galley to see what there was for him to eat. Most of the fridge was taken up with meats, cheeses and other dairy products, but looking through the dry store cupboards, he found some cereals, helped himself to a bowlful and sliced a banana on the top. Pouring some UHT milk from a carton over the top, he was ready.

Ten minutes later, with Skip snugly tucked up in his berth, Chuck started to outline his thoughts and plan to Dom.

"I know I've been a bit subdued these last few days Sis, maybe it's delayed shock, I don't know. But I finally got my head together on my last graveyard watch and I have decided what I need to do."

"I'm glad to hear that, Bro. I have been worried about you: It's not like you to be so withdrawn."

"Sorry about that, but some things have been preying on my mind. The more I think about it, the more certain I am that Global Energy *was* behind the incident on the WAIS. They are the only ones undertaking any exploratory activity in that part of the ice sheet and while their routine drilling and blasting generates spikes on the seismograph, there was nothing scheduled for that day Dom – it was a Saturday. The spikes I saw are unexplained by their routine operations," he finished.

"So, it must have been a natural cause then, or do you think they were aftershocks associated with the previous day's drilling?" she queried.

"Doubtful. There have never been any aftershocks before and the read-outs didn't look like an earthquake to me. Dom, if I tell you something, can you keep it to yourself? It might even be dangerous for you to know."

"Of course, you can tell me anything Chuck, you know that. And for your information, I can look after myself."

"Okay, but maybe you should fill Skip in later. When I was in McMurdo just before my last tour of duty out to the Global Energy research station, I wanted to see Graham Platt, my line manager, so I went along to his office. He wasn't there so I thought I'd leave him a note. When I was writing it, leaning on his desk, I noticed that the file on which the notepad was resting had a title of 'PROJECT UNDERMINE' and was marked 'CONFIDENTIAL'. I know I shouldn't have, but I couldn't resist looking to see what it was about."

"So, what was it about? It all sounds very cloak and dagger," commented Dom.

"It was a top-secret report about an experimental and unproven approach to extract methane gases that have been trapped within the ice using something called sonic blasting. And from what the report said, Global Energy have jumped the gun and started some unofficial but limited use of this approach on the WAIS. I remember the schedule of blasting I saw suggested they were active on the day of the tremor, so I reckon it must be connected."

"Crikey Chuck. Does anyone realise you saw that report? You could be in deep water if they know you did," said Dom.

"No, I was really careful. I made sure no-one saw me, and I haven't ever discussed it, so I don't think anyone knows. Certainly, no-one has inferred they do. But the fact remains that I *do* know, and if it was the cause of the quake, then the programme has got to be stopped before even more damage is caused. Oh, and there was one other thing Dom."

"What on earth now?"

"Well, you know I told you they took my laptop away, and that I had taken a copy of the data on a USB stick? Global Energy don't know I have it."

"Thank God, Chuck, you'd be a big threat to their reputation if they knew. Please tell me you won't tell them. They'll fire you if they ever find out."

"No, I won't. Something made me hold back in the meeting when I could have told them. I don't know if they suspected anything as they did offer counselling and hypnotherapy to help me overcome my trauma. Do you think they were hoping to find out more information from me when I was under?"

"Who knows, but one thing I do know is that you mustn't ever let on to anyone that you have that data Chuck," Dom replied.

"But equally, I can't just keep quiet if they're putting the Antarctic at risk. There could be consequences for the world that we don't know about. What I need to do is fully analyse the data on the USB stick and compare it with output from genuine earthquakes to see what the key differences are. Once I've done that, I will be in a much better position to know whether Global Energy are culpable in this."

"Well I agree you shouldn't jump to conclusions before you're sure of your facts, or at least as sure as you can be. Let's see what you can glean from the data you have on your laptop in the next day or two."

---- 17 ----

Friday 14th September
IVSO HQ, Washington DC

"So, let me get this straight," said Ken Brooke, CEO of IVSO, "you're telling me the data analysis has shown that the incident down on WAIS on 1st September *wasn't* a natural occurrence?"

"That's correct, Ken," responded Keith Mortimer IVSO Chief Scientist. "In my opinion, there's no way that tremor was the result of an earthquake or plate shift."

"And that means what exactly?" Ken queried.

"Well, it means someone, or something, triggered the event and that also means that they could easily repeat it. Whether it was done knowingly, or it was an accident, we can't be sure."

"I can't see what benefit it gives anyone for it to be deliberate, unless we're dealing with some crazy terrorist threat. Do you think that's at all likely?"

"I've absolutely no idea on that front, but I would have thought that if a terrorist organisation was behind it for some ill-gotten means, they would have declared their hand by now. It is, after all, nearly two weeks since the event took place and there has been nothing similar since."

"Hmmm," commented Ken, "that would seem to suggest it was an accidental occurrence which is by far the lesser of two evils. That's not to say we don't need to find out what and who was behind it to ensure we don't have a repeat performance. Have we got a full assessment of the direct results of the event yet?"

"We have been continually monitoring the situation, largely from the air and by satellite as the incidence of crevasses on both the WAIS and the adjacent Ross Ice Shelf makes it too dangerous to send any land-based reconnaissance out. What we're seeing from above is that the front edge of the Ross Ice Shelf has moved over ten miles into the sea in the last week and continues to do so, which is many times quicker than normal. As you know, the ice shelf acts as a 'brake' for the glaciers flowing off the WAIS and controls the extent to which the icebergs calve. Our best estimates at this stage suggest that we might see an increase in the number of icebergs calved this season but nothing more. When the snows come at the end of the warm season next year, I think the crevasses should fill and re-freeze and the status quo will be regained," Keith explained, "but quite what will happen during the summer months I really don't know."

Ken thought for a moment, then said, "I think we should put something in this month's *The Scientist* magazine for the scientific community. We need to counter Global Energy's somewhat spurious article with more definitive information based on scientific fact rather than mere speculation. Can you pull together an article for it, Keith?"

"No problem Ken. The deadline is end of play today and publication is Monday, so I'll get straight on it. But how do we identify who or what was behind it?"

"That's a difficult one. If it was a man-made event, then the only organisation that undertake any sort of activity down there is Global Energy, but I just can't see what they would possibly gain from this kind of thing. They've been drilling on that part of the WAIS for two years with nothing unusual to report so far, so I just can't see it being anything to do with them. I'm sure that they know they will lose their licence if they do anything untoward. I'm at a loss to be honest. I guess I could give their CEO a call and discuss the matter with him as a first step," said Ken.

"There is also one other factor to ponder as well," he continued. "The Southern Ocean Weather Buoy has recorded a noticeable increase in sea level. Do you think this is anything to do with the WAIS tremor?"

"Possibly. Our data shows that the air temperature over the WAIS has remained average for this time of year so there is no reason for us to see a noticeable increase in sea level. Maybe it *is* connected, although there haven't been any more tremors."

"Well, we'd better continue to monitor the situation in the weeks to come. We don't want anything unexpected happening and biting us on the backside," closed Ken.

---- 18 ----

Monday 17ᵗʰ September
mid Atlantic

1300 miles from New York, Chuck, Skip and Dom were having to manage without a cooked meal and were dining on soup and sandwiches instead. After several days of light winds, the Atlantic had hit back with a vengeance. High winds, gale force 8, and big seas had come out of nowhere making for a hard sail. Things that were not fastened down securely were flying around the saloon and galley on *Aztec*, including the crew members if they didn't always maintain a firm hand-hold. One of the basic rules of sailing 'one hand for the boat, and one hand for yourself', was forefront in their minds. The one good thing coming from the bad weather was that the wind had veered to the south; still not the south-westerlies they'd been hoping for but a damn sight easier to sail in than the easterlies they had been experiencing to date.

"How're you doing Dom?" Skip asked as he came up into the cockpit to take his next three-hour shift on watch. "I've been better," she replied. "The sea state is too much for the auto-helm and so I've been steering manually for the last three hours, and I'm shattered."

"Well, I'll take over now so get down below for some shut-eye," instructed Skip. Gratefully, Dom undid her safety harness that tethered her to the cockpit, unzipped and slipped out of her life-jacket, and carefully made her way to her bunk. With Chuck coming on watch in three hours' time she could get her full six hours of sleep unless something untoward required her presence on deck to respond to an emergency. She nestled down into her sleeping bag and rolled against the lee cloth for stability. "Do I really like sailing?" were her last thoughts before sleep rapidly overtook her.

She returned to the cockpit five and a half hours later to relieve Chuck just before the end of his watch and was pleased to have a chance to catch up with him. The impact of the watch rota system and sudden deterioration in the weather meant they hadn't really had much chance to continue their conversation of last week.

"Wow, the last eighteen hours have been a bit of a roller-coaster ride, haven't they?" she opened. "How are you feeling Chuck?"

"You know me Sis, I'm a bit queasy to be honest, but it's not too bad if I stay on the helm. Well, either that or flat on my back asleep!" Chuck teased. "I do find the solitude and personal challenge very cathartic though," he continued, "a great chance to reflect on things and clear the mind. Before the storm came I spent my time very productively over the last few days looking at the data. I'm now certain Global Energy's mysterious sonic blasting activity is to blame."

"Cripes, Chuck. So, what next?"

"Well there's not much I can do from the middle of the Atlantic, but when we get back, I've got to do something. At the very least Global Energy have got to stop their sonic blasting programme before the whole ice sheet fractures into pieces. The big question is: Do I tackle Global Energy directly and risk them ignoring me, swatting me away like an irritating fly, or try for a more indirect approach through a scientific body, or even the press?"

"If you adopted the latter approach, who would you contact that would believe you?" asked Dom.

"Well, with the data I have on the USB stick, plus the somewhat grainy photos I have on my phone, I have the evidence I need to back-up my findings, but I would need a copy of the 'PROJECT UNDERMINE' blasting schedule to tie things together. Whether I'll be able to get my hands on it without raising suspicion is the million-dollar question. I'd need to go back to McMurdo to try to get it, and that would be a difficult exercise. I'm sure it will be securely locked away if it even still exists given what has happened. I know I would certainly 'deep six' it if I was responsible. As to who to contact if I was able to get my hands on the file, I'm not sure: I don't really have any contacts in either the press or the scientific community."

"Skip might be able to help you there, Chuck. Do you remember his friend Julie Grant from university? I think you might have heard him talking about his former heartthrob, tall, slim, pretty with dark hair … you get the picture! She read Ecology and Geology? Well, she didn't exactly follow a research career but, instead, she went into science journalism and is now the Science correspondent for *The Telegraph*. She could be an ideal person to speak to. What do you think?"

"Perfect," said Chuck. "I'll continue to work on the data as we go in readiness for meeting her when we get back. When do you think that will be by the way?"

"Hard to say Chuck. We've completed about 1300 miles of a 3100-mile journey and so much depends on the weather. If the winds stay from the south, or even better swing around to the south-west, we should make much better progress. So maybe another twelve days or so?" Dom suggested. "Whatever the weather and however long it takes us, I don't think you should put the cat among the pigeons this soon."

Chuck accepted this viewpoint and, being at the end of his watch, decided to head below to steal some sleep, leaving Dom to wrestle with the end of the storm as it passed over them.

---- 19 ----

Tuesday 18th September
London

Ray Bergman was fuming. His Director of Research, Digger James, had just brought him the October issue of *The Scientist* and there on page 3 was an article by Keith Mortimer, IVSO's Chief Scientist, refuting Global Energy's opinion that the recent earthquake incident in Antarctica had a natural cause.

"How the hell dare he, the bearded idiot?" stormed Ray, poking at the photograph of Keith that accompanied the article. "That jumped up little bastard is going to knock millions off our share value with this throw-away piece of crap that is wrapped up neatly to look like fact. Who the hell has been talking? Jayne!" he barked at his PA. "Get Jeff Ramsey in here right now!"

Jeff had been in a meeting with Global Energy's Director of Operations, but when Jayne interrupted them he knew he needed to jump to Ray's command and terminated his meeting. Walking into Ray's office he was greeted by a barrage of questions. "Have you seen this article Jeff? It completely undermines all the good work we did last weekend in one stroke of the pen. Those interfering bastards at IVSO have concluded that the tremor on WAIS was man-made. And guess who they've put firmly in the cross-hairs? Yes, you've got it, us!" he ranted. "What the hell do we do now?"

As ever, Jeff, after another of Ray's outbursts, spoke calmly and reasonably, trying to diffuse the tension in the room. "Ray, there's not a lot we can do now as the article is already out there. If we publish a response as a knee-jerk reaction it could only serve to make us look guilty. My suggestion would be to get the legal department to read the article and see whether anything that has been written is libellous. If so, we can consider demanding a retraction, otherwise I think we might be better riding it out and hope that the popular press don't pick up on it. It is only in a scientific journal after all."

Jeff's calm, considered, common-sense approach as ever soothed Ray's raw nerves, and after a minute or two he called down the company lawyer to start the ball rolling.

Sadly, for all at Global Energy, Jeff's common sense was bordering on the naïve on this occasion, and it wasn't only the scientific community that had read the publication. Julie Grant had read the article in *The Scientist* too. Her gut reaction was that there might be more to this than originally appeared from the Global Energy announcement in the press a week earlier. She printed out the two articles and laid them side by side on her desk. Clearly from the content being so widely different, some further questions needed to be asked. Her instinct was telling her that there was a real story here. She picked up the pages with her highlighted sections and went into her editor's office to discuss it.

Mary Roberts was no pushover. She was a successful editor with years of experience and, despite being a feisty five feet two in her stockinged feet, she would take on anyone who stood in the way of a good story. Listening to Julie's ideas she gave no comment, simply reading the articles that Julie had placed on the desk before her. Julie sat patiently, saying nothing. She knew how Mary operated, and she had to give her time to make up her mind. After a few moments, Mary leaned back in her chair and said, "Well done, Julie. It's got legs. There might be something worth pursuing here. Let's poke a stick into a few holes and see what bleeds."

"OK, thanks Mary. How much time do you want me to spend on it?"

"You can have a week, then report back to me with anything you find, and we'll take it from there."

Retrieving her reports from Mary, Julie went back to her desk and set out her draft action plan. She had spoken to Keith Mortimer of the IVSO before on earlier articles he had written and already had his contact details in her address list, but Global Energy's people had been off her radar until now. She Googled 'Global Energy' to find their homepage as a starting point in her research. She would need to know as much as possible about the company's various mining activities in Antarctica, and the names and contact details of all the right people to talk to.

---- 20 ----

Thursday 20th September
London

Julie Grant arrived in the Victoria offices of *The Telegraph* bright and early. She had a conference call scheduled with Keith Mortimer later that afternoon to allow for the time difference between London and Washington DC, and in the meantime was going to try to get hold of Ray Bergman and Henry "Digger" James at Global Energy to try to get their comments on the discrepancies in the two articles.

She'd already found out a lot of background information in the last few days: On Global Energy's Antarctic activity, and its board of directors, and she knew that Ray Bergman wouldn't be an easy nut to crack if his reputation was to be believed. Still, she'd dealt with a lot of difficult individuals in her career and she had something of a reputation herself for winkling out information from those people who didn't want to give anything away. She liked a challenge, and this would certainly be one of those.

Tall, slim, and attractive with lustrous dark brown hair tumbling over her shapely shoulders, she wasn't your usual newspaper hack. Several of her interviewees had completely underestimated her in the past, mistakenly seeing her as a well-dressed woman and not recognising the intelligence behind the smoky blue eyes and naturally long lashes. Her career had very much curtailed her private life, and on occasion she did regret the lack of a partner, but today wasn't one of those days. She was firing on all cylinders and ready to lock horns with Global Energy if need be.

"Good morning, could you put me through to Ray Bergman please?" she asked the friendly receptionist answering her call.

"Can I ask who's calling please?" came the reply.

"Julie Grant of *The Telegraph*."

"Hold the line please and I'll transfer you to Mr Bergman's PA, Jayne Grey." Julie made a note of Jayne's name. It was always better to be able to address the PA personally.

Jayne Grey came on the line, as coolly efficient and inscrutable as ever. "Good morning Ms Grant, I understand you would like to speak to Mr Bergman. Could I ask you what it is in connection with?"

"Good morning to you too, Ms Grey. It's concerning Global Energy's recent article in the *Independent*, and the subsequent report published in *The Scientist* by the IVSO." She knew she would get nowhere with the PA if she didn't tell her what the call was about: CEOs routinely wouldn't accept calls without a clear picture of what they were about to be questioned on in this age of the free press.

"Hold the line please Ms Grant, and I'll see if Mr Bergman is available."

Julie was kept hanging on the line for several minutes before Jayne Grey smoothly came back to her with apologies for the delay in locating Mr Bergman and saying she would put the call through now.

"Ms Grant, Ray Bergman here. I understand you want to speak to me?"

"I do, it's in connection with the article you published on the 8th September concerning the incident down on the Western Antarctic Ice Sheet. You know the one I mean?" she enquired mildly.

"Yes, yes, of course I do. A terrible natural disaster which we felt Global Energy were obliged to bring to the world's attention. As you know, we, at Global Energy, have the sole drilling rights for that area on the WAIS and we suffered great losses in the incident, nearly including the life of one of our valued scientific personnel," Ray continued without pausing for breath.

Julie let him spew, recognising his need to establish the upper hand in the conversation by attempting to dominate it, and her. She wasn't going to play ball.

"Yes, I read your article with some interest at the time, but I have had reason to revisit it following the more recent report in *The Scientist*. What are your views on this contradictory article?"

"That report was just one man's opinion on what may or may not have happened based on data from remote seismic stations. We, at Global Energy, have the data from the actual tremor zone itself, and our scientists are equally as qualified as anyone at IVSO to know what happened. I'm afraid IVSO are commenting without understanding the full picture."

"So what response are you planning, if any, to clarify the matter?" she pushed.

"We feel there is no need for a reply. As I say, the article in *The Scientist* is just one man's opinion based on incomplete data."

"A mutual exchange of data would therefore seem to be in the public's interest I would have thought. When are you planning to share your findings with IVSO?" Julie knew the value of asking open questions, ones that couldn't be answered with a straight yes or no. "Maybe, it would be a good idea to form a joint working party?"

Ray's temper was near boiling at this point – she had him cornered, not something he was used to – and he didn't know how to respond other than, "No comment." He needed to buy himself some time to get Global Energy's story straight. The legal team had confirmed that there was nothing libellous in the IVSO article, so he had to tread carefully to avoid any repercussions coming Global Energy's way.

As soon as she got Ray's 'no comment' Julie knew she had him on the ropes. There was definitely something being withheld: A man with a clear conscience who is confident in his own results doesn't fall back so quickly to a 'no comment' response.

"Oh? I'm sorry to hear that Mr Bergman. I thought it would be in everyone's best interest to have full transparency of data on this occasion. It's not as though the IVSO are your competitors after all, is it?"

"I said no comment, young lady, and that's all I will say," came the terse reply.

"I'd very much appreciate the opportunity to explore this subject with you some more face to face Mr Bergman. When would that be possible?"

The response was a click on the line: Ray Bergman had hung up on her.

"One down, one more to go," she thought.

After a restorative cup of coffee and a blueberry muffin - a late breakfast really - Julie picked up the phone again to try Digger James, Global Energy's Director of Research. Unlike his CEO, it was unlikely he would have had the same media training, so she was hoping to winkle some choice facts out of the conversation.

Surprisingly, the receptionist put her straight through to his office without questioning her on the reason for the call.

"Good morning Mr James. My name is Julie Grant of *The Telegraph* and I'd like the opportunity to chat to you about the recent incident on WAIS. I have a masters' degree in Geology and am intrigued by what has been going on. What's your take on the whole thing?"

"Good morning, Miss Grant, and may I say how nice it is to speak to a young lady with an interest in a subject which is close to my heart," rumbled Digger. "It was certainly an unusual occurrence," he continued, "and one to which I'm afraid there are no definitive answers. Analysis of our data to the best of our in-house abilities suggests it was a naturally triggered disaster, but as usual with these events, it is not conclusive."

"And would that data be available to an interested party? I would find it fascinating to have the chance to look at it."

"What a good idea," Digger responded in a non-committal sort of way. "I'll see what I can do."

"That would be so kind of you. While I've got you on the line, and not wishing to sound at all impudent, what did you make of the IVSO article?" she probed.

"On a scientific level I do have some sympathies with Dr Mortimer's finding, he is after all an esteemed authority in his field."

"What does that mean, exactly?" Julie wondered, but before she had the chance to pose the question, Digger came back on the line.

"Well my eleven o'clock meeting has just arrived. It's been a pleasure talking to you, Miss Grant," and with that, Digger was gone.

"The crafty old devil," Julie thought, "friendly and charming but giving nothing away. Damn, he's obviously had some media training after all."

Pushing back from her desk, Julie stared out over the grey rooftops of Victoria Station and pondered her next move with Global Energy. Maybe a call to McMurdo was a good idea: They certainly wouldn't have had any media training down there!

---- 21 ----

Thursday 20th September
Washington DC

Sitting at his desk in the IVSO head office, Keith Mortimer was dealing with his administration, something he tended to put off for days on end as it was his least favourite task. He was pleased with how the article in *The Scientist* had turned out, and he felt it presented a far more balanced viewpoint to that published by Global Energy. The feedback he had received from the scientific community had been very positive indeed. That was one of the benefits of working for a "not for profit" organisation ... accuracy and fact were all important, and not shareholder value. He had dedicated the best part of his working life to IVSO and now, in his late fifties, he was a respected and personable figure in his field.

He was just pondering the next task on his list when his phone rang.

"Dr Keith Mortimer here," he answered.

"Hello Dr Mortimer, this is Julie, Julie Grant, from the UK *Telegraph* here. I hope you've got a few minutes to talk to me?"

"Lovely to hear from you Julie. How is the weather over on that side of the pond? I know how you Brits like to talk about the weather!"

Swallowing a grimace, Julie laughingly responded, "We're not all the same you know! And just for your information, it's rather grey over here today. But that's not why I called you. I wanted to speak to you about your article that was published in *The Scientist* earlier this week concerning the tremor down on WAIS."

"Ah yes, I thought it might have caught your attention."

"The thing is Dr Mortimer, I've been comparing your article to that written by Global Energy the week before and there are some fundamental differences between the articles in the interpretation of the seismographic data. May I ask how you drew your conclusion that it wasn't a natural disaster?"

"That can be simply answered my dear, and please call me Keith: Dr Mortimer is so formal. I compared the seismic readings with those of every other polar earthquake on record, and the fact is that the two sets of data bear no resemblance whatsoever. A natural disaster has a far longer build up and dissipation than this event showed. It was a spike that had to be caused by man."

"I don't know if you remember Keith, but I have a masters' degree in Geology and I would be very interested in seeing your recorded data from the tremor if you would be prepared to share it with me? I'll undertake not to publish anything without speaking to you about it first," she reassured.

"Well Julie, on that basis, I see no problem with you having a copy. Give me a day or two to tidy it up and I'll send it over to you attached to an email."

"That would be great, thank you! One last question Keith: Are IVSO still monitoring the situation down on WAIS and, if so, can you tell me what the latest position is?"

"We are indeed keeping a close eye on developments, and apart from a shift in the position of the Ross Ice Shelf and a noticeable increase in sea level, there is nothing else to see. Plus, we haven't recorded any further seismic spikes of note. Does that answer your question Julie?"

"Yes, it does, and thank you again for your candid views Keith. Goodbye," Julie replied as she rang off.

---- 22 ----

Saturday 22nd September
mid-Atlantic

"We're over halfway home!" Skip shouted from the navigation station as *Aztec* continued her eastward passage toward the UK. They'd made good progress during the last week and they had even sighted a cruise ship heading in the opposite direction one night, lights all ablaze. Chuck had been on watch and had woken Skip to check if there was anything he needed to do in the circumstances; change course, fire off a flare, or anything like that. It had made Skip smile.

"Chuck my boy, you did the right thing waking me up. We don't need to do anything at all really, apart from keep a watchful eye on things. They probably picked us up on their radar and are fully aware that we are here. What we will do though, is call them up on the radio, have a chat, and ask them for the latest weather report."

The cruise ship happily obliged, and Skip got his weather forecast for the following forty-eight hours. It was a bonus he hadn't expected, and the good news was that there were no more storms in the offing.

They'd enjoyed a good few days sailing, bowling along at an average six and a half knots with the wind finally veering to the point where it was coming from slightly behind them. Even though it was getting cooler at night, the sun was still shining during the day and the cloud-free skies after dark were filled with myriad stars. And that was usually after the most spectacular sunsets.

The crew of *Aztec* were completely settled into their onboard routine now, and they were working well as a team. Dom was creating some tasty meals in the galley, and Chuck was looking tanned, healthy, and relaxed. He'd been studiously reviewing the seismic data during the last week, looking at it from every angle possible to test out his hypothesis that Global Energy had caused the disaster. His conclusions were still the same: The blame was laid firmly at Global Energy's feet.

Now that he was certain he was right in his findings he was keen to start the ball rolling by challenging Global Energy about their secret sonic blasting. He had convinced Skip and Dom that he should phone Julie Grant once they got back to England to tell her what he suspected and get her involved in exposing Global

Energy. It might mean the end of his job with them, but his conscience was telling him he had to do this. In the meantime, there was nothing much to do apart from watch the constantly moving sea and look out for the dolphins and whales that were frequent visitors to the yacht.

---- 23 ----

Monday 24th September
London

True to his word, Keith Mortimer had compiled a file of the IVSO findings and had emailed it across to Julie over the weekend. Opening the attachments, she reconciled herself to at least a full day of analysis to try to make sense of the material. Typical of scientists Keith, or someone, had made small annotations in spidery handwriting against the graphs and plots that covered every page. She would suffer from eye-strain after this.

"This is going to take an age. I'd better update Mary on progress before I make a start."

She'd reflected on her conversations with the Global Energy directors over the weekend and felt it was pointless trying to get a face-to-face interview with either of them – they were unlikely to grant her one. And they were even more unlikely to give anything away, but she wanted to run this by Mary for a second opinion. Maybe a phone call down to McMurdo might be a good idea, where people might be less reticent to share information? Global Energy's article had talked of the dramatic rescue of one of its scientists off the ice sheet, without naming any names. If she could at least find out the name of the scientist who had had the lucky escape, and engineer an interview with him or her, she would have struck the mother lode. Collecting her thoughts, she set out for Mary's office.

"Good morning Mary. Have you got a few minutes for me to give you an update?" Julie asked from the doorway to Mary's office after tapping on the door frame.

"Yes, come in Julie. How was your weekend?"

"Fine thanks Mary. I used the time to get my thoughts together on the Antarctic disaster situation in the light of my conversations with Keith Mortimer, the Chief Scientist from IVSO, and a couple of the directors from Global Energy. I have to say, Keith Mortimer was far more forthcoming than Global Energy. Both Ray Bergman, the CEO, and his research cohort, Digger James gave me the run around. In fact, Bergman hung up on me in a bit of a strop ... it could be a sign of a guilty conscience."

"Sounds like it could well be," affirmed Mary. "What are you planning next?"

"Well, that's what I want to run by you. My instinct tells me I'll get no further with the Global Energy head office. I've asked for a copy of the seismic data that they recorded from the disaster, but I have basically been told I can't have it. The IVSO have, however, emailed over their data, and I plan on studying that today, but to make this investigation stick, I really need to get hold of the comparative data from Global Energy."

"Agreed. Do you have any ideas of how to get it?"

"Well I was wondering about trying to contact some Global Energy staff down at McMurdo. Their article talks about the dramatic rescue of one of their scientists, conveniently unnamed in the article, by the company's helicopter pilot. And presumably there must be someone from the communications side of things in the know, maybe the radio operator? There can't be more than one or two pilots down there, and probably only one or two radio operators, and so if I can contact them, I might be able to get the name of the rescued scientist and track them down. What do you think? Is it worth a visit, or at the very least a phone call?"

"Well the budget can't support a visit at this stage, but it can certainly run to a few phone calls. Good idea … get on to it Julie." Mary picked up her pen and looked down at the articles she was editing on her desk: Julie's five minutes were over, and she made a tactical withdrawal.

Back in her office, with a mountain of IVSO data in front of her, Julie decided to put off making a start until after she'd tracked down phone numbers for the McMurdo station. There would probably be no land lines or mobile phone reception down there, so satellite phones would likely be the answer. She'd get one of the paper's researchers to contact the satellite companies to start the ball rolling and make a start on the data analysis while she waited for the number.

Five hours later, somewhat cross-eyed, and with a brain that felt as though it would burst, Julie got the first glimmer of hope since starting the analysis of the IVSO data. From everything she'd studied for her degree and her experience in the years since, the conclusions drawn by Keith Mortimer appeared to be sound. It would take some very convincing contradictory evidence to demonstrate it was, in fact, a natural disaster. She really needed to speak to someone down at McMurdo, and fast.

Checking her email, she was pleased to see a message from the paper's research team giving her a primary contact number for the communications room at McMurdo. "Perfect," she thought. "I wonder what the time difference is down there?"

Looking on Wikipedia Julie determined that McMurdo was eleven hours behind GMT, but with almost constant darkness in the Antarctic winter months, she did wonder whether time differences really mattered. Maybe she should leave it until 6pm UK time meaning it would be 7am in Antarctica, or possibly 6am since the UK was in British Summer Time.

"Christ, this is complicated!" she thought.

Glancing at her watch, she saw it was close to 3pm, and she hadn't had any lunch. Stretching her arms above her head to ease the knots in her neck and spine, Julie decided to pop out for a sandwich and drink. That was one of the joys of working in London: It was possible to get food and drink virtually twenty-four hours a day.

Returning to her desk an hour later, Julie realised she had two more hours before trying to contact McMurdo and so decided to work on the questions she wanted to obtain answers to. Careful wording and open questions were the order of the day.

---- 24 ----

Monday 24th September
McMurdo Station

Life appeared to have settled back down into its usual routine at McMurdo after the drama of over three weeks ago. After the loss of their research station on WAIS there had been no call for anyone at Global Energy to head out over to the west side of the Ross Ice Shelf until the replacement unit arrived, and so no-one had. Routine drilling and blasting had continued north of the ice shelf but the secret sonic blasting behind 'PROJECT UNDERMINE' had been halted for the time being.

In the communications room, Greg was getting towards the end of his shift. He was feeling tired and was ready for bed. The radio room was manned 24/7 in three shifts and this week he was on midnight to 8am, his least favourite shift: He was by no stretch of the imagination a night owl. Nothing much happened on the night shift, something that made it even harder for Greg to stay awake, even with a plethora of video games to amuse him, so the ringing of the SatPhone jolted him out of his reverie.

"Good morning. McMurdo communications centre. Greg speaking," he answered.

"Oh, good morning Greg. My name is Julie Grant and I work for *The Telegraph* newspaper in the UK. I was hoping to contact the helicopter pilot who made the dramatic rescue mission of the scientist off the WAIS a few weeks ago. He sounds like a bit of an unsung hero to me and he has been nominated for a courage award by our readers, so I wondered if I could speak to him?" she queried. She'd decided her strategy would be to play to male pride rather than a direct line of questioning.

As a friend of Bill Bond, the helicopter pilot, Greg was delighted. He, along with several other staff, did feel Bill deserved some recognition for what after all had been an incredible rescue achievement.

"Yes of course, Julie, is it? That's wonderful news. Bill Bond is a great friend of mine and we were all very proud of him rescuing Chuck so bravely, with no real concern for his own safety," Greg opened, and Julie quickly noted the two names Greg had inadvertently given away in his pleasure for Bill. "Actually, I was the radio operator on duty that day and took the call when then whole thing kicked off," he continued, wondering if he might also get a mention.

"Bingo," thought Julie, "it works every time. The opportunity to get your name in the press always opens mouths."

"It must have been a very tense situation," prompted Julie.

"You're telling me," came the immediate reply. "Chuck came on the SatPhone talking about a sudden earth tremor and asking to be airlifted off the ice sheet, and within minutes the whole thing seemed to be fracturing around him. We scrambled the helicopter as soon as we could, but it was touch and go whether Bill would make it in time or not. I wouldn't have wanted to have been either Bill or Chuck in that situation, I can tell you."

"Chuck is a rather unusual name for a scientist," Julie commented. "Is he American?"

"No," Greg laughed. "It's all to do with his travel sickness. Chuck ... he regularly throws up, do you get it? His real name is Charles, Charlie Fallon."

"Ah, I see. Well I'd better ask you to put me through to Bill Bond if you don't mind, but, would it be possible to contact you again if I need a quote for the article?" she asked.

"No problem at all Julie. The name's Greg Norman by the way, you know, like the golfer? I'll put you through to Bill now."

While he was a pleasant and polite man, Bill wasn't quite as forthcoming as Greg. Obviously pleased that his achievement had been recognised, he was more circumspect in his comments and Julie rang off having gleaned little more from him than she already knew. The lack of information from Bill didn't really bother her: The supposed article she was writing was a ruse anyway to find out the name of the scientist involved, and she'd got his name without really having to ask for it. Result! Now the real work could begin.

---- 25 ----

Wednesday 26th September London

Julie had been busy the whole of Tuesday, writing up her notes and completing her analysis of the IVSO data. Her conclusions remained the same as those of Keith Mortimer. She'd also enlisted the help of one of the paper's researchers again to track down Charlie 'Chuck' Fallon and couldn't believe her eyes when his contact details and family history were emailed through to her. Good old 'Chuck' was only the brother-in-law of Skip, her old boyfriend from university days. "What a small world," she thought.

Having tried Chuck's home number several times to no avail, she decided to try to get hold of Skip instead and was rifling through her old telephone book to find his number. She hadn't spoken to him for over five years and hoped the number she had would still be valid.

"Oh well, best give it a try." Dialling the number, she had no great expectation of anyone answering and was surprised when a female voice said, "Hello?"

"Oh, hello. My name is Julie Grant. Is Skip there? We're old friends from university days."

"I'm afraid the owners of the property are away. I'm their tenant," came the reply.

"Oh, do you have a contact number for them?"

"My only contact is through the letting agents. I can give you their number if you like?"

Having noted down the number she called the letting agents. Julie had to content herself with the agents agreeing to forward a message to Skip with her contact details, asking him to get in touch. There was no more she could do until she heard back from them or him.

Picking up her file on the case, Julie went along to give Mary her report. She had after all been given clearance to spend one week on the matter and that was now up. Entering Mary's office, she found her boss habitually busy and with a frown on her face.

"Yes," she barked out, "what have you got for me Julie?"

"Some good progress actually Mary. You know I got nowhere with the Global Energy executives and so I planned to call the McMurdo station instead? Well, I went with a 'your pilot has been nominated by our readers for an award' approach and hit pay dirt with the first person I spoke to. None other than the radio operator who handled the emergency calls on the day, and who is a close friend of the pilot. In his pride for his buddy, he inadvertently told me the name of the scientist involved, the only information I was really after. And, it gets better! It turns out the scientist is the brother-in-law of an old friend of mine. I haven't managed to contact either of them yet, but I'm on the case,"

"Good work, Julie," Mary said, suddenly appearing in a far better humour. "I'm assuming you're still standing by your opinion that the disaster was caused by man?"

"Undoubtedly. I'd still like to see the Global Energy data before I go to press on this, but from the data I've seen so far the cause is unequivocally man-made."

"Okay, stick with it for another week. It definitely sounds as though there is something underhand going on here. Do you have any reason to suspect Global Energy of deliberate sabotage?"

"Actually no, I don't Mary. From what I can see the only ones who suffered losses in the incident were Global Energy, and they were also the only ones who stood to lose their drilling licence. So, no, I can't see what they would have to gain. I can only conclude it was an accident of some description. But what I don't understand is: Why would they try to cover up something like this if they were just undertaking their licenced drilling activities?"

"Well maybe that is the crux of the matter. What if what they were doing contravened their licence, and it was this activity, whatever it might have been, that caused the tremor? Global Energy would have a lot to lose if they were proven to have flouted the terms of the Antarctic Treaty ... it carries heavy penalties for non-compliance plus an automatic expulsion for the guilty party. If Global Energy were found guilty, they would lose their Antarctic drilling rights which would cost the company a fortune in lost profits and wipe billions off the share value. In that situation, of course they'd try to cover up any scandal."

"I think you might have hit the nail on the head Mary. Let me try to establish contact with this Chuck Fallon chap and get his take on it. In the meantime, I'll keep digging into Global Energy's background to see if they have ever stepped across the line before."

Leaving Mary's office, all of Julie's instincts screamed that they were now on the right track. This could be the scoop of the century if she could just get the evidence to back it up.

---- 26 ----

Friday 28th September
1100 miles to go

Aztec was still making good progress on her homeward passage averaging one hundred and fifty miles per day, not bad in the prevailing lighter wind conditions. "At this rate I reckon we'll be home in about a week," said Skip. Crew spirits were on a high. There was still plenty to eat and drink, they were getting enough sleep, and the weather was pretty good with sunshine most days. They were beyond the Azores now, having passed slightly north of Faial, which could have been a port of refuge if poor conditions had necessitated it, and they were now on the last leg. Next stop Falmouth.

Unusually, all three of them were sitting in the cockpit, with Dom officially on watch, when the SatPhone rang. Picking it up, Skip pressed the connect button and moments later he heard the voice of their letting agent back in Devon.

"Hello there, Skip, this is Mike Partridge here. How are things going?"

"Just fine thanks Mike. What can I do for you?"

"We've been contacted by a Julie Grant, claiming to be an old friend of yours and asking that we give her your contact details so that she can call you. Is that okay? We wanted to double-check with you first."

"That's fine Mike, Julie and I are old friends. Please give her this number and ask her to give us a call."

Seeing the perplexed expression on Dom's face, Skip turned to her and explained the gist of the conversation.

"That's spooky, but it's a bit of luck!" exclaimed Dom. "I wonder why she wants to speak to you again after all this time? Maybe she's found out about Chuck's involvement in the WAIS disaster and wants to speak to him."

"Well whatever her reason, her timing is spot on. I wonder when she'll phone?" Skip replied. "Chuck, have you got everything straight in your mind for when you speak to her?"

"No worries, Skip, it's all in my head. I'll hear what she has to say and probably suggest we meet as soon as we're back in Blighty to fill her in on the details."

"Sounds like a plan to me."

---- 27 ----

Friday 28th September
London

Julie had just put the phone down after Mike Partridge had given her Skip's satellite phone contact number when her door opened, and Mary walked in.

"I'm just wanting an update on what's happening, Julie. Have you managed to speak to Chuck Fallon yet?"

"As good as. He's still not been answering his home number, but I've just got the satellite telephone number for his brother-in-law and was about to give him a call."

"Excellent. Let me know how you get on," Mary said, exiting Julie's office.

The connection time to the SatPhone seemed to take forever but finally it started to ring and was answered after four rings. There was a lot of wind noise on the line, but Julie could make out Skip's voice.

"Hi Skip, it's Julie, long time no speak. How are you?" she opened.

"Good to hear from you Julie, very well thanks. We're mid-Atlantic on our return sail to Europe after three years away. How are things with you? And what can I do for you?" asked Skip.

"Wow, that's quite some trip," came Julie's reply. "I've been trying to contact your brother-in-law Chuck, Skip. Have you any idea where he is or how I can get hold of him?"

"The answer to both those questions is yes," laughed Skip, "he's sitting right beside me. I'll pass you over."

"Thanks Skip."

"No problem Julie. Hold on, here's Chuck."

"Hello Julie, nice to speak to you and quite a coincidence too. I was going to call you when we got back to the UK to talk to you about the recent incident down on WAIS: Dom and Skip felt you would be a good person for me to chat things through with."

"I'd be more than happy to meet you Chuck. I've got quite a few questions for you on the same subject."

"Can I ask how you know about it, and me? Nothing seemed to have hit the press before we left."

"Quite a lot has since. And conflicting reports: One article from your employers claiming it was a natural disaster and talking about their losses and your dramatic rescue, and the other by the IVSO refuting

Global Energy's opinion that it was naturally caused. I've been doing a bit of digging myself and tend to be on the side of IVSO," Julie outlined.

"Me too," said Chuck. "I've studied the data long and hard, and I can't see how it could have been an earthquake."

"What do you mean, studied the data? Have you got a copy?"

Julie was on the edge of her seat as she waited for Chuck's reply.

"Off the record, actually I have," Chuck hesitantly responded. "I managed to secrete a copy of the downloaded data onto a memory stick without Global Energy knowing before they impounded my laptop. Please keep that under your hat as they would go ballistic if they found out."

Julie punched the air in delight. "YES!" she thought.

"No worries there, Chuck. I've tried to get hold of a copy from your head office but with no luck. The IVSO was more than happy to provide their data, which I've studied, but I needed the Global Energy data as well to be able to draw any firm conclusions. Look, I know you can't stay on now, but when do you think we can meet? The sooner the better as far as I'm concerned."

"Skip reckons we'll be back around the 5th October so any time after that. Our first landfall will be

Falmouth, so you could always travel down there to meet us if time is of the essence," Chuck suggested.

"Leave it with me and I'll be back in touch to get an update on your ETA next week. I'm so glad we've managed to touch base," she closed.

"Me too. I've got a lot to tell you. Bye for now then."

It had come to Ray Bergman's attention that Julie Grant had been in contact with McMurdo. A message had come through from Graham Platt via Jeff Ramsey concerning a throw away comment Bill Bond had made to him about being nominated for an award by *The Telegraph* readers. Jeff had forwarded the information on to Ray by email immediately. Ray was concerned about this development: He knew from experience how tenacious reporters could be once they had the bit between their teeth, and it was certainly looking as though this Julie Grant had got it firmly between hers. Maybe he'd been a bit unwise when he slammed the phone down on her last week.

Seeking advice from others on the best way forward was not something Ray did easily, he was too unilaterally minded for that, but he recognised that he didn't always have the finesse that his number two, Jeff Ramsey, did. Sighing he picked up his phone.

"Jeff, can you join me for a few minutes. I want to discuss this *Telegraph* journalist with you – I told you she'd been in touch with me, and Digger, last week?"

When Jeff walked into his boss' office he thought he'd never seen him looking so angry in the fifteen years they'd worked together. Ray launched straight in. "What's going on down at McMurdo Jeff, I thought we had closed all the gossip down?"

"That woman has not only been hassling you and Digger, but it turns out she has now also spoken to Bill Bond about some trumped up story that he's been nominated for an award," Jeff explained.

"She's getting too damned close for comfort in my book. We need to close the meddling bitch down, before she gets any closer." Ray took a moment to think. "How did you find out she'd spoken to Bill?"

"Graham Platt sent me an email immediately following a casual conversation he had had with Bill, it's the one I forwarded on to you."

"If she's going to play dirty, Jeff, we need to play dirty too."

"What do you have in mind Ray? Remember we don't know the extent of what she has discovered yet, so we don't want to be too heavy handed, it will just smack of having something to hide."

"I was thinking of asking our Head of Security, to do a bit of digging into her background .... see if there are any skeletons in her closet that might give us some leverage. Can I ask you to handle it with Ian Smith for me?"

"No problem, Ray, leave it with me."

Secretly, Jeff was rather relieved it was left to him and not Ray: It meant he could keep a bit of control on his hot-headed boss who was just as likely to take matters into his own hands without worrying too much about legalities.

---- 28 ----

Saturday 29th September
London

Julie decided that she would call the radio operator at McMurdo again and see if she could pump him for any more information. She rang the number and Greg answered. "Hello Greg, this is Julie Grant from *The Telegraph* again. Do you have a moment to talk to me please?"

"Oh, hi Julie, how are you?"

"Fine thanks. This is just a brief follow up call from the other day, but this time it is you I would like to talk to if you have the time?"

"Sure," said Greg, "as long as you don't mind me cutting you off every so often to field calls for my day job!" he chuckled.

"No, not at all, work has to come first."

"OK, fire away."

"Right, first of all: When Chuck Fallon made his initial call for help on ... which day was it now?"

"I can help you there, it was Saturday the first of September," Greg jumped in.

"Yes, thank you, Saturday the first of September. Was there anything unusual that you are aware of that had already been noticed by the staff within McMurdo?"

"A good question," said Greg. "Obviously I'm not in the science lab, but I do get to hear what goes on around here. There had been a couple of seismic spikes reported on the seismographs apparently, but nothing that seemed to have caused any concern down here. Usually, when anything strange or unexpected kicks off, everyone rushes around in a bit of a panic and the whole centre seems to know about it."

"But that didn't happen on the first?"

"No, not really."

"Why did you send the rescue helicopter then, if there wasn't an emergency?"

"Well, Chuck called in from the remote station and he had just experienced a shaker first hand. He was adamant there had been an earthquake, but it hadn't triggered any alarms back here at base at the time. He wanted taking off the sheet immediately. I told him that it was on his head, but that I would scramble the helicopter to pick him up and confirmed it to him. Once I had done that, I kept watch on the comms station for further contact. It never came, because it turns out that the SatPhone Chuck used went down the crevasse with the remote station, and because I was focused on the comms activity, I didn't know what was happening in the labs here until Chuck got back to base."

"What happened then?"

"It was the talk of the base. Chuck was something of a walking miracle. He probably should have been dead. It's only because he had some sort of premonition that he got out of the remote station before it went down. Normally, the Health and Safety instructions are that you don't go outside until it is absolutely necessary, in which case he'd be several hundred feet below the ice now in a deep freeze."

"Did you get the chance to talk to him after his return?"

"Only briefly, just to say welcome back. He came to thank me for sending the chopper to get him, even though it wasn't properly sanctioned by management. I just felt it would take too long to get approval for it, and so I acted on my own initiative. You know how it is sometimes, it's better to ask for forgiveness than permission."

"Did he say anything else other than thanks?"

"He didn't really get the chance. He was whisked off to the station manager's office where he was debriefed, then he was ordered to the medical centre for a complete check-up. After that, apart from taking a call from Ray Bergman the CEO that I patched through to him, he was resting in his bunk until the next morning when the company jet arrived and whisked him off to London. Everyone on site was jealous that he got to ride home first class in the Lear. "

"He flew back in the company jet? Is that normal?"

"Not on your life! We travel to the nearest commercial airfield and then we must make the rest of the way by whatever public transportation means are available, sometimes even by cargo plane. How Chuck wangled that one is beyond me. I would love to be pampered in six-star luxury for a few hours just once in my life. No, I guess he just struck lucky, although I wouldn't have wanted to go through what he did. Jeff Ramsey, Ray Bergman's number two, flew down to McMurdo just to have a nosey round for an hour, talk to the station manager down here, and give us minions a pep talk. Then he took Chuck back with him, and we haven't heard anything from him since. It's as if he dropped off the world. Maybe they fired his ass for leaving the remote station in direct contravention of the safety rules. I dunno. It's all a bit odd really."

Julie let the significance of this sink in for a moment, then asked, "Was there any comeback on you for the helicopter scramble?"

"No, it seems like they applauded the move, but they did stress that I shouldn't do it too often if I wanted to keep my job. I got the message loud and clear. Another thing, no-one seems to be talking about Chuck any more, it's like he doesn't matter, and now he's not here, nobody cares. Life just goes on."

"Well, thanks again for your help. Goodbye Greg," Julie closed, ringing off.

After she had replaced the handset on her phone, Julie leaned back in her chair, smiling. All the pieces were falling into place now and she realised that Chuck was the missing link. With the Global Energy data that he had in his possession, she was certain that the cause of the catastrophe could be placed firmly at Global Energy's feet. "I'm just going to have to be patient and sit on it for another week," she thought, "there's not much else I can do until Chuck gets back to the UK."

---- 29 ----

Sunday 30th September
London

Jeff Ramsey was enjoying a rare leisurely breakfast at home with his wife, his two daughters, and the Sunday papers when the phone rang. He sighed aloud and looked across the table to his wife who had rolled her eyes at the ringing sound, knowing that it would be work calling.

"I'm sorry to be disturbing you on a Sunday morning Jeff," opened Ian Smith, Global Energy's Head of Security, "but I've found out some information on Julie Grant, and thought you'd want to know soonest."

"No problem Ian," Jeff said, secretly resenting the loss of his one morning of relaxation in the week. "What have you found?"

"Well, it turns out our Ms Grant was quite the radical in her university days and was arrested following an eco-rally when two members of the public got crushed to death. Ms Grant was taken into custody and charged along with four others, with conspiring to incite a riot and involuntary manslaughter for the two deaths, but the case against her was dropped."

"Really! Do we know why it was dropped?"

"It looks like someone alibied her at the eleventh hour. A chap called Paul Whitehead claimed she was in bed with him at the time and not at the rally."

"Interesting," mused Jeff. "One of the country's leading scientific journalists has a bit of a murky past. Leave it with me Ian and thank you for letting me know."

At this point Jeff couldn't really see how he could leverage this information to deflect Julie Grant but he'd ponder on it: It seemed to him that having a track record for being a revolutionary might even stand in her favour with the more radical factions within the gutter press, it was the way of the world in journalism. He would have to dig deeper than this to find a real leverageable skeleton in Julie's closet. There had to be something somewhere that would identify some weakness in her that Global Energy could use to fight back with and discredit her, or even silence her.

Ray Bergman typically didn't differentiate between weekdays and weekends – every day was a working day as far as he was concerned. He'd also been wondering what to do about Julie Grant, maybe using

161

slightly less orthodox methods than Jeff Ramsey was considering, but ones that would probably be more successful in closing her down ... permanently. The whole situation was driving him crazy – he couldn't allow an interfering glory-seeking journalist to become the catalyst in the downfall of one of the world's greatest energy companies. He had put his life's effort into making Global Energy a world leader, and he wasn't about to let it go lightly. He would do whatever it took to save his reputation, his job, and the company. No, he decided, whatever action was needed to save Global Energy would have to be taken, and soon. He would make a few calls in the morning to start the process.

Early the next morning, Ray made a few phone calls to some of the less desirable characters he knew and was given the number of a contact who could put pressure on uncooperative individuals. He dialled the number and it was answered on the second ring.

"Yes?"

"Hello," said Ray, "I have been given your name by Lance Cooper as being someone who offers a special service."

"Could be, at a price, depends on what it is you need."

"Yes, I realise that," Ray continued. "How much to discourage someone from pursuing an enquiry?"

"You want them to disappear?"

"No, just to be frightened off, and we'll see what happens from that point onwards if we are unsuccessful."

"Give me the details then."

Ray related Julie Grant's name, address and telephone numbers for home, mobile and work.

"How persuasive do you want me to be?"

"Enough to make her want to drop her current investigation."

"You just said investigation – is she a cop?"

"No, she's a nosey good for nothing journalist."

"OK. The price will be two grand. Give me a couple of days to get things underway. What number can I get you on?"

Ray gave him the number of the untraceable prepaid mobile phone he had acquired specifically for the purpose, and the contact rang off. Ray smiled to himself. That no-good, interfering bitch was going to get more than she bargained for.

---- 30 ----

Tuesday 2nd October
London

Julie Grant had had a frustrating day in *The Telegraph's* offices, researching the history of and wrestling with theories as to why Global Energy might have wanted to trigger, or had triggered, the WAIS event. She'd dug deep using her journalistic skills, but she still couldn't draw any definite conclusions: Global Energy had competed long and hard against stiff international competition to win the exclusive oil drilling licence, so why on earth would they want to jeopardise that?

Finally, at pushing 7pm, she decided to call it a day and packed up her phone, notebook, papers and laptop into her shoulder bag in readiness for heading home. As with most London residents, public transport was her chosen mode of transport, involving a short walk to the tube station and a journey of about twenty minutes on the hot and sweaty tube back to Clapham where she lived just off the common.

Leaving the building, she waved goodnight to the security guard and stepped out into the pre-dusk evening, pleased to be outside again after a long day indoors. Turning left along Buckingham Palace Road, she headed for the Victoria tube station to pick up the central line heading west. It was reasonably quiet at that time of the evening with most office workers already home for the evening or enjoying an after-work drink in town with colleagues, often in Covent Garden. Tonight Julie just wanted to head straight home, have a refreshing shower, a bite to eat and a glass of chilled white wine before getting an early night.

As she passed an alleyway leading off Buckingham Palace Road, a man stepped out behind her. Julie barely glanced at him, but thought he looked an unlikely type for the area being somewhat unkempt but thought no more than that. With London having become such a multi-cultural city she simply ignored his presence and continued her journey home. She went into the tube station, passed her Oyster card over the sensor to open the passenger gates and rode the escalator down to the platform.

Standing waiting for the first train to arrive, Julie noticed the same unkempt man standing just along the platform from her. There was something about his swarthy colouring and crumpled beige clothing that sent a shiver down her spine, but, with all the other people on the platform with her, she laughed internally at her overactive imagination - he wasn't carrying a bag, so he was unlikely to be a terrorist bomber. A train soon pulled in and Julie stepped aboard, pleased to note that the strange and unnerving man had entered through a different door from her, albeit in the same carriage. She swiftly put him out of her mind and took out her book to read on the journey home.

Just over ten minutes later Julie's tube slowed for the approach to Stockwell station where she needed to change onto the Northern Line for the final stop to Clapham Common. Julie put her book back in her bag and moved to stand close to the doors with her back to the direction of travel. Several other passengers also assembled near the doors in readiness to leave the carriage. As the train stopped she leant forward to press the button to open the sliding doors. Before she was able to stand upright once again and regain her balance, a hand gave her a firm push in the middle of her back and she found herself lurching forward, falling face downward to the floor, narrowly missing the gap between the train and platform. Her bag and its contents tumbled onto the platform as hands from benevolent strangers reached down to help her back to her feet.

"Oh, thank you, thank you," she stuttered to the helpful passers-by as she slowly clambered to her feet and then shouted, "Hey! Stop that man! Hurry, he's stealing my bag," as the unknown stranger grabbed the shoulder strap and loped off down the platform, turning the corner to join the rest of the commuters who were changing platforms. "Please! Someone call the police, that man has just robbed me!" Julie screamed. "Quickly, before he gets away!"

As he turned the corner her assailant had slowed his pace to match the other travellers and in all the confusion he was able to make a clean getaway. Julie, bruised and dirty, had no option other than to report what had happened to the Transport Police who quickly attended the scene. Despite being sympathetic, the officer taking her report told her that these occurrences were frequent, and that he didn't hold out much hope she would recover her bag. "Damn!" she exclaimed, "all my analysis and research are on my laptop which is in the bag. All that work wasted." Dejected and disheartened, Julie had no choice other than to continue her journey home.

An hour after leaving the office, Julie found her hidden spare key and put it into the lock of her front door. She was grateful to be safely home after being mugged on the tube. "I suppose it's a sign of the times," was her rueful conclusion to the evening's attack. She resigned herself to having to reobtain the information from Keith Mortimer and reanalyse it all before she met up with Chuck around the 5th October in Falmouth. Or at least that was her thought until she opened her front door and stepped into the hallway. All the pictures were askew, the drawers in the hall table had been thrown to the floor, and papers were strewn all over the wooden planked floor. "Oh my God! I've been burgled too … whatever next?" she thought, not immediately associating what appeared to be a break-in with the incident on the tube. Stepping cautiously into the lounge Julie was met with a scene of utter chaos: Furniture upended, valuables smashed, cushions slashed, feathers everywhere. She went to pull out her mobile phone from her bag to call the police, only to realise she hadn't got it after the mugging, so she turned tail and dashed from the house to run to her neighbour and raise the alarm.

Sitting nursing a cup of tea that Moira Edwards, her neighbour, had kindly made while she dialled 999, Julie waited for the arrival of the police wondering why *her* house, one of many identical terraced homes on a leafy street in Clapham Common, should be targeted on the very same day she was apparently mugged on the tube. It was too much of a coincidence.

Thanking her neighbour for her help, she returned home to see what, if anything, had been taken before for the police arrived. Nothing. Absolutely nothing.

Why would anyone break into someone's home, wreak havoc and yet take nothing?" she wondered. "What is the point? Do I have anyone who hates me so much? Have I written anything in *The Telegraph* which would merit such destruction?"

Suddenly a disturbing thought entered her mind. "No, I haven't reported on anything controversial in recent times unless …. unless my current Global Energy investigation is rattling a few cages?"

Minutes later, two officers from the police arrived, one male, one female. The male officer walked through the house making sure that there was no-one still in the place, while the female officer noted down all the details of the break-in. With nothing stolen there wasn't much more they could do other than to advise Julie to change her locks and be vigilant, maybe to stay with a friend that evening and come back to tackle the chaos the next day.

Unnerved now that night had fallen, Julie decided to take their advice and drive over to stay with Ali Walker, her best friend, for the night. She picked up the phone, dialled Ali's number and left a message on her answerphone to say that she would be coming over, and would it be OK for her to stay the night? She would fill Ali in on the details later when she got there.

Gathering up her sleepwear, toilet bag and a clean change of clothing from the detritus in her bedroom, Julie pulled the front door closed behind her to walk the few hundred metres to her car that was parked further along the street. As with most of the terraced homes in this part of London, there was no off-road parking and so Julie, like all her neighbours, had to park her car in a residents' permit space on the street as close to her house as she could find a space. It was a constant competition to find a parking place close to home, and it often meant that vehicles were left unused and unmoved for days on end. But tonight, she couldn't face using public transport to reach her friend's home in Balham and so she had decided to drive the short distance.

Approaching her vehicle from the rear, Julie noticed glass on the pavement. Closer still, she saw her tyres had been slashed and they were all flat. Whoever had broken into her home had obviously not restricted their efforts to that alone: They had also worked over her car as well.

Now, standing out on the quiet residential road in the dark, Julie was really scared and afraid. She ran quickly back to her neighbour's house once more to phone the police again. Hammering urgently on the door she called out, "Moira, Moira, let me in! Hurry, please! My car's been broken into as well. Someone is obviously trying to scare me. Please, let me in!"

Moira slid the bolt and opened the door. Julie leaped inside before it was opened more than a crack and stood in the hallway, panicking. "Quick! Close it! There might be someone outside watching," she whispered. Moira locked the door and called the police again.

This time, the police were far more concerned … the combination of the tube attack, break-in and car vandalism gave them grave cause for concern and they returned with a full retinue of scene of crime officers. While the officers dusted for fingerprints, the lead investigator questioned Julie at length: The work she did, whether she could think of any reasons why she might be being targeted, any enemies she might have, recent relationship break-ups, all these topics and more. By midnight, thoroughly exhausted and too terrified to remain alone, Julie borrowed some cash from Moira and took a taxi to her friend Ali's house. Once safely inside, she collapsed into a fitful sleep as soon as her head hit the pillow. It had indeed been one hell of a day.

---- 31 ----

Wednesday 3rd October
Bay of Biscay

With 300 miles to go to Lands' End, *Aztec* and her crew had just endured a raging storm as they approached the northern limits of the Bay of Biscay. The Bay is notorious for big seas and tricky winds, exacerbated by the sudden uprising of the Atlantic seabed to meet the continental shelf, causing a big upsurge and swell. Skip had set a waypoint to cross the continental shelf at the place where the water was deepest, and they were battling their way towards this in Force 8 gales and pelting rain.

"Quite a contrast from the sunny Caribbean," he fumed as, wrapped in his extreme wet weather waterproofs, he wrestled with the helm in the raging seas.

Chuck and Dom were resting down below, dry and cosy in their bunks, neither of them relishing the prospect of taking over from Skip when their watch was due. Not that Skip would really rest in these conditions: As skipper of the boat, and with three lives in his hands, he took his responsibilities very seriously. While he might go down below at the end of his watch to rest, he certainly wouldn't fall asleep and he always had an ear listening for any unusual sound – a flapping sail, a vibration, anything. There was too much at stake and he was damned if anything bad would happen in the last few hundred miles of what had been an eight-thousand miles journey since leaving Antigua in the spring.

Back on dry land, Julie awoke surprisingly refreshed after the horrors of the night before and had that split-second comfort of not remembering what had happened before the events of the previous day all flooded back to remind her.

"Christ," she thought "what do I do now?" Recognising she needed to keep a low profile until the police had completed their investigations, she realised she must update Mary on what had happened, and then make the necessary arrangements to get out of London to somewhere safe. The obvious and safest place to go to was Cornwall, to meet up with the returning crew of *Aztec*, but before committing to anything she wanted to brief her boss.

As ever Mary Roberts was busy and focused on the task in hand and on answering her phone took a few seconds to recognise who was on the line and what investigation they were working on. "Julie, give me a status report on Global Energy," she snapped.

"Mary, I need to update you on what's happened since I left work last night. In the last fifteen hours I've been mugged on the tube on my way home, my house has been ransacked and my car vandalised."

"My God!" exclaimed Mary, instantly concerned for her valued employee. "Are you all right? Where are you? Why have *you* been targeted for God's sake?"

"I'm okay Mary, I think, and I've spent a long time pondering that very question, along with the police. I can't think of anything that could have prompted a trio of attacks on me with one possible exception: My current investigation into Global Energy and the happenings in Antarctica."

"Why would you think that would be a reason to attack you Julie? It's not as though you've even put anything in print yet."

"I know, but I have been in touch with Keith Mortimer at IVSO who has reported on the situation in a scientific journal and was very helpful. By contrast I also contacted two of the directors at Global Energy following their press release last week and both gave me the run around, politely in the case of the Research Director, but rather curtly in the case of Ray Bergman, the CEO."

"So, are you suggesting the attacks have been initiated by Global Energy? And why on earth would they sanction such behaviour? They must know we would put two and two together?"

"That's what I don't know the answer to, but I'd like to continue with my investigation to get to the bottom of it."

"But won't that put you in risk of physical danger Julie?"

"Potentially Mary, but if I go off-grid while I'm undertaking it, hopefully I can keep out of harm's way. I need to speak at some length to the scientist who was rescued once he returns to the UK later this week, and I was thinking of heading down to Falmouth to meet him on his return from an Atlantic crossing with his sister and her husband. Do I have your approval to go down to Cornwall for the foreseeable future?"

"If that's what you want to do, then go for it, but please keep me informed of what's happening on a daily basis. And be careful!" Mary implored.

Hanging up on the call, Julie immediately dialled *Aztec's* satellite phone to check on their ETA. As the phone was answered all she could hear was howling wind.

"Skip, is that you? Is everything okay? It's Julie, Julie Grant."

"Yeah it's me. It's blowing a hooley out here Julie. We're battling our way towards the English Channel and the weather just isn't playing ball. But we're okay: Wet, cold and a bit bruised, but fine."

"I need to speak to Chuck, is he there?"

"He's down below in his bunk, staying out of the way of this God-awful storm. I'll pass the phone down to him, hang on."

"Chuck, a call for you, it's Julie Grant," bellowed Skip over the howling wind. Julie waited for Chuck to come to the phone.

"Hi Julie, how are you?" opened Chuck. Julie quickly filled him in on the happenings of the last twenty-four hours, and her plan to come down to Falmouth to meet them on their return.

"Christ!" exclaimed Chuck. "It certainly sounds as though someone's trying to scare you off or something, doesn't it? Are you certain it's Global Energy behind it? I wouldn't have thought a big and successful company would resort to such activities. Or at least I hoped they wouldn't."

"I can't be certain that it is Global Energy Chuck, but I have racked my brain, remembering everything I have reported on so far this year and I can't think of who else it could be. Ray Bergman didn't seem to be a very nice guy when I spoke to him last week. Do you think he would authorise something like this?"

"I really don't know Julie. I do know that there was something suspicious going on under the radar down on WAIS, and if that was illegal then maybe he'd feel he needed to keep it quiet. Your investigations could jeopardise both his and the company's reputation, possibly their mining licence too; not to mention the damage that the loss of that would do to the share price. It would probably bankrupt the company. So maybe you're right, who knows? What are the police saying? What do they think?"

"I haven't exactly explained my theory to them, I wanted to speak to you first, and it sounds so improbable that a captain of industry would put the frighteners on a journalist from a respected newspaper," said Julie. "I don't want to put the cat among the pigeons until I'm sure."

"And how are you going to be sure? And stay safe?"

"Well, I think the first step is for me to get out of London. When do you think you'll arrive into Falmouth?"

"Let me speak to Skip and Dom and tell them what's happened. Can you call me back in a few minutes?"

"No problem," said Julie, "speak soon," and she rang off.

Chuck woke Dom, and the two of them donned their waterproofs and climbed up into the cockpit to join Skip. Chuck filled them in on everything Julie had told him and asked about their ETA into Falmouth.

"With these winds we'll be back on dry land by the 5th, mid-morning I would imagine, but if Julie is being watched or followed then I suggest we head for Fowey and not Falmouth. It's a much quieter port and not somewhere most returning yachtsmen head for, they usually favour the bigger ports of Falmouth or Plymouth where they can pick up spares and provisions if they need them," Skip explained. "Has she booked anywhere to stay yet? She might be advised to check into a small bed and breakfast rather than into an hotel where it would be easier to find her."

"Good thinking on both points," said Chuck, "I'll pass that on to her when she calls back."

Julie called a few minutes later, and arrangements were made between them for Julie to be on the quayside next to the Harbourmaster's office in Fowey in two days' time to meet the returning crew. In the meantime, she would have to find herself some accommodation and then travel down to Fowey using public transport as her car was out of commission. The loss of her cell phone could be easily overcome with a pay as you go phone; the transportation would be more difficult unless she could talk Mary into loaning her a pool car from *The Telegraph's* fleet .... she didn't fancy travelling by train again so soon.

---- 32 ----

Thursday 4ᵗʰ October
London

Ray Bergman was sitting in his office pondering his next steps – he had just put the phone down on Lance Cooper who had called to tell him Julie's bag was now in his possession. Ray considered it a bonus that her laptop and phone were within his reach, certain that the laptop would contain all her research and findings to date, and that the phone would store all her contacts. No doubt her passwords would need to be broken to be able to access the information they stored but that shouldn't be too much of a problem with Lance's contacts.

He had arranged to meet Lance in the Café Nero around the corner from Global Energy's office later that morning. Once there, they found a table in a corner, away from the rest of the customers, and sat down.

"So, do you think your man has succeeded in scaring her off from making further investigations?" Ray wanted to know.

"Hard to know," said Lance. "She involved the police for all three incidents and then we lost track of her when she disappeared off in a taxi."

"So where is she now? Did anyone think to follow her?"

"We don't know, it wasn't in our brief to do so. She'll undoubtedly have gone to ground, but she's bound to keep her boss at *The Telegraph* in the picture. Maybe we should pay her a visit?"

"No. The first thing we need to do before we go off questioning other people is to review what's on her laptop and phone … she's bound to have files on her research findings on the laptop, and details of any recent calls on her phone. Can you arrange for someone discreet to hack into them immediately?" Ray did not want to risk threatening a senior editor of one of the country's leading broadsheets unless it was absolutely necessary.

"Give me twenty-four hours and we should be able to get all the data off the phone and laptop for you," Lance confirmed as he rose from the table with Julie's computer bag in his hand. Ray nodded approvingly, then he finished his double espresso and left the café, returning to the office.

As he walked into the reception area, he was approached by a strikingly beautiful red-headed young woman dressed in a smart black pinstripe suit who was smiling openly at him as though she knew him. He smiled back at her as she approached, always appreciating youthful beauty. "Mr Bergman?" she asked huskily. "That's me," Ray replied, "what can I do for you?" She handed him a letter saying, "This is for you." Ray took the letter and looked down at the plainly addressed envelope. "You've just been served with a subpoena," said the young woman, still smiling. "What?" retorted Ray, incensed that he had been duped. "What's all this about?" "Read the letter and see," replied the young woman as she turned on her heels and strode towards the front door, her job for the day done.

Ray's face was red with rage. He ripped open the envelope and shook out the letter. It was from a firm of solicitors and subpoenaed him to appear in court for a financial hearing in a divorce case between Ian Smith, Global Energy's Head of Security, and his soon to be ex-wife. What the hell was going on here?

He stormed into his office barking at Jayne, "Get me Ian Smith in my office, now!" "Yes sir, right away," said Jayne picking up the telephone handset. Ray slammed his door and stalked across to the window, standing there fuming. A minute later, he was still in the same spot when there was a knock on the door and Ian walked in. "You wanted to see me Ray?"

"What the hell is this?" Ray demanded, waving the subpoena under Ian's nose. "I've just been served bloody papers to appear in court as a witness for your fucking divorce hearing."

"Oh shit!" thought Ian, who had no idea that this was going to happen. His wife's solicitors had already employed dirty tactics to bring him down, putting him under surveillance, and demanding all sorts of financial records even though his wife had access to all the joint accounts. This latest move was another thing altogether. How the hell did she expect to gain from it? It was short sighted revenge that would only serve to damage his career and could ultimately backfire on her in terms of ongoing maintenance. "Look Ray, I can only say I'm very sorry. I had no idea whatsoever that my ex-wife's solicitors would do this. The basic problem is they don't believe a word I'm telling them, and they are just looking for anything to discredit me. I can't apologise enough for what's happened."

Believing that Ian knew nothing about the papers being served on him, Ray eased off a bit. "Look Ian, I've got too much on my mind with all this business down on WAIS to be running around attending court hearings. You need to make this subpoena go away, and fast."

"I'm not sure I can Ray. I don't know how much you know about English law, but if you don't attend, you'll be in contempt of court and could be sent to prison. However, I think you might be entitled to send an alternate if you have a good reason for being unable to attend," Ian explained.

"That'll have to do. I'll get Jeff to sort it out and represent me, but for God's sake, don't bring your personal problems to work like this." Breathing deeply to calm down Ray then asked, "Now, as you are here, tell me what you have found out about Julie Grant."

"Not a lot more than I told Jeff over the weekend … I presume he passed that information on to you?"

"Of course. But I am rather surprised you don't have anything else to report. You've had a few days since then: What have you been doing in the intervening time?" barked Ray.

"I, ah, I …. Well, to be honest Ray, I've been tied up in the financial settlement hearings for the divorce."

"What the fuck do you mean by that? Global Energy has to be your priority! I can't have you losing focus at this critical time. What the hell is going on with you?"

"I - I'm sorry Ray," Ian stammered. "You have my assurance that Global Energy *does* come first but my ex-wife's solicitors are giving me a grilling and taking me to the cleaners: I don't think they'd care if I was left living in a cardboard box with only the shirt on my back providing 'their client' gets what 'she deserves'. I've had to attend court the last two days for the financial hearing and have not had any time to pursue my enquiries," he confessed. "You have my word that I won't let it impact my work going forwards. I'm going to need my job more than ever to recover from the whole debacle."

"It better not. Let's get back to business. Recap for me where we are," Ray commanded.

"As far as we know, Julie Grant is acting independently at the moment, presumably briefing her editor along the way. The IVSO report published earlier this month contradicts our view of the situation as you know, so I assume she'll have spoken to that organisation," Ian summarised.

"We need to find out who was her contact there," stated Ray. "Can we achieve that?"

"Possibly: I could make some phone calls to some ex-forces guys I know who work for the security organisation at *The Telegraph* and see if they can find any of her documents on their intranet server as they do their security audits. I will also try to find out if we have any people inside IVSO too: We can usefully enlist their help to track down calls made in and out."

"Make the calls Ian," directed Ray. "We also need to ensure she doesn't manage to identify and contact Chuck Fallon. He'll be returning to work as soon as he arrives back in the UK from sailing the Atlantic. That must be any day now and he has been told to report in at the first opportunity. If we can get him straight back to McMurdo he will be under our control and out of Julie Grant's way. Can we find out where he is?"

"Not easily on a sailboat unless they have an AIS transponder aboard," outlined Ian who had done some sailing during his years in service. "It sends a positioning signal to satellites and the information received allows the coastguard to map the boats worldwide. We would need to know the name of the boat, and if we did, and they had an active transponder, we could pinpoint them."

"Find him," ordered Ray, terminating the meeting.

---- 33 ----

Friday 5th October
Fowey

Julie was on the quayside bright and early in anticipation of *Aztec's* arrival. She'd been on edge throughout the journey down to Cornwall in the pool car Mary had authorised, constantly looking in her rear-view mirror to see if anyone was following her. It had been a relief to get away from London: She'd phoned her neighbour Moira asking her if she would collect some belongings for her and meet her at a local coffee shop. She took the precaution of advising Moira to enter the house through the kitchen door and not to switch on any lights. Their gardens were linked by a gate in the fence and, Julie reasoned, if anyone was watching her house from the front they wouldn't realise anyone had been inside.

Now, with London and that horrific night three hundred miles away, Julie was beginning to feel more secure, and started wondering whether she'd overreacted to it all.

"Better to be safe than sorry I guess," she mused, "and I needed to meet Chuck as soon as possible anyway, so the trip down here was justified." She settled down in the warm autumn sunshine on a bench seat close to the Harbourmaster's office to wait, scanning the river mouth for arriving boats.

The crew of *Aztec* were very much looking forward to being on firm land again. The last few hundred miles of their journey had been tough, and they were all tired, ready to shed their salt-encrusted clothing, and relax with a mug of tea and a plate of full English breakfast. The storm had abated during the night and the morning dawned bright and clear, almost as though welcoming them home. When at last they rounded Dodman Point to the south-east of Falmouth for their final approach to Fowey they admired the beautiful Cornish countryside, so lush and green with rolling hills descending to towering cliffs, and with quaint fishing villages such as Mevagissey along the shoreline.

"It's good to be back," said Dom. "I'd forgotten just how beautiful the countryside of good old England is, especially on a bright autumn morning like today."

The town of Fowey sits about a mile up river from the sea, a stretch of water lined with pretty coves and stunning cliff-top houses, eventually giving way to the attractive outskirts of the town itself.

"This is just as gorgeous as the Caribbean," she continued.

"It might be Dom, but I bet you wouldn't enjoy the sea temperature quite as much!" teased Skip.

"No, you're probably right there, I won't be swimming today!"

As they approached the mooring field just off the town dock, Skip looked over to the quayside and spotted Julie leaning against the waterfront railings, waving enthusiastically to them all.

"Welcome home!" she shouted, but her voice was lost in the wind to all but a passing seagull. Skip waved back, but then he had to concentrate on tying up to one of the mooring balls in the fairway. Dom took the helm as usual and Skip went forward to the bow. Slipping the dock line through the eye of the mooring ball, he quickly made it fast to one of the bow cleats, then repeated the process with a second dock line and secured that to the opposite bow cleat. They were then safely moored.

Next, Skip and Dom removed the protective rain cover and lowered *Maya*, *Aztec's* tender, into the water and used the onboard hoist to lower and attach the outboard motor to the dinghy's transom. Hopping on

189

board carrying the fuel tank, Skip attached the fuel line, inserted the safety cut-out cord into its socket, and pulled the starter. Once the engine was running properly, he cast off and headed for shore shouting to Dom over his shoulder, "I'll just go and clear in with Customs and then come back for you guys. We'll go and get a cooked breakfast with Julie … the full works!"

While Skip was off dealing with the customs and immigration formalities, Dom and Chuck used the time usefully to stow the lifejackets and harnesses and tidy up the boat's various lines before heading below for a quick shower and change of clothes. They were both eager to be ashore after such a long stretch at sea.

Having greeted Julie on the quayside with a big hug and a brotherly kiss on both cheeks, Skip presented his boat papers and the passports to customs and immigration and was given clearance for them all to re-enter the country. That done, he helped Julie into the dinghy before setting off back to *Aztec*.

"Chuck, let me introduce you to Julie Grant, my old friend and alumnus from Nottingham University. Julie, this is Charlie Fallon, Dom's big brother. We call him Chuck," said Skip, "because he's not a great sailor and is always throwing up!"

"Pleased to meet you at last Julie," said Chuck. "Pay no attention to this big oaf, he doesn't know what he's talking about!"

"Pleased to meet you too Chuck," replied Julie as they shook hands.

"And of course, you know who Dom is, Julie." Dom and Julie hugged each other like old friends.

"Right then," said Skip, "introductions over. I'm starving and really want a full English breakfast. Who's coming with me?" They all nodded their approval. "I need to have a shower first though and wash off all this salt, so I'll be a couple of minutes," he said, already peeling off his outer layers as he headed down the companionway into the saloon. Five minutes later, much cleaner, and wearing a change of clothes Skip re-emerged into the cockpit to find the others waiting patiently. They stepped down onto the stern platform and into *Maya*. Skip fired up the engine once more, and within two minutes they were tied up at the dinghy dock and were making their way ashore to find a café. Chuck and Julie walked together in front. "It's a pleasure to finally meet you Julie. I guess we're going to have a lot to talk about."

"More than you'd think," replied Julie somewhat candidly. "I'm almost convinced that Global Energy are behind things and I am very keen to cross-match my findings when I re-create them, with those you managed to get."

"First things first," said Skip, "we all need a good breakfast to boost our energy levels. Can we postpone our discussion until then?" he pleaded. Chuck and Julie both nodded. "Great! I'm so hungry I could eat a scabby monkey."

An hour later, tucked away in a small café on the high street, with a plate of well-cooked local back bacon, sausages and fried eggs and all the trimmings inside them, their thoughts turned once more to Chuck's lucky escape down on WAIS and the attacks on Julie in London.

"How are you feeling Julie? What a terrible thing to happen. It must have been terrifying for you," Dom said.

"It was pretty surreal to be honest and didn't really register as anything more than a coincidence until I discovered that my car had been vandalised as well. I'm not sure I'll ever feel safe in that house again," Julie explained. "I must say it's lovely down here and seems to be a friendly and sleepy little town. I think I may stay!"

"Do you know who did it? Have the police got any leads?" Skip enquired.

"Not as far as I know, but I have my suspicions as to who was behind it. I've racked my brain thinking of reasons why anyone would want to subject me to these attacks, and still really can only come up with one suggestion: Global Energy. Well, to be more exact, Ray Bergman, the CEO. When I spoke to him on the phone he was very cold and offhand. But it is only a suspicion, I have absolutely no proof."

"Well hopefully, that's something I might be able to help you with," commented Chuck. "I guess we need to have a 'show and tell' session, and then come up with a strategy for the way forward."

"Agreed," said Julie. "We need to find somewhere isolated and off-grid where we can put our heads together to study all the data and findings we have and draw some conclusions. Do you know anywhere down here? I don't relish the thought of returning to London right now."

"We've got three cabins on board *Aztec*, why don't you use her as your base? We can keep moving around from port to port, so it will be difficult for anyone to keep tabs on us. What do you think?" asked Skip.

"Well if you're sure you don't mind, as it is involving you and Dom in this situation, then I think it's great idea," commented Julie. "Do you agree Chuck?"

"It's fine by me. My mobile has plenty of internet access and we can download what we need from anywhere in the UK, so, yes, go and check out of your B&B and collect your things. Welcome to the crew!"

"Okay, thanks Skip, Dom, I appreciate your help and hospitality. I guess I'll have to arrange for someone to come and collect the pool car I used to drive down in," Julie mused. "But that shouldn't be a problem. I'll phone my editor and ask her to arrange it," she decided.

Three hours later, having checked out of her accommodation and with plans in place for the pool car to be collected, Julie was settling into her cabin on *Aztec*. She put her few belongings into the wardrobe and cupboard available to her. "It's really rather spacious," she called through to Skip, who was sitting in the saloon, "I hadn't expected a double bed and good storage facilities."

"Yes Julie, there's no slumming on good old *Aztec*. To be honest, if you're going to be living aboard a sailing yacht, you do need your home comforts. There's no way I'd have convinced Dom to set sail without the promise of a hot, fresh water shower every day, plus a good sound system and plenty of room to be comfortable. It was one of the reasons we chose her."

"Chose who?"

"*Aztec*. All boats are referred to as she," he explained. "I don't know why, it's historical."

"Ah, I see. I'm not surprised this sleek, stylish yacht with beautiful lines is female!" she teased, "but can't see why anyone would think of an old, rusty tugboat as feminine! Definitely more of a male vibe going on there."

"Now, now," said Chuck. "That's enough denigration of the males of the species! And now that you're settled on board, shouldn't we start thinking about deciding what we should be doing next? I have a few ideas about our next steps I'd like to share with you all," he added, steering the conversation back to the matter in hand.

"Fire away," said Julie moving into the saloon to sit on one of the two easy chairs that straddled the navigation table. "I'm grateful for any suggestions. We really do need to agree a strategy for handling this situation."

"Well," Chuck continued, "I think the first thing we need to do is bring everyone up to speed with both sides of the story ... my experience down on WAIS and the subsequent contact with Ray Bergman and the rest of the Global Energy board of directors, and your actions to date including the dreadful events of two nights ago. We also need to re-create and cross-refer your research findings to the data I copied."

"Agreed," said Julie as she took a breath to continue, only to be interrupted by Skip.

"Don't you think we should head out of Fowey and find a remote anchorage first? If someone is on Julie's tail, they'll soon be able to track her to Fowey, but they would struggle to locate us if we are tucked away in a quiet bay somewhere, off-grid so to speak. Why don't you two start the show and tell session while Dom and I grab a few provisions from town to tide us over the next few days?"

With everyone in agreement, Skip and Dom headed back to shore in *Maya* while Chuck and Julie filled each other in on the happenings to date.

"It's incredible you survived!" exclaimed Julie. "And to have the foresight to take a copy of the recorded data was inspired. I imagine it will provide us with the evidence we need to explain what really happened when we compare it to my research findings, especially when coupled with the opinions of Keith Mortimer from IVSO. He feels very strongly that the cause of all that activity down there was man-made, but without proof he says he can't go to press on it. As soon as we're at anchor somewhere and have a few hours to focus on things, we'll do a detailed cross-reference and see what conclusions we can draw."

"Well, Skip and Dom will be back any minute, so we'll be heading off very soon. I wouldn't imagine we'll be going very far: Skip knows the south west coast like the back of his hand and will have somewhere in mind, I'm sure."

"Okay," replied Julie. "Let's leave it for now."

---- 34 ----

Friday 5th October
London

On his way into the office, Ray Bergman's newly acquired untraceable mobile phone rang. It was Lance.

"I've got the information off the laptop and phone for you. Do you want to meet?"

"Yes," replied Ray, "Café Nero, ten thirty this morning."

"I'll be there," said Lance, ending the call.

At ten thirty, Ray was sitting in a remote corner of the café at one of the small square tables with a double espresso coffee in his hands. Lance walked in. Standing in the doorway, he scanned the room until he found Ray, then paced over to his table and sat down opposite him. He handed over a USB memory stick. "That contains everything that has been date stamped within the last three weeks from the laptop and smartphone. Will there be anything else?"

"We'll decide on that when I've had a look at the files. I'll be in touch," said Ray.

Lance stood up, nodded, and walked out of the café. Ray finished his coffee, slipped the USB stick into his pocket and went back to his office. He fired up his laptop, inserted the USB stick and opened the files one by one.

"Shit," he said as he read the analysis document Julie was working on. "She's getting too damned close, she needs to be closed down, but how? I need someone who can take her out of the picture with no possibility of any comeback on yours truly."

Ray recognised his options were limited. Lance and his hired hood could be a possibility, but these guys sold out to the highest bidder and there could be no guarantee of confidentiality. "What I need is someone who owes me," mused Ray, "someone who's loyalty is to Global Energy and not to their pocket."

He leant back in his chair pondering who might fit the bill. Jeff Ramsey's loyalty to the firm was unquestioned, but he was too straight and too much a family man to ever countenance anything underhand, let alone illegal. No, he was a non-starter. It needed to be someone who knew how to handle themselves, and who could also keep a cool head in difficult situations. Someone professional, yet creative. "Ian Smith. He'd be perfect for this," he concluded, "but how can I get him on side?"

Recalling the previous day's row over the subpoena, Ray wondered if he could leverage Ian's current circumstances to his advantage. "Hmmm .... the guy's obviously being cleaned out financially, and with ongoing maintenance payments to meet, money could really be an issue. It might just work."

He picked up the phone and punched the intercom button. "Jayne, can you get Ian Smith for me please? And ask HR to let me know what his annual salary is before he arrives."

Ray wasn't a man known for his compassion unless there was something to gain from it but, having been divorced himself in the past, he had felt something akin to pity for Ian yesterday once his anger had passed and he felt he could put on a credible performance as a concerned boss. Possibly, a friendly shoulder and an offer of support could be of benefit after all.

"Good morning Ian, come in and take a seat," he said looking up from his paperwork as his Head of Security entered his office fifteen minutes later. "Look, I've been thinking about your unfortunate situation and wondered if there is anything Global Energy can do to help you get through it successfully? I mean, do you need any legal help? Compassionate leave or financial assistance to help you get back on your feet? Where are you living for example?"

"Well Ray, as far as accommodation goes, I'm having to rent a bedsit near Kings Cross. It's all I can afford."

"Well we can't have that. You're one of our senior managers and we do try to look after our executive team at Global Energy. If it helps, I'll see about arranging a loan for you through HR, we might even be able to manage a salary increase or long-service bonus or something along those lines."

"Well, a cash injection would undoubtedly be a big help, but it's probably better I don't receive anything until my divorce settlement is finalised … it would only be more for those money grabbing lawyers to get from me," Ian lamented.

"Perfect," thought Ray, mentally rubbing his hands together. "If he can't accept official company money, I can certainly give it to him myself, off the record and untraceable, and have him very grateful to me indeed. Maybe grateful enough to bend the rules a little."

Slapping Ian on the back in an apparent sign of solidarity, Ray exclaimed, "Nonsense! If we can't do it through 'official' channels, then I'll give you the money myself for the time being. How much do you need to make a down payment on another property

201

somewhere? We need to get you out of rented accommodation. Would £100,000 set you on your feet? £150,000? More?"

Ian, shocked by the generous offer, was overwhelmed with gratitude. He didn't even consider the consequences of accepting money from someone he had previously viewed as cold and calculating, and simply couldn't believe his luck. The embarrassment and frustration of having to leave his marital home, a five-bedroomed detached house, to move into a terrible bedsit with no room for his children to stay had been a severe blow. Now this man, his boss, was offering him his pride back. Ray was giving him the ability to buy a small home several years before he would otherwise be able to afford to do so with the extortionate maintenance payments it looked like he was going to have to pay.

"Do you really mean it Ray? I would be eternally grateful, and would of course, pay you back as soon as I could," Ian spluttered.

"Think nothing of it, Ian. It's a sorry state of affairs if we divorced men can't help one another out every now and then. I'll tell you what: Open yourself up a new bank account in whatever name you see fit and let me have the details. No-one else needs to know about it but us. I'll deposit the money into it for you within the week."

Ian nodded gratefully, then stood up and shook Ray's hand. "Thank you Ray, you have no idea how much of a difference this will make to my life."

"Don't mention it Ian. Seriously, don't mention it to *anyone*," said Ray, thinking to himself, "I own you now buddy, from this moment onwards, you're mine."

---- 35 ----

Saturday 6th October
Kingsand, Cornwall

It was more than six hours before *Aztec* was at anchor again: Skip had decided to push on to, and anchor outside, the twin villages of Kingsand and Cawsand, just west of the River Tamar and Plymouth. The dividing line between these two villages had historically been the border between Devon and Cornwall with an inn, *The Halfway House*, straddling that border. In more recent times the border had been defined as following the line of the Tamar, one of England's major rivers and still home to Devonport, one of the British Naval Dockyards. A pretty and sheltered anchorage, Skip felt it was the ideal place to lie low, yet there was the convenience of a major port and city within an hour's sail if needed. Arriving in the dark the previous evening, the crew had decided to turn in for the night and start refreshed in the morning.

"So, if I am understanding you correctly, immediately before the WAIS event, you'd noticed some strange vibrations?" Julie asked Chuck to confirm.

"Absolutely right. I initially thought it must be an earthquake, and a very big one at that. It was only after Bill Bond, the pilot had come out to the sheet and rescued me, and we flew over one of the biggest crevasses, that I really began to question what was happening. I was sure I could see faint reddish threads running at the bottom of it instead of the normal blue-white ice that I would have expected."

"Are you positive about that?" Julie asked. "You'd just been rescued from a potentially fatal situation and could have been having an adrenaline spike which can sometimes distort your perception and vision."

"I know what I saw Julie. Something looked like it was glowing hot, deep down in the ice, so I took out my mobile phone and took some photos through the plexiglass window. Here they are look, they're somewhat grainy, but you can just make out the redness on the image. There's something glowing at the bottom of that crevasse, here, and here. I can only think it was something like a lava flow, but without a volcanic eruption I don't know where it can have come from, and from my research, there is no volcano in that part of the Antarctic. I'm certain it must have been triggered by man, possibly even my own employers. I had discovered they'd been carrying out some under the radar exploratory drilling just before my trip out."

Julie studied the images that Chuck had shown her. She had to agree. There was something glowing red at the bottom of the crevasse. What the hell was it?

"This is all very strange Chuck. My contact at IVSO, Keith Mortimer, could probably shed some light on it. He has been comparing past earthquake seismograph readings against those from the time of the WAIS event, and because they don't correlate he feels strongly that the cause of the event wasn't a natural one. You also just said you don't think it was a natural disaster. You'd better tell me more about this secret drilling activity Global Energy are undertaking down there."

"Well, the details of the project are only available to employees who are way above my pay grade I'm afraid, and not something I really know much about. But I heard on the rumour grapevine that the company had been doing some minor 'off-piste' exploration employing a new type of deep core sonic blasting, a few hundred miles north-west of where I was working. I'd noticed that there had been a few odd spikes on the seismograph in the days running up to the event, readings similar to those I saw on the day in question, now I think of it."

"Wouldn't that have been in contravention of the Antarctic Agreement?" queried Julie. "I thought all drilling and exploration activities were strictly controlled down there. Presumably, Global Energy have only been granted a licence for standard extraction activities, haven't they?"

"Well that's what I would have expected," confirmed Chuck, "but when I saw a schedule for exploratory sonic blasting on my boss' desk, it was the top page in a file marked 'PROJECT UNDERMINE – CONFIDENTIAL', so I'm wondering if Global Energy aren't being as straight with everyone as they should be."

"Let me call Keith Mortimer to see what he knows about this sonic blasting, and why an international energy company might be engaging in that type of activity in the Antarctic."

Julie checked the time and decided it wasn't too early to call Keith, although she realised he would probably be at home as it was the weekend. She dialled his number and turned on the loudspeaker on the mobile phone as Keith answered the call.

"Good morning Keith, it's Julie Grant here from *The Telegraph* in London. I'm sorry to be calling you at home so early in the morning, but I need your help again. Is it convenient to talk?"

Keith put down his cup of coffee and looked longingly at the pancakes and maple syrup on the plate his wife had just put down in front of him. He pushed the plate away reluctantly.

"No problem, Julie. How are you, and how can I help?"

"I'm fine thanks Keith, although there have been one or two strange things happening to me recently so I'm lying low at the moment," she explained. "I think it's all wrapped up with what's going on down on WAIS and wanted to pick your brain again. I've managed to contact the Global Energy scientist who was at the focal point of the activity down there, and he saw something that we're struggling to understand."

"What was that?" queried Keith.

"Well, before I go into any detail, I need your assurance that this conversation is strictly off the record. I know it sounds rather dramatic, but it's possible that lives could depend on keeping things under wraps."

"My God, are you telling me you're in danger? What have you got yourself involved in?"

"I don't think I'm in any real danger at this exact moment Keith, but there is definitely something fishy about Global Energy's activity on WAIS. I'm actually sitting with their scientist as we speak, and he's listening in to our conversation. He's told me something which is very alarming, but before we can go any further with our investigation, we need to understand what it was that he saw and what might have caused it."

"You have my word that I will treat everything you tell me in the utmost confidence Julie," Keith assured. "And I must say, you've certainly piqued my interest."

Julie proceeded to explain to Keith the happenings in the run up to the event, including the secret memo about exploratory sonic blasting, and what Chuck both saw and recorded from the helicopter on his return trip to McMurdo.

"I can't believe Global Energy are undertaking sonic blasting in the Antarctic. They must know it's forbidden!" he exclaimed, "but I am certain that could be the cause of the event. An artificial stimulus or resonance sent down to the earth's core which might have triggered a series of earthquakes and explosions deep below the earth's mantle. That could very easily have caused a tear in the earth's crust and as a result magma could be escaping. I'll check on our satellite imagery to see if it can shed any light on what's happened, but rest assured, if there is a tear in the crust and it doesn't seal itself quickly we could be facing a global disaster. I would really need to flag this to my colleagues as a matter of urgency, Julie, if the imagery shows anything untoward."

"I understand your position Keith, but please speak to me before you bring anyone else into the discussion. Why do you think Global Energy would take such a risk?"

"Well, that's fairly straightforward. You're aware that global oil reserves are depleting and are in danger of running out, and that energy corporations are having to look for alternative sources of energy for the future?"

"Of course," confirmed Julie.

"Well many of them are looking at solar and wind power, others are exploring the harvesting of gas trapped within shale, popularly known as fracking," he explained. "A few of the big players have also been researching the possibilities around extracting methane hydrates from ice but the general conclusion in the industry from the early tests results is that the extraction techniques needed to do this could jeopardise the fragile ecosystem at the Poles, the only areas where there are sufficient volumes of ice to make it worthwhile. It sounds as though your Global Energy friends have decided to ignore the potential dangers and side effects and get ahead of the game and their competition."

"So, do you think Global Energy are just doing this to protect their bottom line and increase shareholder value?" asked Julie. "Surely they wouldn't go against scientific advice and endanger the whole planet! Keith, I'm going to involve Global Energy's scientist, Chuck Fallon now. Chuck, you've been listening to our conversation: Does any of this make sense to you?"

"First of all, I'd like to say good morning to you Keith. Well, referring to your conversation, it sounds plausible I guess, and anyone getting in at the outset could make massive profits. Ray Bergman, the CEO, is totally financially focused, and a recognised risk taker, so it wouldn't surprise me at all."

"They've got to be stopped! And their activities brought out into the open," Julie stated, incensed. "Keith, you have to somehow publish a paper to name and shame them!"

"Just wait a minute Julie," said Keith, trying to calm things down a little. "You're forgetting the fact that we haven't got any evidence of foul play. IVSO can't risk a libel suit unless we're absolutely certain about the facts."

"You're right, Keith. Leave it with us and we'll try to secure that evidence for you. In the meantime, please keep what we've discussed under your hat," she implored.

"Of course, I will my dear. You have my word on it. I'll wait to hear from you before I do anything else, but any evidence you can obtain will have to be rock solid if IVSO are to go to press."

Julie and Chuck said their farewells to Keith and hung up the phone. Julie looked across the saloon table at Chuck, Skip and Dom. "What do we do now?" she asked. "Without the schedule you saw in McMurdo Chuck, we've got nothing to prove that the spikes on the seismograph correlate to the sonic blasting schedule you saw. We've got to get our hands on it somehow."

"You were only given a month's paid leave weren't you Bro?" queried Dom.

"That's right. I'm supposed to contact our Head Office as soon as we make landfall, which I guess I need to be doing round about now I suppose."

"Do you think they'll send you back to McMurdo or pension you off in head office?" Skip asked. "If you're to stand any chance of getting your hands on that schedule, you need to get back to McMurdo and take up your old duties as soon as possible. Do you think you can convince them that you're still an innocent and loyal company man who just wants his old job back?"

"Well I certainly haven't said or done anything to make them think anything other than that."

"Okay, that's great. I know it's not really my battle, but to my mind you need to establish contact straight away to start this ball rolling, if you're sure you want to," outlined Skip.

"I don't really see I have a choice," said Chuck.

"Absolutely not," agreed Julie. "We've got to take these people to task. If they get away with this, who knows what else they'll think they can get away with to bolster their bottom line."

"We can't send Chuck back to McMurdo without some form of back-up," said Dom, ever the concerned sister. "Is there any way you could get *The Telegraph* to pay for you to go down there too Julie? Didn't you mention you'd used some awards ploy in garnering information from the staff down there? That could you be your entry ticket so to speak."

"I can give it a go. It would mean taking my editor into my confidence, but I think she can be trusted."

"So, it looks like we have a plan coming together," said Skip. "Tomorrow, Chuck, you should take a train up to London from Plymouth, and phone into Global Energy first thing on Monday morning to arrange a meeting with whoever you need to, to get your old job back. You, Julie, need to contact your editor and get clearance to travel to McMurdo."

"But we can't expect Julie to return to London after what's happened to her, Skip," Dom stated quite categorically. "Who knows whether Global Energy have got the stations and ports being watched?"

"Well she can hardly fly to Antarctica from anywhere else than London!" Skip replied.

"She can from Paris though, can't she?" Dom suggested. "We could sail her over to Calais and she could pick up the Eurostar from there, sneak her out from under Global Energy's noses."

"A great idea," agreed Chuck. "Are you okay with all this Julie?"

"It's my story and if you're prepared to go back to McMurdo Chuck, then I guess it's the least I can do to come with you. I'm sure Mary will give me the go ahead, but I'll need to buy a new mobile phone before I call her … my old one was stolen last week when I was attacked," she reminded them.

"We can get one in the morning when we take Chuck over to Plymouth," said Skip. "We'll go into Plymouth Yacht Haven and take the ferry from Mountbatten across to the Barbican where we can find a phone store."

On that note the four of them climbed into the dinghy to go ashore and sample the culinary delights of *The Halfway House* inn.

Monday 8ᵗʰ October
London

At 9am Chuck picked up the phone and dialled the number for Global Energy's head office and asked for Barbara Seeder, the HR Director. She came on the line after a few seconds. "Seeder."

"Hello Barbara, this is Chuck Fallon here, just wanting to let you know that I am back in the country after crossing the Atlantic, well rested and fully recovered from my ordeal, and ready to start work again."

"That's great to hear," said Barbara, "can you come into the office today to discuss your options? I'm free all morning."

"No problem, I can make it into the office by mid-morning if that's OK?"

"Yes, that will be fine: I'll block out some time at 10:30 for you, just come up to my office when you get here," she replied, knowing it gave her plenty of time to speak to Ray Bergman to see how he wanted the company to redeploy Chuck.

Chuck replaced the handset on its cradle and picked up his jacket. He didn't expect to be doing much actual work that day, and anyway, there was no point taking a laptop bag with no laptop to put in it! Picking up his keys, he walked out of the front door and headed towards the railway station.

Arriving at the office just after 10:15, he signed in at the front desk, was given his visitor's badge and ushered towards the lifts. He stepped inside and pressed the button for the sixth floor, where the HR department was located, and was shown straight into Barbara's office.

"Welcome back, Chuck," she opened. "Please come in and sit down. We're all delighted you're feeling rested and well after your ordeal. Are you experiencing any flashbacks that are causing you distress?"

"Nothing at all, I'm pleased to report. The four weeks at sea gave me plenty of head space, time to reflect on many things and get everything into perspective. It was the ideal antidote. No contact with the world at large. It was just perfect," he explained.

"That's good to hear, Chuck. We've all been concerned for you. We'll be heading up to Ray Bergman's office in a few minutes: He's keen to have you back on board and hear about your Atlantic adventure," she continued.

"Interesting," thought Chuck, "the CEO wouldn't normally welcome a middle manager back into the fold in person. Let's see what he has to say."

Ray Bergman was full of welcomes and bonhomie, and he showed an apparent great interest in the crossing. "So, you're telling me you had no contact at all with the outside world? Incredible. I would have thought in today's technological world you'd have been online all the way across," he probed.

"Nothing like that at all, Ray," Chuck explained. "We had a satellite phone on board for absolute emergencies, but as it is so expensive to run, the skipper kept it strictly for that purpose. No idle chit chat allowed!"

"Well I'm staggered. Anyway, it's good to have you back Chuck, and I gather from Barbara you feel fit and able to resume your duties. I'm pleased to tell you that there haven't been any more earthquakes down at McMurdo, it looks like it was a one-off event down there. Unfortunate that you were caught in the middle of it."

"Just one of those things I guess," Chuck replied, "but I'm really keen to get back to work, I feel lost when there is nothing concrete for me to focus on."

"That's what I like to hear. Barbara, get this good man booked on a flight for Antarctica straight away. We need his expertise back at the front line," directed Ray. "And now Chuck, if you'll excuse me, I have other matters to attend to."

Standing up, Ray extended his hand to Chuck to close the meeting.

Two hours later Chuck was on his way home again, with flight tickets for the following day, and a new laptop and mobile phone in his new company bag. "Step one completed," he thought.

A few miles away at *The Telegraph* offices, Mary Roberts had just picked the phone up to take a call from Julie Grant.

"Good afternoon Mary, it's Julie."

"Julie! Thank goodness you called. I've been trying to contact you on your home and mobile numbers but couldn't get any reply. Where are you?"

"Somewhere in the English Channel on board a sailing yacht. I'm on my way to France, Mary," Julie explained.

"Whatever for? Never mind. At least we've re-established contact."

"That was one of the reasons for my call. I've had to buy a new mobile phone following the attack last week and wanted to give you my number."

"Of course, I'd forgotten you'd had it stolen. Give it to me now before we forget." Mary scribbled the number down on the pad in front of her on her desk, fully intending to enter it into her phone contacts as soon as they'd finished speaking.

"My laptop was stolen too. Mary, I really think that Global Energy were behind everything and that brings me on to my second reason for calling: I want to go down to McMurdo Research Station and I need you to authorise the trip."

"What on earth for?" asked Mary.

"Well, I've established contact with Global Energy's scientist, the one who was caught up in the disaster, and he says there is evidence of illegal blasting activity down there. He's trying to be sent back to Antarctica himself, so he can try to get hold of it, and I would like to go down to support him if you'll give me the go ahead."

"Under what guise Julie? Won't the arrival of a *Telegraph* reporter raise a few eyebrows and sound alarm bells if there is anything untoward going on?"

"I've already established a reason, well sort of," explained Julie. "When I was trying to identify who had been airlifted away and wanted to speak to the helicopter pilot involved, I did mention we were looking to give an award to the 'brave pilot' who had made the rescue. I could use that as my reason."

"It's a bit improbable but I suppose we could swing it. I'd need to authorise a few dummy articles in support of your story … readers award for corporate bravery or something along those lines. It would mean me deploying manpower up here, and possibly a photographer to join you there to make it stick, but if you and your scientist are correct in that one of the world's biggest energy companies is undertaking illegal activities, then it would be worth it. It could be the scoop of the century." Mary paused for a few seconds, weighing up the pros and cons. "Okay Julie, you've got my clearance to go. I'll email the travel department asking they arrange tickets for you. Heathrow, I presume?"

"Actually Mary, can we make it Paris. I don't want to come back to London in case Global Energy are on the lookout for me. If I can arrive in McMurdo unannounced, it could give me a couple of days to scout around before Ray Bergman and his cronies get wind of it."

"Ah, so that explains your current location. Okay Julie, we'll have tickets waiting for you at the Air France travel desk in Charles De Gaulle airport by the morning. Good luck and keep me posted."

"Will do, and thanks Mary," Julie replied, ending the call.

---- **37** ----

Thursday 11th October
McMurdo Research Station, Antarctica

There aren't many flights to Antarctica and most of those originate from South America or South Africa. Cape Town was the favoured hub on this occasion, there being more flight connections from Europe. For that reason, Julie and Chuck found that they were booked onto the same flight for the leg of their journey from Cape Town to Wolf's Fang Runway in Queen Maud Land, and both welcomed the pleasure of having company on it.

On the flight, they exchanged their new mobile phone numbers, and talked about how they would communicate with each other in Antarctica, arranging daily schedules at differing times so that no pattern would be evident to anyone else.

Chuck was carrying straight on to McMurdo, where he would go and see his boss to get his new work schedule. Once he had that in his hands, he would call

Julie and pass the details on to her, so that she would know where he was at any given time.

Being a reporter from *The Telegraph*, Julie had arranged to stay in the White Desert Hotel on the promise of writing an article about it while she made the necessary arrangements for her own transport to, and accommodation in, McMurdo Station. Once there, she planned to hold interviews with Bill Bond and anyone else involved in the rescue on the sheet. It would be a viable cover, and hey, she might even get a story with mileage from it as a bonus.

Chuck joined the McMurdo transport shuttle and flew to the base. On arrival he presented himself to the company stores department and picked up a new set of cold weather gear to replace the ones that were damaged during his plight on the WAIS. He was given a new red high visibility Parka, more up-to-date hi-tech boots and gloves, and a new pair of salopettes. He went to his quarters with the new equipment and settled himself back in, unpacking the holdall that he had brought with him from the UK. Most of his stuff was exactly as he had left it when he boarded the company jet after the near disaster on the sheet; as far as he could tell, only the cleaner had come in and disturbed the room as she passed through vacuuming and dusting. There were clean sheets on the bed and fresh towels ready for him in the bathroom.

Despite being tired after the journey Chuck needed to get things moving forwards in terms of gleaning information about 'PROJECT UNDERMINE' as soon as possible, which necessitated getting into his boss' office. He wandered across from the living quarters, through the internal corridor to the admin part of the complex and arrived at the office wing. He asked the receptionist if Graham Platt was in. "Yes, he is. Go on in," came the reply.

Chuck went to the office door, knocked and waited. "Come in," said Graham.

Chuck opened the door and put his head around into the gap. "Hi Graham, I'm back from my travels and ready to get back to work. Is this a good time for you?"

"Hello Chuck, good to see you back here again, I heard you were coming. Yes, it's a good time, come on in."

Chuck walked in and sat down on one of the visitors' chairs in front of Graham's desk. He said nothing for a few seconds, milking the silence. He wanted Graham to open any dialogue.

"So, how are you?" Graham enquired.

"Fine thanks Graham. I'm glad to be back in the fold and eager to resume my duties. I don't suppose there has been much monitoring activity in my absence, and I would like to get started downloading and analysing the data that has accumulated for the last month or so; it's going to take me a while to catch up, so the sooner I start, the better. Has a new remote station been set up to replace the one that dropped into the abyss?"

"Yes, it has. It was only finished last week, so the timing of your return couldn't have been better. We have just finished siting the new station and its living quarters several miles north of the location of the old one, well away from the crevasse. We'll be stocking up the stores tomorrow - why don't you go out with the helicopter, and oversee the commissioning activities in person?"

"Right, I will. Thanks. What time is the transport leaving?"

"Eight a.m. sharp. Don't be late. You've got all your new survival equipment?"

"Yes, I have, I'll be ready first thing in the morning."

"Great," said Graham, "go and get some food, rest up for the afternoon, and be outside the transportation office first thing to meet Bill Bond."

Chuck wasn't ready to go back to his quarters just yet. He wanted to catch up with some of his colleagues, starting with Greg, the radio operator who had coordinated his rescue. He wandered along the corridor to the telecoms centre, peered in through the glazed panel in the door and saw Greg busy on the radio. He opened the door and stuck his head around. Greg was just finishing a broadcast. "Chuckmeister!!" he shouted. "How goes it dude? Long time, no see."

"Yeah, hi Greg, I'm fine thanks, you?"

"Fine? You know what that stands for don't you? Fucked up, Insecure, Neurotic and Emotional. Does that fit the bill?"

"Pretty much! I can't wait to get back to work, I've been idle too long."

"Not what I heard," said Greg. "Word is you just sailed the frigging Atlantic! How awesome is that?"

"Yeah, well, I crewed the boat, but that's all. My brother-in-law was the skipper, he and my sister did all the difficult stuff. I just pulled on ropes when I was told to, kept a lookout, and the boat did all the rest by herself."

"Whatever dude, I'd still like the opportunity to do it. Anyway, not much has been happening down here since you left, no more exciting rescues for me to coordinate."

"Glad to hear it, can't have you being the hero too often."

"Nah, but hey! I did get a call from a cute reporter about the rescue operation, she wanted to know what happened. Seems like Bill is in line for some sort of reward; maybe there'll be a little something in there for me too, being as I was the lynch-pin of it all."

"Well, I'd put you up for an award, you stuck your neck out for me and I appreciate it. Who was the reporter?"

"Some cute-sounding woman from *The Telegraph*, I forget her name. I've been looking online at the electronic version of the paper every day since, but there's no record of anything so far. It's quite disappointing really, I thought I might at least get a mention in dispatches somewhere." Chuck realised it was Julie who had spoken to Greg, but he didn't react.

"I'm sure you'll have your moment of glory, Greg. Anyway, changing the subject away from your long-distance lust affair with a reporter, who's been collecting the remotes in my absence?"

"Uh, actually, no-one has Chuck. Without the remote station, no data can be retrieved, it's all there waiting for you, my friend. You're going to be somewhat busy for a while till you catch up."

"Great, just what I didn't want to hear. An extended period out in the field seems to be on the cards. Oh well, 'c'est la vie', someone's got to do it, and I guess that's me."

"Yeah, bummer isn't it? Never mind mate, I'll catch you when you get back, and we'll down some beers, OK?"

"OK Greg, I'll look forward to it. In the meantime, I'll be in touch on the radio or SatPhone. Cheers."

Chuck backed out of the comms room and went to the dining room. He was hungry after his trip and wanted to get a good, freshly-cooked meal inside him, it might be the last one he would have for a while. He ordered his food and sat down on his own to eat it. He needed to think. If he was being sent out to the remote station tomorrow, and he was likely to be there for some time as the data collections hadn't been done in his absence, he would have to make a move on getting the information on 'PROJECT UNDERMINE' sooner than anticipated. It would have to be tonight. He would need to break into his boss' office and copy the file details. He couldn't risk stealing the original as it would be missed, and all hell would break loose. He didn't want that to happen. He was going to have to break-in and give himself time to get the information before anyone realised what was happening or arrived on the scene. He didn't want to be anywhere near the place when the break-in was discovered.

"OK," he thought, "how am I going to achieve this without being caught?" His boss didn't tend to lock his door when he was elsewhere, Chuck had been in there on his own before now, so it wasn't difficult to get inside the office itself. However, the file was no doubt going to be in a locked drawer, especially now that there had been the 'incident' on the ice sheet. He would have to make a bit of a mess finding the file, then copy it, and put it back where he found it, breaking a few other locks too, just as a distraction. He didn't want anyone to know what the burglar had been after.

He waited in the dining room until a few more people arrived and had noticed his presence, then, once Graham Platt appeared, he slipped out, leaving his tray of half-eaten food on the table so that it looked as though he had gone to the bathroom. He took a knife from the cutlery tray as he passed and slipped it in his pocket.

Walking smartly along the corridor to Graham's office he looked around him. Nobody there, the corridor was empty. He opened the door and slipped inside, quickly crossing to Graham's desk. No file on the desktop, so he went around to the drawers, his heart pounding in his chest. "What the fuck am I doing?" he thought to himself. "If I get caught here, I'm certainly straight out on my ear."

Dismissing that thought, he attacked the first drawer. The knife was sturdy, and he had soon forced the lock. He pulled the drawer open and rummaged through the contents. No file. "Shit!" He attacked the second drawer in the same manner. Just as the drawer came open, he heard a noise from the corridor, someone was outside the door talking. He heard someone say, "I'm just going to put a file on Graham's desk," and again, he thought, "Fuck!" He quickly moved Graham's office chair to one side, ducked down behind the desk and crawled into the kneehole pulling Graham's chair in behind him, hardly daring to breathe. The door handle rattled, the office door opened, and someone walked across the carpet to the front of the desk and placed a document on the desktop. Thankfully Graham's desk had a full modesty panel that continued down to the floor, or Chuck would have been seen.

After a few seconds, the unknown employee turned around and Chuck heard their footsteps retreating, then the door closed. "Oh God! What the hell am I doing here? That was scary!" he thought, his adrenaline levels spiking. "Better get back to it, though. Thank God I closed the top drawer." He pulled the second drawer open and rifled through the documents. Still no file. "Double Shit!" With one eye firmly fixed on the doorway, he shifted his attention to the top drawer on the other side of the desk. "Please let it be in here!" he pleaded. As the drawer came open, he saw the file. Lifting it out, he laid the file on the desk, took out his mobile phone, photographed the cover first, then every page inside it. Once the whole file was copied, he replaced all the pages in their original order and closed the folder, putting it back in the drawer exactly where he had found it. He didn't want to make it too obvious what had been looked for. So, for good measure, he forced the final drawer lock, and then, slipping the knife back into his pocket, he retreated to the office door.

He turned the handle and opened the door a tiny crack, paused for a moment, straining to listen for any movement in the corridor, then on hearing nothing, opened the door a little more. He listened for a few seconds longer, popped his head around the door jamb, saw there was no-one there, then walked into the corridor and back to the Gents' toilet off the dining room. He went into a cubicle and waited a minute until someone else came into the facilities, then he flushed the toilet and went to wash his hands. He made a point of referring to an upset stomach to the other occupant, and then returned to his place in the dining room to finish his half-eaten meal. No-one appeared to have taken any notice of his absence. As he left the dining room a short while later, he purposely stopped by another table to chat to two of his co-workers and Graham Platt, just to reinforce his alibi, then tagged along with some others that were leaving at the same time to return to their quarters. He felt that he should be above suspicion now.

Once back in his room, Chuck looked at the photos of the pages he had taken of the 'PROJECT UNDERMINE' file. It was clear from the schedule that blasting was ongoing, despite the earlier disaster. He copied the images onto a memory stick and encrypted the file, not wanting to put any clandestine information on his laptop that could be taken from him again at any time if the company suspected him of anything after the break-in. He hid the stick on the bottom shelf of the bathroom cabinet above the basin in his bathroom, behind a can of shaving foam, and closed the door. He would get the data to Julie as soon as he could without drawing attention to himself but couldn't risk emailing her as all mails were routinely scanned by the company. Once the file was in her hands, she could compare the blasting schedule with the recorded data he had downloaded onto the USB stick and which was now on his laptop in her care. After that, it was up to her how she handled things. In the meantime, he would do his job as normal, and just keep his head down until the shit really hit the fan. Who could know what he was going to do afterwards? Would he still have a job? Would they suspect him and fire him? Well, time would tell, and there was no point worrying about something that might never happen.

Back in the White Desert hotel, Julie was making her arrangements to travel out to McMurdo. She had tried calling Chuck on his mobile but there was no service, so she realised that any contact would have to be made in person when she was there. She had booked her accommodation on site very easily; it was normal for journalists to visit and report on the various research activities in the complex. She had also scheduled her shuttle flights and was focussing on getting skidoo transportation organised so that she could go out and visit the ice shelf, but she needed to report in to the office first. She picked up the hotel phone and dialled Mary's direct number. The call was answered on the second ring.

"This is Mary," she heard.

"Mary, it's Julie."

"Hi Julie, I hope you have got an update for me as you are spending most of my travel budget?"

"I'm sorry I haven't called earlier, but you know, things are pretty hectic here, getting meetings arranged."

"OK, you're on the line now, give me your number there so I can reach you, and then tell me what's going on."

Julie relayed the direct dial number for her hotel room, then said, "Well, I'm safely here in Antarctica. I have arranged a visit to McMurdo for a two-night stay from tomorrow and am in the process of organising a skidoo and guide to take me out to the ice shelf to see what is happening there for myself."

"OK but be careful. Make sure you let people know where you are going, I don't want to lose one of my brightest senior reporters. I have high hopes for you."

"Thanks Mary, I'll be careful. When I am there, I will be meeting up with the rescue pilot, to cover the interview as planned, but mainly to hook up with my scientist on the inside. He is trying to get me the vital evidence we need to bring this story to the forefront and implicate Global Energy. He says he will be in touch as soon as he has anything for me."

"How long do you think this will take Julie? I've got other stories you could be working on that would be much cheaper to fund the research for."

"I'll be as quick as I can Mary, I don't like the cold so much and would rather be back in the UK. I reckon a few days will do it here."

"Keep me posted, send me your notes as you type them up."

"Will do Mary. Bye." She hung up.

Unbeknown to Julie, all visitors to McMurdo were listed by the reception office daily and sent to the various security departments of the companies housed on site so that clearance and visitor badges could be provided. Clearance was merely a matter of administration and was rarely refused, just an approval message that was returned by the security officer on duty.

At Global Energy a copy of the list was also routinely sent to Ian Smith for his records. On this occasion work had long finished for the day and he had already left the office when the list arrived in his email inbox.

---- 38 ----

Friday 12th October
London

Ian Smith had not slept well. The emotional pressure of his divorce hearing was beginning to tell on him, and not being able to sleep was exacerbating the problem. He simply didn't know what his ex-wife's solicitors were going to throw at him next. The financial hearing was already several days long, and he was due back in court at 10:30am for the next session. "Tomorrow should be the last day," his barrister had informed him yesterday. Well, they couldn't get anything else out of him, he was already cleaned out of what they knew about. The towel was wrung completely dry, except for the £150,000 cash that Ray Bergman had put into his newly opened secret bank account.

In·a state of reconciled defeat, he decided he might as well get something out of the day and call quickly into the office on his way to court to see if there was anything urgent to attend to. Stepping into his office he picked up the pile of papers that his secretary had printed off for him and placed in his in tray, put them in his briefcase, and left without looking at the contents. These papers could wait, there would be time to deal with them later when he was waiting to start his next session at the courthouse.

He arrived at the County Court with fifteen minutes to spare. Entering the courtroom, he sat down next to his barrister who was busily poring over some papers. Not wanting to interrupt his barrister's train of thought, Ian opened his briefcase and looked at the papers inside. The standard list of scheduled McMurdo visitors was low down in the pile. It contained a short list of five names, and the fourth was Julie Grant from *The Telegraph*. He suddenly went pale.

"Oh my God!"

"What?" asked Jon Grimes, his barrister, suddenly looking up from his papers.

"Oh, it's just something work related. I have to make a quick phone call," he said getting up.

At that exact moment the judge entered the courtroom and court was officially in session. There was no escape now, and Ian was panicking. He couldn't leave the courtroom until the first break which was going to be lunch time, and he urgently needed to let Ray Bergman know what was happening in McMurdo.

"I have to make an urgent call," he whispered to his barrister.

Jon Grimes shook his head, "Not a hope Ian, you're in the witness box. You should have done that earlier."

"I couldn't! I've only just discovered something important and I need to get a message out now."

"Write a note, and I'll get it delivered," Jon said.

Ian quickly scribbled a note addressed to: 'Ray Bergman, Global Energy: Ray, JG checked into McM today for 2 nts. Ian S.' He passed it to the supporting solicitor's clerk and said, "This is urgent, please would you deliver it asap?" The clerk looked at the barrister, who nodded surreptitiously. He begrudgingly took the note from Ian and left the courtroom as Ian made his way to the witness stand to face yet more probing questions.

The note was delivered by hand to the receptionist at Global Energy at 11:00am. By 11:10am it was passed to Jayne, who took it straight in to Ray Bergman. He took the note from her, opened it and read it. It took a couple of seconds for him to realise who JG was, and the rage took half that time to consume him as the red mist came down.

---- **39** ----

Friday 12ᵗʰ October
Antarctica

Chuck just stood on the ice and slowly turned through 360 degrees, marvelling at the glistening whiteness all around him. He'd been dropped off by Bill Bond in the helicopter earlier that morning. Now that Bill Bond had flown off again, he was all alone in the wilderness, back very near to where his misadventure started six weeks ago. He couldn't see the crevasse that had opened and swallowed the old research station, but he knew it wasn't far away and that thought sent a shiver down his spine.

He was tasked with commissioning the newly sited replacement station, a collection of insulated metal pods, housing the high-tech seismology and scientific equipment and accommodation unit, plus a generator. They had all been recently delivered to site on the back of trucks equipped with snow tracks, taking a rather circuitous route to avoid the crazed ice surface on the ice shelf. As soon as he had the equipment up and running he would also have to check the radio links to the satellite data stations that were spread out on WAIS. Only then, when everything was fully functional, and the satellite station data collected for the last six weeks had been downloaded, would he be able to determine once and for all what Global Energy was up to. He would have his work cut out.

"Better get to it," he thought resignedly, entering the largest of the pods which housed most of the technical equipment. Once inside and insulated from the cold, he started firing up the equipment.

Julie arrived at McMurdo two and a half hours after Chuck had departed for the ice sheet and went straight to the press quarters where she had reserved a room. After checking in, receiving her press pass and a map of the facility clearly indicating any areas which were 'off limits', she was shown to her room. It was basic but clean and warm, an immense relief after the sub-zero temperatures outside. It was her first experience of a proper research station, and she marvelled at the never-ending pristine white landscape in the distance and the people who chose to live for months on end so far away from civilisation. "This definitely wouldn't be for me," she thought.

Recognising her need to keep up appearances, her first port of call was the radio room to build on her acquaintance with Greg. She picked up the phone and rang through to the communications room. "Greg here," he answered.

"Greg. Hi, it's Julie Grant from *The Telegraph*," she paused to let the name sink in for a couple of seconds, "… we spoke on the phone two weeks ago …"

"Oh yeah, I remember, Julie. Yeah, how are you? Wait a minute, you called internal!"

"Very well, thank you. Yes, I'm down here in McMurdo to complete my story about the rescue, and was wondering if you could spare me a few minutes later this morning? After all, you played a vital part in coordinating the rescue operation and you certainly deserve to be quoted."

"Absolutely! I would be delighted to input to your article Julie, it would be an honour indeed," Greg responded enthusiastically, imagining his name in print, "any time at all would suit me."

"That's great, thank you. I'll pop over in an hour before I try to meet with Bill Bond. Will I need any special clearance to reach you?"

"Your press pass should suffice but if you have any problem just call me."

Bill Bond was a harder man for Julie to track down. According to the air traffic controller he was in the air, returning from dropping a scientist off on WAIS, and would be back by just after lunchtime. She decided that she would wander over to the transportation office on the off-chance he was there after talking to Greg and find out whether the scientist in question who had just been dropped off was Chuck.

Greg was a very willing interviewee. He was more than happy to share his memory of the rescue, and his opinions on most other topics, but it was obvious he didn't know much about any illegal blasting activities from her gentle probing. He was a straight up and down sort of guy, but he had to be spoken to if her cover was to be maintained. Thanking him profusely for his time and assuring him that his invaluable insights would provide very good background in her story, Julie headed over to the airfield in the hope of catching Bill Bond.

Bill was back from flying out to drop Chuck at the new station and he was enjoying a late lunch in the airport canteen when Julie arrived. She didn't recognise him, having only ever spoken to him rather briefly, and had to have him pointed out to her by a passing airport worker. Approaching him from across the canteen she observed a weathered, middle-aged man sitting alone and quietly eating his lunch. "Hmm, he looks rather self-contained," was her first impression, "he could be a difficult nut to crack."

"Excuse me, Mr Bond? Could I interrupt you for a couple of minutes please?" she asked, deciding a more formal approach might be best. Bill looked up from his lunch, holding her in his steady gaze. "Hello, my name is Julie Grant, from *The Telegraph* newspaper in London. We spoke a few weeks ago about your recent rescue mission."

"Hmmph," was the rather taciturn reply, "I'm in the middle of eating my lunch."

"Yes, I'm very sorry to disturb you, but I just wondered if we could arrange a mutually convenient time to meet to discuss the award our readers would like us to bestow on you."

"I'm not interested in any award. It beats me how they even knew about anything in the first place."

This was obviously not going to be at all easy she realised: She needed to back off from the whole award idea and engage him on a different topic. Maybe appealing to the man as opposed to the pilot might be more successful, much as she disliked using her femininity for that purpose.

"I really am sorry, and understand your viewpoint, I really do. It's just I've been tasked by my editor to cover this story and need to be able to prove my abilities as a journalist to her. It would help me a great deal if you could find half an hour to speak to me," she implored, playing the 'poor little me' side of things to the hilt.

Bill looked at her standing in front of him. She seemed to be a nice young woman from what he could see, who had been thrown a dud story down in the back of beyond, and so he relented, and decided he'd give her some time after all.

"Sit down then," he said in between mouthfuls of his food. "I've only got thirty minutes before I'm in the air again, so you'd better make it quick, and please excuse me for continuing with my meal, breakfast was early this morning."

Julie eased into the chair across from him and quickly prioritised her questions in her mind.

"Many thanks Mr Bond."

"Call me Bill."

"Okay, Bill. You outlined the basics of the day of the rescue when we spoke before, but I'd like you to describe to me in more detail the conditions you experienced, what you were feeling at the time, and maybe what you noticed on the rescue flight if you don't mind?"

"There's not a lot to see out there, just a white wilderness," came the reply. "It was incredible that I found him really, the whole research station had disappeared into a giant crevasse that had opened up beneath it. Bloody impossible to land: The surface of the ice was fractured like crazy paving. I had to hover just off the ground and Chuck Fallon had to grab my landing skid to be lifted off. I had no idea whether or not he would be able to hold onto the skid long enough for me to carry him across the crevasse to firmer ice, and even then I wasn't able to put any weight on the ground, I just had to maintain the helicopter's lift and hope to God he had the strength and good sense to let go and climb aboard quickly. It was a hairy moment for both of us, I can tell you."

"It must have been, it certainly sounds it. So, I guess that is the end of that research sub-station then?"

"Yes and no," came the reply. "That actual one is long gone but the company have since shipped out a replacement station. In fact, I'm just back from dropping off the same scientist out there, and he is going to be recommissioning the equipment in the new station over the next couple of days," Bill explained.

"The same scientist as before? Wow! It would be great to meet him to get his side of the story."

"It is the same guy and I can see why you'd like to get his take on the rescue too. Look, my flight this afternoon is back out to the WAIS research station to take out more supplies …. there's a spare seat up front with me, so you're welcome to come along for the ride if you'd like to," he offered. "It would have to be off the record of course."

"That would be great," Julie interjected before he had time to change his mind. "Just let me grab a few things and I'll be right back."

In the helicopter Julie couldn't believe the sights below her, mile after mile of rippling white snow and ice, glistening in the sunlight. "It's spectacular," she commented to nobody in particular, "I can totally see why it is one of the planet's last pristine wildernesses."

The flight out to Global Energy's research substation took little more than two hours and Bill Bond was soon setting the helicopter down gently on the icy surface next to the newly installed station. Julie couldn't wait to get out of the cockpit and onto the ice and she turned to open the door. Bill put his arm on hers to stop her.

"Wait until the rotors have stopped turning before you take off your seatbelt," he yelled over the noise of the slowing blades. Julie nodded her assent and waited patiently.

Chuck had heard the helicopter approaching from within the main technology pod and had donned his outerwear to go and collect the supplies that Bill had just flown out. He was very surprised to see that Bill had a passenger aboard, especially given it was Julie. He had no idea what might have been said between them on the journey, so put on a perplexed look and waited for Bill to make the introductions.

"Welcome to Global Energy's new WAIS research substation," he said, extending his hand in greeting once Bill had introduced them.

Julie was breathless with the extreme cold despite her Antarctic-wear and quickly shook the hand in front of her. "Thank you but is there any chance we can get out of this freezing air?" she asked. "I'd welcome the opportunity to have a chat with you before Bill needs to head off."

"Go ahead and take her indoors while I offload the supplies," said Bill. "We'll need to be on the way back pretty soon though if we're to make it in daylight."

"Happy to oblige. Will you have time for a quick coffee before you need to leave Bill?"

As soon as they stepped inside the accommodation pod, Julie and Chuck exchanged a clumsy embrace, hindered by all their sub-zero gear. "Let's get out of this stuff and I'll show you around. I'm in the process of commissioning all the new equipment and re-establishing links to the satellite data recorders," he explained. "Once everything is back on line, I'll be able to cross-reference the data to Global Energy's sonic blasting schedule."

"You've managed to get it already?" exclaimed Julie. "That was very quick work."

"Well I didn't have much choice, given my boss told me I was being shipped out here the morning after I arrived, so I had to act quickly. I can't believe I had the gall to do it – I had to break into the drawers of his desk with a knife while he was eating dinner!" Chuck explained. "But I found the confidential file in question and photographed the pages. It's downloaded onto a memory stick that I've hidden in the wall cabinet in my bathroom."

"Way to go Chuck. I feel surplus to requirements now though!"

"Actually, you can play a very important role Julie. All our emails are routinely scanned down here so I didn't dare send it to you and leave an audit trail behind for either of our sakes. I had been hoping to see you before I came back out here, but my immediate deployment rather put me off the grid, so to speak. At least you can now perform your own bit of breaking and entering and collect the USB stick from my room."

"Happy to Chuck, but don't we also need the data you're collecting in the next couple of days to provide the categoric link between Global Energy and the disaster? If we can't communicate safely electronically out here, I need to hang around with you to collect it in person. Do you think Bill Bond will come back to pick me up in a day or two?"

Bill walked through the door at that precise moment. "Is that coffee you promised ready Chuck? I'm frozen through."

"Coming right up Bill. Thanks for bringing all that stuff in for me. Julie and I have been using the time productively – she's blown away by the dramatic beauty of the scenery out here and I was telling her the only way to feel at one with it is to make an excursion into the wilderness. I've got to go out and check on one or two things tomorrow and have suggested she accompanies me, that is if you're prepared to make another trip out in two days' time to collect her?"

"Well, I'll be coming out on Monday anyway to collect you, so why not make a weekend of it?" Bill suggested. "That's assuming you've got everything you need to do so?" he queried, looking at Julie.

"I always carry the essentials for a couple of days with me in my bag, Bill. We journalists never know when we may need to stay somewhere unexpectedly, so that will be fine."

Finishing his coffee, Bill stood up to leave Chuck and Julie with the parting comment and a grin on his face, "Right then, behave yourselves kids, don't get up to anything you shouldn't. I'll see you both on Monday."

---- 40 ----

Saturday 13th October
Antarctica

It was the complete and utter silence that Julie found the most astounding. That, and the uninterrupted view in every direction. "How can you stand being out here on your own for days on end Chuck?"

"Look at it this way Jules, it has its advantages: No pollution, plenty of time for reflection, and as you are now discovering, absolute peace, at least when the weather is calm. That said, I'm always glad to return to McMurdo for a bit of conversation … too much of your own company can becoming wearing!" he laughed. "Anyway, we need to tog up properly now and head out to one of the more remote satellite data stations: It's the only one I haven't managed to re-establish a data link with and it probably needs a manual reboot. The trip will kill two birds with one stone, so to speak. Reconnect the station and give you your Antarctica excursion, avoiding the crevasses of course."

"How far away is it? And do we have to walk there?"

"My God no Jules, it's fifty miles away. We'll use the skidoo and be there in no time at all. I've checked the weather and we're clear to go."

"Ooh, exciting! Can I drive?"

"Not a chance, it's man's work, like barbecuing! Surely you know about boys and their toys?" Chuck teased.

Clad in their full survival gear, Chuck mounted the GPS unit on the handlebars, checked the fuel and oil levels, packed his tools and equipment in the panniers, then started up the skidoo and they set off west into the white wonderland. Their helmets were equipped with intercom radio mikes and Chuck was able to provide a running commentary on the geology of the area; the depth of the ice and the microscopic organisms trapped inside it that tell us so much about climate change; the melting and calving of the glaciers, and much more.

Arriving at the remote data station, Chuck was soon able to diagnose the problem causing the communication failure with the research substation and replaced the offending faulty panel from the box of spares on the back of the skidoo. He ran his diagnostic checks, and when they came back clean, he was satisfied all was well again.

"Right, now that's sorted, let's head off and explore. Providing we're back at the base by mid-afternoon for the routine radio check-in, we've got time to have a bit of an adventure. I'll even let you have a steer if you behave yourself!" he joked.

Heading off in the opposite direction from which they'd come, Julie marvelled at the sights passing by her eyes, nature at its rawest yet most beautiful. "Will we see any penguins?" she shouted into her helmet mike, "or polar bears?"

"The answer to that is no and no: First we're too far inland here for penguins to be able to feed, and secondly polar bears are only at the North Pole," Chuck explained.

Suddenly, Chuck swerved to the right and stopped. "My God!" he exclaimed "Can you see that?" he asked, pointing into the distance.

"What? Where?"

"Over there, it looks like a lake but I'm pretty sure it's a massive hole in the ice sheet. We're miles away from the original crevasse so I don't think it can be connected to that but I daren't go any closer, the ice may not take our weight."

"Are we safe here?"

"I'm not sure Jules, we'd better get out of here, but let me take a couple of photos and our GPS co-ordinates first, so we can study things later."

Armed with the photos and location, Chuck turned the skidoo around and hurried them back to the research substation where he fired up his laptop to download the photos.

"I should be able to zoom in and get a clearer view. Maybe we can make out what it is we saw." Armed with the enhanced images on the laptop it became very clear that there was indeed a gigantic hole in the surface of the ice, and what looked to be another behind it in the distance.

"Have you ever seen anything like this on the ice sheet before Chuck?"

"Never, and I've been working out here for nearly ten years. I know people talk about global warming, but the effects from that take decades to be felt and, trust me, those holes were not there two months ago."

"Do you think it's all connected to what happened six weeks ago?"

"I can't see what else it could be. And if it was all caused by Global Energy's sonic blasting programme, then any further continuation of the blasting project is only going to exacerbate the situation."

"We need Keith Mortimer to see these photos as soon as possible," said Julie. "It looks to me as though the ice sheet is melting, and if that's the case, he needs to know. Surely it would mean sea levels would rise dramatically if something the size of WAIS melts."

"It would mean disaster Jules. I read somewhere that if the Ross Ice Sheet melts it would increase global sea levels by almost sixty metres. That would wipe out most of the capital cities in the world, not to mention the loss of power and impact on the food chain. It would cause a global disaster, possibly extinction."

"We've got to do something Chuck. Global Energy's sonic blasting programme has got to be halted."

"You're right. They've got to be exposed in the world's media and pressure brought from the highest level to make them stop. It will most probably cost me my job, but if the world is in danger what job would there be left for me anyway? We've got to get this information back to civilisation soonest."

"Will Bill come back and get us straight away?"

"I think it would be best if we left the plans as they are and don't stir things up just yet. That way we won't be alerting anyone at Global Energy to what we've discovered here. And let's face it, one more day is not going to make much difference anyway."

Saturday 13th October
London

Knowing Ian Smith wouldn't be attending court over the weekend, Ray summoned him into the office.

"Ian, we have a problem," was his opening remark as Ian walked into his office, "something I need you to deal with as a matter of urgency."

"Is this connected with Julie Grant's presence at McMurdo?"

"Too bloody right it is. That woman is getting too close Ian and needs to be closed down before she blows our cover story."

"What do you mean by 'closed down' Ray? And what cover story are you talking about?"

"I'm going to take you into my confidence Ian, completely off the record. Global Energy's profits have been declining in recent years, a slow decline granted, but nevertheless heading in the wrong direction. As CEO I am expected to bolster profits and that means diversification into the field of alternative energy sources. To that end, we have started a programme of sonic blasting down in Antarctica looking to release and harvest the methane hydrates in the ice."

"But isn't that in contravention of our drilling licence Ray?"

"Yes, it is. And that's why we've been conducting the programme under the radar. No-one must find out about this activity: It would mean the loss of our licence which would be the end of Global Energy, and your job," explained Ray. "We can't let this Julie Grant woman stumble onto what we're doing, and the more she digs into our activities, the more likely she's liable to find out."

"But I thought she was just down there to present some award to Bill Bond for his dramatic rescue of Chuck Fallon."

"A handy cover story, no doubt, but that doesn't stack up. No national newspaper would send a top reporter to Antarctica to present a bloody medal to a hero," said Ray. "Trust me, she's up to no good and has got to be stopped .... permanently this time. And you're the man to deal with it."

"What?!" exclaimed Ian. "You want me to arrange an "accident" to happen to her? If that's what you're saying, I'm definitely not your man."

"Oh, but you are my man, Ian, you're bought and paid for. To the tune of one hundred and fifty thousand pounds, remember? I'm sure you don't want to find yourself in contempt of court and with a prison sentence for not declaring all your money in your divorce hearing? You know you ex-military men never get an easy ride in prison," Ray threatened.

"But that was just a temporary loan, and I am going to pay you back!"

"That's as may be, but you haven't, have you? One phone call from me on Monday morning would see you well and truly in deep shit – because don't forget, I have the bank account details and can drop you right in it, so I recommend you do just as I say Ian. What choice do you have?"

"But that's blackmail Ray! You can't do that."

"Well, actually, yes I can, and it looks like I am. If you want to keep your freedom to see your kids, and your job, you'll do exactly as I say."

Downcast and defeated, Ian reluctantly listened to what Ray required. He had to fly down to McMurdo on the company jet that day. He had no choice in refusing, he was truly caught between the devil and the deep blue sea.

---- 42 ----

Monday 15th October
Antarctica

Ian Smith had touched down at the McMurdo airstrip shortly after midnight local time. He'd spent the flight in a state of shock: Even though he'd killed people before during his time in the military on the front line, that had been mechanically easy as he had been trained to do so, and they were always the enemy. He'd never had to kill an innocent person before, and now his job and freedom rested on being able to do it. How could he live with himself afterwards, assuming he got away with it?

Checking into Global Energy's visiting staff wing at the research station, he unpacked his few possessions, sat on the edge of the bed, and put his head in his hands. Maybe risking prison was worth it, better for fraud and contempt of court than for murder. But without his job, and in prison, there was no way he would be able to support or see his children. God! What a mess.

Resigned to his fate, he finally started to think of how he might bring about Julie Grant's demise. To ease his conscience as much as possible he decided he should do it in a quick, clean and the most pain free fashion as possible. "I'll break her neck," he decided. "With no visible marks of a struggle on her body it'll look like she tripped and fell; an unfortunate accident, and, even better, I could leave her body out in the wilderness, somewhere it will never be found."

Later that morning, Julie and Chuck had packed their bags and were waiting for the arrival of Bill Bond to ferry them back to McMurdo in the helicopter. They'd spent most of Sunday analysing the downloaded data from the remote data stations and they now had categoric proof linking Global Energy's illegal sonic blasting activity to the event on 1st September. The evidence of resumed and ongoing blasting since that date presumably had exacerbated the situation, leading to the formation of the giant ice holes they had seen for themselves. Now they needed real-time satellite imagery of the ice sheet and for that, they needed IVSO satellite access and the input of Keith Mortimer to fully understand the extent and implications.

They'd formulated a plan: They would get back to McMurdo, retrieve the USB stick from Chuck's bathroom cabinet and make a hasty exit on the first available flight out of there before they were missed. As soon as they were back to civilisation, they would email the images and data to Keith Mortimer, and contact Mary Roberts to bring her up to speed on what they'd found.

Julie planned to work on her headline story for the paper during their flight and then it was up to Mary when and how to proceed. "It will be largely out of my hands whether or not Mary decides to publish my report. She's been supportive of the story so far, but potentially exposing the details that would cause the collapse of one of the largest energy companies in the world won't be without repercussions," she commented.

The distant beating of the approaching helicopter had them donning their survival gear for the quick run over to the aircraft and then they were up and away, heading back to the base.

"Had a good weekend, guys? Did you get the full Antarctic experience you were looking for?" Bill enquired with a slight twinkle in his eye.

"I've seen more than I could have possibly imagined," was Julie's cryptic reply.

Bill smiled and raised an eyebrow at this response and then focused on his piloting. During the flight, Julie and Chuck chatted to Bill about his flying job and found that he did a regular transport run to Mario Zucchelli Airport to collect travellers and workers from the charter flights out of New Zealand, and the next one was scheduled for later in the day. That would be their quickest way out of McMurdo, and they decided to ask Bill to take them with him. They touched down in McMurdo two hours later having benefitted from a following wind and after thanking Bill, they parted company.

"I'll see you back at the airfield in an hour," Chuck said to Julie as they headed back to their own accommodation.

Ian Smith hadn't been idle. After a few hours of very fitful sleep, he'd awoken feeling stiff and somewhat jetlagged, but as ready as he would ever be to start on his task. His first step was to locate Julie Grant. Then he had to somehow catch her alone and unawares to deliver the fateful blow.

He knew McMurdo had a press accommodation wing and so that was his first port of call. "Good morning, I have an appointment with one of your guests, Julie Grant, but she hasn't shown up. Could you try her room for me please?" he asked the receptionist.

"Of course, one moment please." Ian counted to ten as the phone rang unanswered and then turned to leave. "Would you like to leave a message?" the receptionist enquired.

"No thanks, I'll catch up with her somewhere."

Hurrying to her accommodation to collect her belongings and make arrangements for them to join the next available flight out of Mario Zucchelli Airport, Julie's mind was solely focused on the task in hand and she didn't notice the man coming out of the entrance with his head down against the chill wind until she collided with him, knocking them both to the ground.

"I'm so sorry," she gasped, somewhat winded from the impact. "Are you okay?"

Recognising her and grabbing an unforeseen opportunity, Ian was quick to feign injury. "I think I might have twisted my ankle. How about you?"

"No damage as far as I can tell," said Julie as she slowly climbed to her feet and put out her hand. "Here, let me help you stand up."

Accepting the proffered hand, Ian hauled himself to his feet, wincing as he put weight on his supposedly injured ankle. "Ouch," he exclaimed, "it's more painful than I realised. I don't think I can manage to walk unassisted on this ice: Do you think you could lend me a shoulder to the medical centre?"

Glancing impatiently at her watch, Julie suddenly remembered her manners. She might be in a hurry but had caused the accident in the first place. "Of course. Do you know where it is?"

Having studied the map of the station to try to identify somewhere suitable to strike against Julie, Ian knew the location of most buildings at McMurdo and the medical centre was tucked away beyond the storage depot. He nodded to Julie and put his arm around her shoulder, allowing his weight to bear. "Perfect," he thought to himself as they hobbled away.

Leaning heavily on Julie and favouring his injured ankle, they made slow progress limping in the direction of the medical centre and making polite chit chat as they went. The storage depot loomed in front of them, the large doors shut firmly against the penetrating cold. "Maybe I could get her inside on some pretext," Ian pondered, literally thinking on his feet and surprised how calm he felt now that the dreaded moment was nigh. "It must be all the military training," he mused.

Approaching the pedestrian entrance of the depot he stumbled and cried out in pain. "I don't think I can make it all the way to the medical centre. Can we rest inside here out of this biting cold for a few minutes?"

Cursing her luck, Julie felt she had no option other than to comply to his request however reluctant she was. "Okay. Maybe I can find you a chair to rest on while I go and get some help from the medical centre," she suggested.

Struggling inside she left Ian propped against the door jamb and turned to go and find a chair. "Hello," she called out. "Anyone in here?" Silence was the reply. "I suppose no-one hangs around in here unless they need to," she said, looking back over her shoulder to where she'd propped Ian, but he wasn't there. "What the hell?" she wondered, when Ian suddenly leapt at her from out of the shadows, cannoning into her. She fought to retain her footing as he prepared to break her neck with a single blow, stumbling away from him back towards the entrance door.

Chuck had seen her helping Ian from his bedroom window and had come down to offer his assistance, and then he saw them enter the storage depot. Pushing open the door into the facility he called out, "Julie, are you in here?" as he stepped inside.

"Chuck, help … help me!" she cried falling into his arms.

Pushing Julie firmly behind him, Chuck strained his eyes trying to see into the gloom of the facility only to get a glimpse of Ian disappearing behind some packing chests. "What the hell's happening?" he asked Julie.

"The man I was helping just attacked me," Julie stammered.

"Christ! I probably should go after him, but I'm a scientist not an assassin. Let's just get out of here."

Dragging Julie behind him they stepped back outside. "We need to get away from this place as soon as possible Julie. Have you collected what you need?"

"I never made it to my room, but I have everything important, my laptop and phone, with me here. Let's abandon the rest and go to your accommodation until we can get a flight."

"I don't think my room is a good idea, Jules. I think that man was the Global Energy Head of Security and he knows who I am. I can't be certain, but I think it was him. We'd better head to the airfield … Bill Bond's office will be as safe as anywhere."

"But what about the USB stick?"

"Fortunately, I'd already put it in my pocket before I came down to help you. My laptop is another matter: It's still in my travel bag in my room and we need it. All our data analysis from yesterday is on it. Look, I'm going to take you over to Bill's office and then nip back to get it."

"Be careful Chuck. That guy will be on the lookout for both of us now."

"I will. While you're waiting for me see if you can sweet talk Bill into flying us down with him when he goes to the airstrip at Mario Zucchelli this afternoon. We will be able to pick up a charter flight back to New Zealand from there."

After delivering Julie into Bill's safe keeping, merely asking him to look after her as she'd had some bad news, Chuck set off back towards the Global Energy accommodation block. He didn't spot Ian Smith on the way but knew he wouldn't be far away.

In fact, Ian Smith was more shaken by the botched attack this morning than he would have expected, and he had returned to his room to recover. "I hope that Chuck Fallon didn't recognise me," he fretted. "If he did, I'm screwed, unless I deal with both of them now." Pushing himself off his bed, he stepped outside his room and headed for the stairs. "I'd better find out which room Chuck Fallon is in."

As luck would have it, as Ian Smith headed down one staircase in the accommodation block, Chuck was creeping up the other and along the corridor to his room. The coast seemed to be clear as he edged his way inside and grabbed his bag. Turning to leave, he heard someone outside in the corridor, trying to open the door. "Bloody hell, that's got to be Ian Smith." Thinking quickly of where he could hide that wouldn't be too obvious, the door opened to a woman's cry of, "Housekeeping." Chuck sagged down onto the bed, "My God, I don't think I'm cut out for this."

Chuck's luck remained with him and he made it back to Bill Bond's office unscathed to find Bill fussing over Julie. "She's really made a hit there," he mused.

"This poor woman, to have her home broken into and car ransacked all in one night is beyond belief," said Bill. "No wonder she's upset." Julie had been able to talk with credibility about the attacks and Bill didn't need to know it had been two weeks previously. The important thing was he had believed her and agreed to fly them down to Mario Zucchelli Airport that afternoon. They were almost home free.

Ian Smith had seen that Chuck and Julie were in Bill Bond's office and had been loitering just outside the window. He strained his ears to hear what was being said inside, and managed to string together a few of the words, including 'Mario Zucchelli'. He realised that they were going to do a runner, with Bill Bond's help. He would have to move quickly and decisively. He moved across to the helicopter on its landing pad and walked around the craft. Opening the engine compartment, he looked inside for some means to sabotage the craft. "One extra casualty of war won't make any difference," he thought as he located the fuel hose, took out his Leatherman tool and pushed the end of the knife into the hose. The cut in the pipe was only large enough for the fuel to just seep out, but he knew that as the pump cut in, the flow would increase under pressure. He closed the engine compartment door and walked away from the helicopter. "That'll sort both of you out and get me off the hook with Bergman," he muttered under his breath.

Bill Bond had already registered his flight plan and shortly afterwards the three of them walked out to the helipad, climbed aboard and closed the doors. Bill did his pre-flight checks, and all instrument readings were good. He fired up the engine and increased the power to lift off. The helicopter rose a few feet, then Bill rotated and tilted the joystick forwards, increased the collective and they were off. He rose to 2500 feet, levelled out, and cruised at top speed towards Mario Zucchelli Airport, 250 miles away over the Prince Albert Mountains along the Scott Coast. The weather was good, visibility great, and Julie scanned the area as far as her eye could see.

Bill Bond focused on his instruments and the GPS system, making sure he was on track. All appeared to be going well, just as he would hope. An hour into the journey Bill noticed that the fuel gauge was much lower than he expected. "What on earth can have caused that? I refuelled before we left. There must be a leak in the fuel pipe." He kept his eye on the gauge for the next 5 minutes and noticed a further significant drop. "I don't know about a leak, it looks like the fuel pipe has split." He made a quick mental calculation and realised that they weren't going to have enough fuel to reach the airport. He got on the radio.

"Mario Zucchelli, this is McMurdo1, McMurdo1, over."

"McMurdo1 this is Mario Zucchelli, what can we do for you? Over."

"Mario Zucchelli, we have an issue. My fuel levels are dropping fast, I appear to have developed a break in the fuel line. I am over the ice field and am probably going to have to ditch before long if I can find somewhere even to land. Can you scramble the rescue service for me please? Over."

"Roger that McMurdo1, what is your position? Over."

"Mario Zucchelli, I am currently 100 miles south-south-west of you, current speed 120mph altitude 2500 feet, but dropping down to 500 feet. I have survival gear aboard if we have to ditch, but I would appreciate some speedy assistance. Over."

"Roger McMurdo1, scrambling the rescue chopper now. Stay on this channel and give me updates every minute. Over."

The fuel levels continued to plummet. Bill looked back to his passengers sitting in the rear and pressed the intercom switch. "Look guys, I'm sorry, but we have a problem."

"What is it?" asked Julie, looking at Bill and gripping Chuck's arm. Chuck had been dozing but was instantly awake. "What's up?" he said.

"Fuel is leaking out fast, we don't have much left, so I need to reduce altitude in case the engine fails and try to preserve what we have remaining. That means slowing down, something I am reluctant to do but have no choice. I'm hoping we have enough to get us to some even ground."

Julie looked down on the jagged ice field and shivered. "What if we don't find anywhere?"

"Well, we'll have to do the best we can. The land below is a mass of ice peaks and crevasses but there are a few plateaus if we can reach one. We're all wearing survival gear, so we'll be OK for a while. It won't be pleasant, but I have already got the rescue service on its way. So, let me tell you what will happen, and I ask you do exactly what I say at all times."

As he reduced the helicopter's height and speed, keeping an eye on the fuel gauge, he relayed the safety instructions to Julie and Chuck and asked them if they understood everything. They both nodded their assent, clinging on to each other for dear life. The engine started to cough and splutter, air was getting into the system and causing the motor to misfire.

"Hang on folks, this is going to be rough!" Bill wrestled with the collective and the joystick trying to maintain level as the misfiring continued and the helicopter started to lose control. Down and down it went towards the ice field. Bill put out a Mayday call on the radio:

"Mayday, Mayday, Mayday, this is McMurdo1, call sign 2BFX0. Mayday. My position is 76.15 degrees south 162.50 degrees east, I have motor failure and require immediate assistance. I have three persons on board, I am losing power and having to ditch."

He scanned the ice field looking for anything flat that he could set the chopper down on. After a few moments, he had made up his mind. He aimed the craft towards a small plateau between two crevasses that looked reasonably flat on the surface and the helicopter careered towards it. Chuck realised what was happening and braced for impact.

"Bill! You can't be serious!" he shouted.

"No choice! It's this way or nothing!"

Chuck grabbed Julie and clutched her tightly to his body. "Hang on Julie, we're going to land."

"How? Where?" I can't see anything to land on."

"Look, over there. There's a plateau…"

Julie's hand flew to her mouth, her eyes standing out on stalks in horror. "Chuck, hold me tight …"

The helicopter finally lost power as it reached the plateau. It dropped the last 30 feet onto the icy surface, bounced twice on its skids and settled into a sideways slide, heading towards the crevasse. Julie screamed, Chuck could see the edge getting ever nearer, and Bill was trying everything in his skillset to stop the helicopter. The edge of the chasm got closer and closer, it looked as though their impetus would carry them over the rim and down into the icy depths. Bill threw the joystick over and the rotors, still turning, tipped into the ice. They bit into the surface, folding and crumpling as they struck, and slewing the helicopter round, but gaining enough purchase to slow it down. Finally, right on the ridge with the tail hanging out in fresh air, it came to a halt. Bill breathed out a sigh of relief. Julie was in tears, and Chuck, who was closest to the edge, had shut his eyes in anticipation of the worst.

"Out! Now!" ordered Bill. They opened the door on Julie's side of the cabin and climbed down onto the ice. Bill reached inside behind the pilot's seat and passed the survival bag down. He opened the bag and took out the handheld VHF radio, then called Mario Zucchelli Airport to let them know what had happened, and once again he gave their GPS position. A few moments later, with a grinding crunching sound, the weight of the helicopter crumbled the edge of the plateau and it tumbled over the edge and into the crevasse. "God, that was close!" said Bill.

"Once again, I owe you my life Bill, thank you!" said Chuck. Julie ran across, threw her arms around Bill's neck and gave him a big hug and a kiss on the cheek. "Yes. Thank you, Bill, I'm so glad you were our pilot. I wouldn't be here otherwise. How did you know to tip the rotors?"

"It was a gut reaction. I've never been in that situation before, and it now looks as though we'll never know the reason this happened, with the helicopter hundreds of feet below us."

Julie said nothing, she just looked at Chuck. He raised his eyebrows as if to say, "I know who's behind it, bloody Ian Smith and Global Energy."

"Right," said Bill, "we need to spread out the red flag and get the flares ready so that the rescue helicopter can find us in this godforsaken ice hell."

They took the flag out of its bag and pinned it to the ice. Bill handed an orange smoke flare to Chuck and continued calling on the hand-held radio, guiding the rescue crew towards their location. A few minutes later it hovered over them and a rope ladder was dropped down for them to climb. Julie went first, then Chuck, and finally Bill. The rescue crew helped each of them aboard, wrapped them in survival blankets, and closed the door. Bill was on such an adrenalin rush that he couldn't rest and went forward to talk to the pilot and relayed the situation to him. Julie watched from her seat at the back and noticed Bill was gesticulating wildly, clearly upset about what had happened. She leaned across to Chuck who was sitting silently, still in something of a daze. "You OK, Chuck?"

"No, not really Jules. You?"

"Me neither, I can't believe what just happened," she said, leaning against him. Chuck put his arm around Julie and said nothing more. He sat there thinking. Two helicopter rescues in quick succession was more than the average person could ever expect in one lifetime. Mercifully, he was unscathed, no thanks to the efforts of Global Energy. "Well," he thought, "screw them. They'll get their just desserts now."

Back at McMurdo, Greg had heard the Mayday distress call that Bill had put out to Mario Zucchelli Airport just before he ditched, and he had heard nothing since then. He looked up the coordinates that Bill had given on the charts and he could see that it was over the massive ice field, close to the mountains and with nowhere to land. "The poor devils, they don't stand a chance," he thought. He assumed that the worst had happened, and he was in a state of shock. "Shit," he said to himself, "three lives lost! I'd better report this." He left his radio station and went to see the McMurdo manager. Knocking on the door, he didn't wait for an invitation to enter, just opened the door and walked in. "Boss, I've got some bad news," he said sitting down in a visitor's chair.

Andy Mills, the station manager looked up from his paperwork and saw that Greg was ashen. "What is it Greg?"

"I've just heard a mayday call from Bill Bond in McMurdo1. He's had to ditch 100 miles south of Mario Zucchelli Airport, and there were two passengers on board. I haven't heard anything since."

"God, no! Shit, shit, shit. What can have happened? The helicopter is so well maintained, it was only serviced last week, and nothing showed up as being in the slightest bit suspect. You're positive about this?"

"Yes Andy, I logged the mayday call in the book, checked the coordinates Bill transmitted and plotted their location on the charts. It was over the ice field with nowhere to land. Even if they got out of the chopper alive, no-one is going to survive long in those freezing temperatures."

"Right, I'll handle this from here. First things first, we'd better give an announcement about the accident. Second, it looks like we're going to need a new pilot and a new helicopter, otherwise things are going to come to a standstill round here damn quickly. Shit!"

Greg got up and left Andy's office. He needed a drink. He went to the bar and ordered a double brandy, sat on a stool at the bar and wrapped his hands around the glass. "I don't believe it," he said out loud to himself, "Bill, Chuck, and that reporter, whatshername, Julie, all gone."

"Gone where?" asked the bar steward.

"Dead," said Greg.

"How?"

"Chopper ditched on the ice field en-route to Mario Zucchelli Airport. No-one could survive that for long

277

enough to be rescued, and that's assuming they found somewhere to land."

Downing his brandy, he put his head in his hands and wept for the two friends he had lost.

It didn't take long for word to get around the station. McMurdo was a hotbed of gossip at the best of times, and after an incident like this, the news spread like wildfire. Ian Smith was one of the first to hear. He made all the right noises of sympathy to those he met, but inwardly he glowed. His problems had all been solved in one hit. Julie Grant would no longer threaten his livelihood with her investigation, and Chuck Fallon was no longer a witness to his failed attempt to wring Julie Grant's neck. It was a shame about the pilot, but there is often some collateral damage on occasions such as this. He went back to his accommodation and picked up the phone. The call he made to Global Energy's head office was answered immediately by the switchboard operator. "Ray Bergman please," he said. He was put through to Ray's office. "Bergman."

"Ray, it's Ian Smith. Just calling to let you know that Julie Grant and Chuck Fallon met with a flying accident and crashed into an ice field as they fled McMurdo. They shouldn't bother us anymore."

"That's great news Ian, well done," replied Ray, punching his fist in the air. "Yes! Got you, you nosey little bitch. That'll teach you to meddle in my affairs." He collected his thoughts for a moment. "Listen Ian, you'll need to stay down there and tidy things up a bit. I heard there was a recent break-in attempt at Graham Platt's office, you need to get to the bottom of that, find out what was stolen and try to determine who was involved, there aren't that many people there who could have done it."

"Actually Ray, it was a bit of a coincidence that Chuck Fallon had just returned to McMurdo, and I suspected that maybe he had something to do with it. However, I have asked around already, and he appeared to have a solid alibi. He was seen in the dining room that evening and only left his table to go to the toilet, and he was witnessed in there too. Apparently, he had an upset stomach. As he left the dining room he was accompanied all the way to his quarters, and by the time he got there, the break-in was already reported."

"Well find out what was in the office that was sensitive."

"I already have, the 'PROJECT UNDERMINE' file was locked in his desk drawer. Even though the desk was ransacked, the file is intact, and the photocopying facility is monitored for access and recharging, and Fallon didn't use it."

"OK, if he was involved in this, it's academic now if they have crashed and burned. There's not much more you can achieve down there I guess so get yourself back here to London."

"Will do Ray," said Ian as he ended the call.

He rang through to transportation to find out when he would be able to leave McMurdo. "Not until we have a replacement helicopter," came the terse reply.

"Bugger! I'd forgotten about that," he thought. "Oh well, please book me onto the first flight out whenever it is available."

At Mario Zucchelli Airport, Bill Bond, Chuck and Julie were shepherded off to the police department to give their accounts of the helicopter crash. They were kept apart and interviewed separately, then after a while they were released once the police had checked their stories and realised that they were all the same. Chuck and Julie made their way to the ticket desk in the departure area and booked themselves onto the first flight out. Bill found some accommodation nearby and went to get some rest. He was mentally and physically exhausted after his ordeal, and the shock of the incident was beginning to tell on him. He would rest first, then report back to McMurdo.

Unbeknown to him McMurdo had no idea that he was still alive: The range on the handheld radio he'd used hadn't been powerful enough to reach the communications centre. They weren't expecting a call from him anyway.

---- 43 ----

Tuesday 16th October

By the time Bill had made his call to McMurdo the next morning Chuck and Julie were already on their way back north. They had decided that they were going to visit Keith Mortimer in America to show him their findings, and to try to tie everything together. Julie had called Mary to let her know what was happening and to get funding for the flights for her and Chuck, since he was now officially involved on the investigation. Chuck gratefully accepted the gesture; it would ease the burden on his bank account, and as he had now effectively left Global Energy by departing from McMurdo in rather a hurry, it wasn't likely that a pay check would be coming his way on payday.

Bill's call to Andy Mills, his boss in McMurdo, had created a real stir. Having taken the call from Bill, the word was soon out that the passengers and pilot were safe, despite the loss of the helicopter. Ian Smith was devastated when he heard. Now what was he going to do? There was a good chance that he had been

282

identified as the would-be assailant, and it wouldn't take much to put two and two together to make four about the sabotage. He called through to London to speak to Ray Bergman.

"Yes Ian," said Ray, somewhat upbeat.

"Erm, Ray, I've got some … bad news …"

"What?" said Ray, suddenly becoming serious.

"They somehow all escaped the helicopter crash and were rescued."

"Shit. That puts us right back in the mire. Who knows what you did down there?"

"Chances are that they reported the incident here, and it's only a matter of time before someone in authority comes looking for me. I need to get out fast."

"No. You stay there."

"But Ray, I'm a sitting duck here."

"Tough shit. You screwed up big time. You only had to do one thing and you blew it. Sort your own shit out," snapped Ray slamming down the phone.

Ray sat still for a few moments. He needed to move fast now that Fallon and the reporter were obviously working together, and who knew where that would lead. He picked up his prepaid mobile and dialled Lance Cooper.

"Yes?"

"We need to meet, same Café Nero, one hour."

"I'll be there."

One hour later, Lance turned up at the café. He found Ray waiting for him by the door. "Let's walk," said Ray, "I don't want us to be overheard." They headed towards the nearby park and passed through the entrance gates.

"What happens going forwards is just between you and me."

Lance nodded his agreement.

"We need to escalate our activity, and that includes the elimination of certain parties. Are you up to the job?"

"It will be expensive, but yes, I'm up to it and ready to roll."

"Good. Here's what I want you to do."

---- 44 ----

Wednesday 17th October
Washington DC

It had been a long haul. The journey had taken them by a SAFAIR charter plane from Mario Zucchelli Airport to Christchurch, New Zealand; and then an onward Qantas flight to Dulles Airport in Washington DC. Julie and Chuck had both managed to grab a few hours' sleep on both the planes and in the airport on the way. Surprisingly, given the events of the last 48 hours, they were remarkably upbeat and glad to be back in civilisation, if not their home country. Washington DC was glowing under an autumnal sun and all the trees in the park surrounding the Lincoln Memorial and Washington Monument were turning the wonderful golden hue of the Fall.

"Isn't this an amazing sight?" commented Julie as they crossed the bridge over the Potomac River and could see the Washington Monument standing tall in the distance.

"Yes, it is. I only wish we had enough time to explore," replied Chuck. "Maybe we could visit here again when this is all over? That… erm… that's if you'd like to," he stammered, somewhat embarrassed to find himself thinking along those lines.

"I'd love to," affirmed Julie, squeezing his hand, "in fact, right now, I can't think of anything I'd enjoy more."

"That's a date then!" exclaimed Chuck, feeling on top of the world.

Their cab stopped in front of the IVSO offices, and after paying the cabbie his fare, they got out to walk across the forecourt.

"Wow look at the height of this building. Very impressive! IVSO obviously have either a very generous budget, or wealthy investors," Chuck commented.

"They get a lot of government and private funding, but only actually occupy a small part of this building," replied Julie. "They're a relatively small, but highly respected, organisation and have the ear of a lot of world leaders. If we can get Keith on our side, we'll have a direct line to the President."

"Well, let's go and show him what we have and take it from there."

Keith Mortimer welcomed them warmly as he showed them into his office on the fifteenth floor, and Julie formally introduced Chuck to him. After shaking hands with Keith, Chuck moved across the office to the plate glass window to look out. The views over the city were outstanding.

"How do you manage to get anything done with views like that?" asked Chuck. "I think I'd just lean back in my chair and watch the world go by."

"It is pretty special I have to admit, but I manage to keep my mind on the task in hand most days, well for a large proportion of them at least!" Keith joked. "But, from what you two said to me on the phone from Christchurch Airport, you haven't come here to admire the view."

"No, we haven't," said Julie. "We've brought some data and photographs with us which we believe prove that Global Energy have been undertaking illegal sonic blasting on WAIS. Very worryingly this has triggered some sort of chain reaction, which has led to several enormous sink holes developing in the ice sheet. We'd like to show you what we have, explain our analysis, and benefit from your experience to really understand what's happened, and potentially is still happening."

Keith gestured to the conference table in his office and requested refreshments from his secretary before joining Chuck and Julie at the table.

"Okay, show me what you have."

Chuck fired up his laptop and displayed the analysis spreadsheet he'd compiled showing the seismic readings, timed and dated, from his work on the WAIS including the readings on the 1st September and in the weeks since.

"As you can see Keith, the magnitude of the readings on the 1st September was significantly higher than anything that had been previously recorded. That's what led me to believe initially that it was an earthquake. That is until I remembered the schedule for sonic blasting I'd seen on my boss' desk," Chuck explained, "but with the drama of the rescue I rather put it to the back of my mind. It was only after I was fêted by the CEO of Global Energy that I began to think about it all again and wonder whether there was more to things than I'd originally thought. They took my laptop with all the data on it from me and didn't give it back, which seemed rather odd, but fortunately I had copied it onto a memory stick without their knowledge."

"That's where I come in," commented Julie. "By putting our heads together over the data Chuck had copied, and the research I'd collated, including your report Keith, we realised there was something very fishy going on, but without proof there wasn't much we could do about it. So, we decided to return to the Antarctic and collect the evidence we needed to expose Global Energy's underhand activities: We got rather more than we bargained for though."

"What do you mean?"

"Well apart from the attempts on our lives, we discovered large holes in the ice sheet and we also managed to gather some hard evidence showing that Global Energy had continued with their sonic blasting," she continued.

"Yes, if you cross-match the information on this confidential blasting schedule, you can see that it directly matches the spikes in the seismic activity from the data recordings," Chuck pointed out. "We believe this proves that Global Energy's activities have triggered some subterranean imbalance which has resulted in these giant holes forming."

Keith took his time to study the spreadsheet analysis and photos laid out before him. "The only way this kind of hole can form is if the ice is melting from below," he said, "but that would require enormous heat and would also result in a rise in sea levels over and above that we would normally expect from the thaw when Antarctica heads towards summer. We had noted higher than average sea levels a few weeks ago, which might tie in with all this, so let me get the latest data from our oceanographic monitoring stations in the southern hemisphere, and we can start to verify your hypothesis."

"Don't forget about the photos Chuck took when he had been rescued and was flying over the fissures as well. He could see something glowing red at the bottom of them: That surely shows there was a heat source doesn't it? Julie pointed out.

"An interesting observation, it could well do," replied Keith.

"And have you got access to real-time satellite imagery as well?" Julie asked. "We need to find out the extent of these giant holes on WAIS."

"Yes, I have. It takes a little time to organise as satellites typically don't pass over the poles very often, so I suggest we break now so I can get the satellite repositioned for imaging, and we'll reconvene back here later in the day when I will hopefully have it available. In the meantime, I suggest you two go and get some rest, or enjoy the sights of Washington DC."

"I vote for a bit of sight-seeing," said Julie. "Okay by you, Chuck?"

With several hours to kill, Julie and Chuck wandered around the National Mall and Memorial Parks, admiring all the great memorials along with the thousands of other visitors. "I almost feel like a tourist," Julie said, "but then the memory of everything that's happened comes flooding back."

"I know what you mean. I can't really focus on anything other than what's happening down on the WAIS. Do you mind if we postpone our exploration to another time? I could do with a good meal and freshening up before we see Keith again this afternoon."

"No worries. Mary has booked us into the Embassy Row Hotel near Dupont Circle. We can take the DC Metro to it from what I can see," said Julie, studying the metro map on her mobile. "I hope they have an express laundry service: I could do with a change of clothes."

"If they don't, I'm sure we'll be able to buy something in America's first city!"

Five hours later in the late afternoon, showered, fed, and wearing hastily bought new clothes, Julie and Chuck returned to the IVSO offices, eager to see what Keith had found. They entered his office to find the conference table covered with satellite images.

"Chuck, Julie, come in. Let me introduce you to my colleague Malcolm Steel who heads up our satellite control department." They all shook hands. "I asked Malcolm to reposition our satellite to get images of the area we are interested in and these are the images we have just received. Given it is such a large area of interest, I took the opportunity to print them out, so you can see them side by side at a reasonable scale. As you can see, there look to be numerous holes across the eastern half of the WAIS."

Turning to Malcolm Keith said, "Thanks, Malcolm. It would be very helpful if you could continue to obtain images of the area for the next few days and let me have any images you have for the same area from the last few weeks."

"And what about the sea levels?" queried Julie.

"Well they *have* increased and, looking back at historical data, the increase is above average. It's not enough to trigger any alarm bells at this stage but there has been a definite increase over and above what we would expect from the summer thaw. I am unaware of any other global phenomenon that has occurred to cause it, so it does seem very likely that the increase is attributable to the meltwater from the WAIS. What we don't know at this stage is whether the size and number of these sink holes is the sole cause of the increase: If they are, then that would suggest whatever subterranean activity is causing them is continuing. If Malcolm can dig up any other satellite images we have of the same area for the last month, we'll get a very good idea about the state of play."

"So, what should we do now?" asked Julie. "If there is a continuing melt of the WAIS, what does that mean?"

"I'm afraid it could be very bad news Julie. The WAIS is over two million cubic kilometres of solid ice and there are several possible disastrous outcomes if it disintegrates. A lot depends of course on the form of the disintegration. If it is meltwater, then we are talking increased sea levels which would flood large parts of the planet making billions homeless. If it were to fracture and effectively calve an iceberg, then depending on the size of that iceberg, it could potentially tip the earth's axis if it drifts sufficiently far north," Keith explained.

"It sounds as though the world is potentially screwed, whatever happens," said Chuck. "And all because Global Energy are trying to maintain their profitability."

"Possibly," agreed Keith, "but before we flag this as a global disaster, we need to understand whether the ice holes are still expanding and calculate the possible risk of fracture."

"And how do we do that?" asked Julie.

"IVSO needs to send a team of scientists to WAIS to see first-hand what's happening. We need to lower probes into the holes to determine depth, temperature, and collect samples at differing levels to understand the composition of the ice," explained Keith. "That will give us a rate of disintegration, and also, some valuable images of what's really happening at the bottom of these things."

"How soon can you get a team together Keith?" Julie queried. "It sounds as though it needs to be sooner rather than later."

"A couple of days to assemble everyone, pull together the necessary equipment and make travel arrangements. We'll use military aircraft to fly direct to McMurdo and be based there, and then we'll have to set up a camp out on WAIS near the holes. So probably four or five days in total," calculated Keith.

"Maybe Chuck and I could be the advance party?" suggested Julie. "We can arrange the ground transportation and accommodation for everyone."

"That would be ideal. This is your discovery, after all, and you know the terrain Chuck. We'll get you both on the next flight down, but from what you have told me about the attempts on your lives, are you sure you want to do this?"

"Absolutely!" they replied in unison. Keith nodded his assent, then picked up the phone and got his secretary to arrange the flights and have their tickets sent over to the hotel. Going to a cupboard in the corner of his office he pulled out a satellite phone and handed it to Julie.

"You should take this and use it as our main means of communication: You have my direct line. Call any time night or day, the call will be patched through to me."

"Thank you, Keith, we really appreciate your help on this."

"My pleasure, Julie, just be careful from here on out, OK?"

"We will. We'll keep in touch," she replied.

45

Thursday 18th October

At an altitude of 38,000 feet above central South America, Julie was midway through writing her report for Mary Roberts, hoping to be able to email it to her from Punta Arenas airport before their flight back to McMurdo Station. Despite feeling jetlagged from all the different time zones that they had been in during the last few days, she and Chuck had decided that the exposure of Global Energy, and especially Ray Bergman, should go ahead straight away, even though the true outcome of the sonic blasting was still unknown.

To their minds there were now two stories to report: One was the exploits of Global Energy and the lengths Ray Bergman seemed prepared to go to to safeguard his position; and then secondly, the mind-boggling global disaster that was potentially looming. While the two were directly connected, Julie had pointed out that even Ray Bergman couldn't have imagined the disaster scenario that his sanction of illegal sonic blasting could cause.

"He's a thoroughly evil and unpleasant man, totally focused on Global Energy and his position, but I doubt even he would have started this chain of events solely for the purpose of world domination or some other such objective," she observed.

Her report for Mary covered the happenings down on WAIS, the illegal blasting activities and the subsequent appearance of the giant sink holes in the ice sheet. The attempts on her and Chuck's life wouldn't be an element of the story at this stage: They had decided to make full statements to the police on their return and leave it to the authorities to deal with Ray and his cohorts. It was a criminal matter, and publication in the press could jeopardise any trial.

Touching down in Punta Arenas in Chile, they had a four-hour stopover before their flight to McMurdo Station.

"Good timing," said Julie, "this gives me time to proof-read my submission and send it to Mary."

"Would you like me to read it?" queried Chuck. "I might be able to add a bit of background for you."

"That would be great, thanks. The more detail and accuracy, the more credible the story."

Julie passed her laptop over to Chuck who sat quietly reading the article. She'd covered all the salient points in a very clear and pragmatic manner. No over-dramatization, just hard-hitting and damning facts.

"This could be the end of Ray Bergman, you know?" he said. "Global Energy will undoubtedly lose their drilling licence for Antarctica, and will probably face a heavy fine, but the company will no doubt survive based on their existing oil drilling activities elsewhere to see another day. At least that should safeguard the jobs of the innocent employees."

"That's what I was hoping for. I don't want to be responsible for the loss of livelihoods, but whatever happens to Ray Bergman, both professionally and criminally, is fine by me."

Having fine-tuned the article, Julie saved the latest version and attached it to an e-mail to Mary. She hit the SEND button and watched it progress to the sent mail box. As the file reached Mary's inbox, Chuck and Julie climbed the steps to the small plane flying them down to McMurdo.

"I hope there's not too much turbulence as we fly over Cape Horn," said Julie. "I'm not really a fan of flying, especially when it's in a small plane."

"We'll be fine. After everything we've survived in the last few weeks, we'd be bloody unlucky to be killed in a plane crash now!"

As it happened, the flight was smooth and uneventful, and the plane touched down safely on McMurdo some hours later.

"Here we go," thought Chuck as they taxied to the terminal, "back into the dragon's den."

They'd decided to keep as low a profile as possible at McMurdo, not wanting to advertise their return in case Ian was still around and might make another attempt on their lives. Fortunately, McMurdo is a large research base and Keith Mortimer had secured them accommodation under the IVSO banner so hopefully no-one connected with Global Energy would register their presence.

"Passing through the airport could be tricky: We need to keep our heads down and not draw any attention to ourselves," directed Chuck.

Having collected their bags from the hold, they headed straight across to the accommodation section reserved for them by IVSO and dropped their bags in their rooms. "Right, we need to head over to the ground transportation unit and arrange all the survival equipment and transportation to get it and the IVSO team out to WAIS," said Chuck.

"Do they know you over there, Chuck? Or do I need to front it on behalf of IVSO?"

"No, they don't. All my previous travel arrangements were handled by Global Energy, so we should be okay going over together. We'll need to work out how many skidoos and accommodation pods we need for the team, plus shelters, food and drink supplies and clothing. How long did Keith say we'd need to spend on the shelf to collect the information?"

"He didn't say. I guess if we provision for ten days, that should amply cover it."

The Ground Transportation team were very helpful, and arrangements were made to head out the following morning with three caterpillar tracked trucks delivering Chuck, Julie and all the necessary equipment and supplies to establish a temporary base camp. The IVSO team weren't due to arrive for another few days yet, giving them plenty of time to have things set up and be ready in time for their arrival.

46

Thursday 18th October
London

Ray Bergman had outlined what he wanted Lance to do: Find Julie Grant and kill her. He wasn't clear at this stage what Chuck Fallon's role was in the whole scenario, but he had decided it would be advisable to rid himself of that potential threat as well. The biggest problem was going to be finding them both: They seemed to have gone to ground since the helicopter crash on the way to Mario Zucchelli Airport. He presumed they had headed back to civilisation, but in what part of the world he didn't know. As yet Lance and his contacts hadn't managed to track them down. He'd suggested Lance should have his people hack into *The Telegraph's* intranet to see whether their location was mentioned in despatches and Lance's man was on the case.

On the other side of the city, Mary Roberts had just received Julie's article and was reading it with great interest. She could see the headlines, "Global Energy:

One of the UK's biggest international energy corporations involved in illegal blasting in Antarctica," a coup for any newspaper reporting what had been happening.

Without stating the reason for it, Julie explained that she and Chuck Fallon were on their way back to McMurdo at IVSO's expense, and that they would be in touch soon with an update. In the meantime, Julie proposed that Mary should go ahead and publish the article immediately.

Tempting as it was to run with the article as it stood, Mary knew from experience it had to be cleared by the Legal Department before anything appeared in print. Forwarding it on to them, she decided to call it a day, shut down her laptop for the night, and went home. She would call the guy in Legal first thing tomorrow to see if they could go to press with it.

Later that night, Lance's hacker was still having problems breaking the security on *The Telegraph's* intranet server. He'd spent several hours peeling it away layer by layer and was now close to finding a way in. Eventually, the last layer of protection had been by-passed. "Bingo! I'm in. Now to search for references to Julie Grant," he thought. It didn't take long: The search engine on his machine was powerful and soon picked up Julie's article. "I've hit the payload here," he thought, "maybe there's even a bonus in it for me."

Early the next morning, Ray Bergman was reading the article and the accompanying report delivered to him in person by Lance. "Ah, they're heading back to McMurdo then. Right. You need to get down to McMurdo straight away. I'll authorise the company plane to get you there faster: If anyone asks, you're on a special assignment for Global Energy, and if pressed, tell them it's a classified security issue and you can't say anything more. When you arrive, hook up with Ian Smith who will give you whatever assistance you need."

"Understood," was the brief reply.

Ray picked up the phone to his secretary asking, "Jayne, can you find out if Ian Smith is still in McMurdo and if so, get him on the phone for me?"

"No problem Mr Bergman. I'll get onto the base straight away."

In no time at all, she was patching through a call to Ray. "It's Ian Smith on line one."

"Ian, Ray Bergman here. My apologies for my somewhat curt communication the other day. What's the latest situation down there in McMurdo?"

"Well, I'm still a free man," said Ian, thinking, "no thanks to you, you bastard."

"Great. I knew you'd be OK, especially as I have had no feedback to the contrary up here. Anyway, I'm calling to let you know that an associate of mine is heading down to McMurdo and I'd like you to give him every assistance when he arrives. His name is Lance Cooper and he knows to contact you on his arrival. Is that all clear?"

After the sharp exchange and his immediate abandonment by Ray several days earlier, Ian was surprised to hear from his boss. "He still needs me more than I need him, maybe I can come out of this unscathed after all. This time I know that Ray Bergman is only interested in covering his own backside: He's not going to find me quite as gullible," he thought.

"Yes, OK, that's crystal-clear Ray, I'll keep an eye out for him."

"Good man," said Ray, and hung up the phone.

---- 47 ----

Friday 19th October
Antarctica

Julie and Chuck were ready to depart McMurdo with their assembled scientific and survival equipment early in the morning. The three tracked vehicles that would carry their kit across the ice cap to the chosen camp site had been warmed up and were sitting with their engines idling. They had all been lashed together for the journey across the heavily crevassed ice shelf: If one fell in, the other vehicles would be able to pull it out. They climbed aboard the leading truck, donned their safety harnesses, and within minutes, they were on their way. Julie leaned against Chuck. They were firm friends now having been through so much together and it seemed a perfectly natural thing to do. Chuck slipped his arm around Julie's shoulder and enjoyed the moment. They would have a great deal of physical work to do soon out on the WAIS, but for now they could relax and enjoy the scenery.

The journey out to WAIS from McMurdo by ground transport loosely follows a route running parallel to the Transantarctic Mountains for several hundred miles, before turning west to cross the full width of the Ross Ice Shelf. Chuck knew this would be slow progress and would take approaching two days of travelling whenever light permitted, avoiding crevasse fields, and camping in the short periods of darkness. It was the only way to realistically get the equipment they needed for the IVSO team into place.

"It's going to be a long, cold journey Julie, over very uneven ground, especially seeing as we now need to avoid the crazed area of the ice shelf. I hope you don't suffer from travel sickness!"

"Well I haven't to date, but I've never actually travelled in a tracked vehicle like this before. They seem to have a very high centre of gravity: Are they stable?"

"I certainly hope so! The size of the tracks spreads the load significantly so that these trucks can cross thinner ice than you or me on foot, so fingers crossed!"

The cavalcade had pulled out of McMurdo heading northwest over the tediously flat terrain. Low cloud had soon settled in, reducing the horizon many kilometres away to an inch-high slit of light held between identical walls of dull white snow and sky.

The lead vehicle set the pace with the others following in its tracks. The drivers swapped every two hours: Maintaining concentration was of paramount importance and driving in these conditions was very tiring.

Camp that night involved erecting very heavy-duty tents, designed to retain any heat from the sun's rays, with camp beds on top of insulated matting to keep them protected from the penetrating cold of the frozen floor. Despite the fact the temperature would dip to around minus twenty degrees Celsius overnight, the combination of their protective clothing, hi-tech sleeping bags and tents ensured that Chuck and Julie felt snug and warm.

"This feels like an amazing adventure," Julie confided from the depths of her sleeping bag. "I can't believe we are in the middle of a frozen plateau, miles from anywhere, but as cosy as can be."

"You'd have to pay a fortune as a civilian to experience something like this," Chuck agreed. "If we could forget about the reason we're out here, we'd consider ourselves very privileged indeed."

After a surprisingly good night's sleep, the transport leader woke them in the Antarctic dawn to get on their way. With luck they would reach their destination by the end of the day, thus having to make and break camp only one more time. The cloud base had cleared, and the rising sun created a dazzling display on the frozen wilderness.

"This is breath-taking," said Julie, looking out of the truck's window at the jagged mountain range dividing the Ross Ice Shelf from the south pole.

"On a fine and bright day, the air is so clear it's possible to see for hundreds of kilometres," replied Chuck. "It's amazing to think that Roald Admundsen traversed this area over one hundred years ago without any of the hi-tech equipment we're relying on now."

The convoy pressed on throughout the day, and just before civil twilight, they reached the chosen destination for the IVSO camp site.

"Phew, I'm glad to be here," said Chuck, stretching as he exited the cab of his vehicle. "Just the tents to erect and another meal of freeze-dried food, and we'll be all set!"

Unloading the tracked vehicles would be left until the morning and then the ground team would depart to return to McMurdo.

---- 48 ----

Sunday 21st October
WAIS

Julie watched as the last of the tracked vehicles disappeared over the horizon before turning slowly in a full circle to view the polar landscape all around her. They'd erected all the accommodation tents, together with the separate food tent and kitchen, and had stowed all the scientific equipment away neatly. As far as they knew the rest of the IVSO team would be arriving on Tuesday by ski plane, giving them two full days to begin their explorations.

Loading up the equipment he needed into the spacious paniers on one of the skidoos, Chuck fired up the engine. He called over to Julie, "Come on Jules, we should head out to locate as many of the sink holes as we can. We've got the satellite photos which we can cross-match to this map to provide us with a point of reference."

"OK, I'm coming. I just want to grab my camera first," she replied, disappearing into their tent.

Five minutes later they were heading out further into the barren WAIS, away from the Ross Ice Shelf. Chuck negotiated around the uneven ground keeping a close lookout for crevasses.

"We've got about twenty miles to cover before we should see the first of the holes," he said into his intercom microphone. "We couldn't sensibly establish camp any closer than we have done, just in case the ice was unsafe."

Their skidoo covered the distance in little more than an hour. Chuck turned off the ignition, and turning to Julie said, "Okay, we'll head due north from here on foot and see what we find."

"How close to the holes dare we walk?"

"While it's just the two of us, we'll keep a safe distance, but we'll rope ourselves together and carry ice picks just in case," instructed Chuck. "We can't be too careful; the surface of the ice may be cantilevered out over a void."

Having loaded some tools into his rucksack, Chuck lead the way. They set out cautiously, checking their handheld GPS and placing a waypoint that would ensure they would be able to find their way back to the skidoo. It was hard going over the uneven terrain, but Chuck set them a steady pace. Julie managed to keep up with him for the first hour, but then the extreme

310

cold and unfamiliar exertion made her flag, slowing down their progress. They sat down on an ice mound and rested for a while, but their inactivity caused their body heat to drop quickly.

"Come on Julie, we need to keep moving."

Picking themselves up, they trudged on towards the first sink hole. As they approached it cautiously, Chuck tried to estimate the size of the hole. He guessed it to be somewhere around 150 metres by 250 metres, a sizeable elliptical crater. He drove an ice screw into the ice at his feet and attached a battery powered winch connected to a safety line to it, clipping the other end to his harness.

"Stay here Julie, I need to get closer to have a look and I don't know how stable the edge will be. The safety line is my insurance."

"Be careful Chuck, I don't want to lose you." Instinctively he stepped forward and gave her a kiss.

"I hope that's not a kiss goodbye."

"Not a chance, I'll be back for more of the same soon," he said grinning at her as he moved off towards the edge of the hole, paying out the safety line as he went.

He soon reached the edge, laid flat on his stomach and slid forward so that his head was stretched out over the void. Looking down, he could see that the bottom of the hole was several hundred feet below, and at the bottom there was a steady flow of blue ice-cold water, but no lava.

"That's a relief," he thought, "I was expecting to see something hot down there."

Sliding his phone out from his pocket, he switched on the camera and took several photos, picking out the hole from various angles so that he and Julie could examine them later back at the base. It would give the IVSO team something to look at too, enabling them to plan their own examinations better. At least they would have some idea of what they would be facing out here. He backed his way away from the edge a few yards, then gingerly stood up and walked back to the anchor point where Julie was waiting for him.

"What could you see?"

"A bloody great hole with lots of flowing water at the bottom, about three to four hundred feet down. No lava. I took some photos, which we can look at back at camp."

"Can I have a quick look now?"

"Okay, but quickly, we need to keep moving," he said handing over his phone.

Julie opened the gallery app and looked at the photos. "Wow! That's huge! If they're all like this, then there has been more ice melting than we thought. This is really serious!"

"Well, we'll know in the next few days when the team get out and explore the area more fully. We need to send these photos to Keith as soon as possible to help them with their planning and preparations so let's head back. And, besides, I'm getting hungry again. Fancy some Irish stew tonight? It's particularly good when reconstituted with Antarctic ice from dried ingredients."

"Sounds perfect," said Julie ironically, wrapping her arm through his as they retraced their steps to the skidoo.

Back in the camp they emailed the photos to Keith via the IVSO SatPhone and then downloaded the photos to the laptop and displayed them one by one, poring over each in minute detail, making sure that they had missed nothing, as they ate. They were able to identify the best point to drop a researcher down into the hole and triangulated it onto a map of the area. At least the first drop should go well, and they would be able to get decent core samples on the way down. Having done all they could, they decided to retire early and get another good night's sleep. It would be a longer day tomorrow visiting other holes further away.

Julie and Chuck woke suddenly, finding themselves unceremoniously thrown out of bed onto the floor of their sleeping tent as tremors ripped through the base station. Items of equipment were hurled across the floor in the neighbouring tents, crashing into other objects and tearing the fabric walls apart. Chuck and Julie clung together on the floor waiting for the quake to subside.

"What the hell is happening?" yelled Julie.

"It's got to be an earthquake. Keep your centre of gravity low and hold on to me. We'll be fine," Chuck reassured a near-hysterical Julie.

"You can't know that! We could die out here and no-one would ever find us!"

"Earth tremors are common in this area, it will subside soon, I promise," he tried again. On this occasion he was right. When the shaking had eased, they unsteadily got to their feet and left their tent to survey the damage. The camp looked as though a bomb had hit it with equipment strewn everywhere, broken and smashed into pieces.

"This looks more serious than I first thought," said Chuck. "Most of the equipment is of no use to us now. Let's check to see what supplies are left. We may have to survive out here for a couple of days before a rescue party is sent. That was a real shaker: I bet alarm bells are ringing all over the world."

Indeed, the impact had been felt over a great distance. Out on the ice shelf the tremor caused the ground below the trucks returning to McMurdo to heave and shift. The lead truck sheared off to the left and half disappeared as the ice below it gave way. Fortunately, the drop was only a minor one and the truck eventually stopped, dangling from its tether to the rest of the convoy. Using the combined power of their engines and the tow lines between them, the drivers managed to regain control and pull the trapped vehicle back up the face of the slope, and out of the hole onto a firm surface. Once back on solid ice, the team checked the tracks and the vehicles for damage. Satisfied that there was nothing untoward, they climbed back in and started up again. The terrain ahead of them had changed: The journey back to McMurdo was going to be much slower than they had expected.

Two hundred miles south of the convoy, there was another more significant outcome from the earthquake: A crack had appeared across the Ross Ice Shelf, running along the line where the ice projected out over the sea bed. With nothing left to support its weight, the shelf sheared along its entire length. One third of the ice shelf had separated from the land, barely missing the station at McMurdo.

Slowly, slowly, the giant 'Rossberg' inched away from the shelf that calved it as its buoyancy found a natural level, until the ocean current took hold and it started to float away from its former position. The world's largest iceberg on record had just been calved; one with sufficient mass to tip the world off its axis.

---- 49 ----

Monday 22nd October

Back in Washington DC Dr Keith Mortimer at IVSO headquarters had been alerted to the latest Antarctic earthquake and was busy reading the seismograph recordings with a feeling of dread. He had been called by one of his staff at the first indication of the massive tremor and he had hurried to his office to monitor the situation. He pulled up the real-time satellite images from the Antarctic and he could clearly see the rift in the ice shelf, together with a massive indentation in the neighbouring WAIS in the proximity of the holes Chuck and Julie had discovered.

"What the hell has happened down there?" he wondered. "It looks like the surface of the ice sheet has collapsed and the ice shelf has split! The two things have got to be linked."

Keith was right. They *were* linked. The flow of molten magma released when the earth's mantle ruptured had caused an enormous honeycomb of caverns to be created beneath the surface ice, scoured out by the meltwater from the lava flows, leaving the surface of the ice sheet supported by narrow pillars of ice. These pillars had developed hairline cracks under the great strain of the weight above, weakening them, until finally they crumbled and collapsed into the abyss below. As the pillars gave way, the surface layers high above the void followed, falling like a house of cards. Within minutes, a major portion of the centre of the ice sheet had dropped by several hundred feet, crashing to the icy floor below. An earthquake hadn't caused the rift on the ice shelf: Global Energy's sonic blasting was the culprit.

Keith was one of the few people on the planet who realised the wider implications of the severing of the Ross Ice Shelf and knew he must brief his boss immediately. The IVSO team sent to join Chuck and Julie was already on its way to McMurdo, indeed might already be there and caught up in the disaster.

"My God, what about Julie and Chuck as well?" he wondered, "they'll be out there somewhere, if they've survived."

He needed to find out what was happening, where all his people were, and implement whatever rescue plans were needed. Picking up his phone he dialled Ken Brooke's extension, "Ken, it's Keith. We've got a major problem. A massive iceberg looks to have calved from the Ross Ice Shelf, one that is big enough to tilt the earth's axis if it travels far enough north. You need to brief the President and other world leaders. The world needs to prepare for the worst; the potential for an impending global shift."

In London, Ray Bergman was working in his office, contemplating Global Energy's future exploration projects, and their potential impact on the company's bottom line profits. He had been basing his forecasts on the continuation of sonic blasting in Antarctica and the projections looked good. He smiled to himself, but his smile was very short-lived. Jeff Ramsey appeared in his office doorway holding a document and looking as white as a sheet.

"You're not going to like this one little bit Ray," he said handing the piece of paper across the desk to him. Ray took it and read the message that had been relayed through from McMurdo. He paled and broke out into a cold sweat as he read the text.

"Fuck, fuck, FUCK! When did this come through Jeff?"

"Just now, I brought it straight in to you. No-one else has seen it yet."

Ray continued to the end of the document. It wasn't good news at all. McMurdo had been almost destroyed by an earthquake down in Antarctica, with several Global Energy employees injured, and three dead. The Ross Ice Shelf had split in two and a gigantic iceberg floated off into the Ross Sea. McMurdo itself was balanced on a knife's edge of falling into the Ross Sea. He knew that there would be no way that Global Energy could dodge the flak from this one if the cause was linked to their resumed sonic blasting activities – fingers would be pointed in their direction from every which way. The shit was really going to hit the fan now.

Ray also knew that Julie Grant was down in Antarctica and if she didn't know already, she would very soon know what had happened first hand. She already had the bit between her teeth on this issue and he was certain that she would have a field day now. It was more important than ever that she was eliminated to stop her going to press. "Hopefully, she was in the middle of the earthquake and killed," he thought, "but with her luck so far, it's unlikely."

He needed to get in touch with Lance who would be on the ground down there to find out the position, but that issue would have to wait. Right now, the board needed a new approach for this problem, and fast. He sent Jeff away with instructions to convene the directors immediately. Once Jeff had left his office, Ray leaned back in his swivel chair with his eyes closed and his hands over his face thinking "Oh fuck! What am I going to do now?" Jayne Grey entered the room, saw Ray was clearly distressed and quietly backed out again. She had seen him like this a couple of times before and knew he was best left alone to his own devices. He would call her when he needed anything.

Lance had touched down at McMurdo on the Sunday evening, literally seconds before the massive earthquake ripped the Ross Ice Shelf apart. The Global Energy jet had slewed across the runway as the tremors rippled the surface but survived intact thanks to the skills of the pilot and crew. There weren't many things that ruffled Lance, but this was one of them and he exited the plane on shaky legs.

"Pull yourself together man," he said to himself, "you're on solid ground, safe and sound. First things first, find Ian Smith and determine the location of Julie Grant and Chuck Fallon."

Striding through the airport building he exited into the research station, staggered at the sight of the collapsed buildings and dazed people wandering the streets with their survival gear hastily pulled over night clothes and bloody cuts and bruises on their faces. Lance realised how lucky he and he crew of the

Global Energy jet had been, but he just shook himself, mentally and physically. He needed to focus on the task in hand.

Ian Smith was one of the people out on the main thoroughfare that ran through the centre of McMurdo. He'd been in his room awaiting the arrival of Lance when the quake hit, throwing things off the table and shelves and upending the chair he was sitting in. His survival training kicked in immediately: Get out of the building and find somewhere safe, free of falling debris. It was chaos everywhere with people stumbling around trying to find colleagues and friends. "I don't stand a chance of finding Lance in this bedlam" he thought when suddenly there was a tap on his shoulder. Turning around he looked into one of the hardest faces he had ever seen.

Cold, cold eyes surveyed him critically. "Ian Smith, I'm guessing?" came the impassionate query.

"Yes, that's me. Who are you?"

"Lance Cooper sent by Ray Bergman. You're expecting me: Is there somewhere we can go to get out of this cold and talk? I'm hardly dressed to be hanging around outside for any length of time."

Turning on his heel Ian led the way towards the Global Energy offices at the far end of McMurdo, inland from the rift. "If any buildings are going to have survived, I think these might have stood the best chance," he said as they walked. They went along silently, side by side, avoiding the bewildered people around them. Turning the corner, they saw their destination a few hundred metres ahead, one of the few upright buildings. "As I thought, we should be okay in there."

Once indoors and ensconced in an empty office, Lance closed the door and window blinds. "Okay, down to business. I need to find Julie Grant and deal with her. Where is she?"

"Somewhere out on WAIS, the last I heard," replied Ian. "But with what's just happened, I seriously doubt she'll have survived. Even if she did, you won't be able to get out to her: The direct route to WAIS seems to be on the move."

"I won't be going anywhere on my own," came the terse reply. "You will be accompanying me. There must be an alternate way out to WAIS. Helicopter? Boat? Maybe a longer overland route?"

"No helicopter, at the moment, and I imagine any boats will be needed for the clean-up operation here," responded Ian. "The best we can do is head north along the foothills of the Queen Elizabeth mountains and then head west when we reach the remaining portion of the Ross Ice Shelf, but we'll need a tracked vehicle and skidoos to get there. There should be some tracked vehicles returning from dropping off Fallon and Grant. Maybe we could intercept and borrow them?" said Ian, warming to the idea - logistical problems were his forte. "We could head north on skidoos, flag them down and position ourselves as a rescue party requiring one of the vehicles and leaving the other two available to return to McMurdo to help with the rescue operation here."

"Sounds like a reasonable plan. Where do we get skidoos from? And I'll need survival gear too," replied Lance.

"No problem on either front. Global Energy have their own skidoos, survival gear and supplies catering for the regular expeditions their scientists make. We can use them if they've survived the earthquake."

"Okay, we'll set out at first light. 4am rendezvous here. That should give you enough time to organise everything we need." With that, Lance leant back in his chair, put his feet on the desk and closed his eyes. The talking was obviously over, and Ian had work to do.

---- 50 ----

Tuesday 24th October

The world was agog, wanting to hear about the calving of the giant 'Rossberg', and the rescue of the people stranded at McMurdo before it fell into the icy seas. The press had got wind of the situation almost immediately after a US newspaper received a tip-off from the relative of a McMurdo station employee who had phoned home to tell his wife what had happened. The newspaper called *Reuters* and they spread the word across the globe almost instantly. Two chartered airplanes were soon criss-crossing the area as cameramen with zoom lenses filmed the holes in the icecap and concentrated on the widening gap between the newly formed iceberg and the remainder of the ice shelf. It was moving ever further away, the gap now close to two miles wide. Scientists around the globe were frantically studying the satellite images of the shelf, looking at the latest weather forecasts and ocean current measurements, and making calculations to try and predict the course that the enormous iceberg would follow and how quickly it would probably move.

Having been apprised of the situation, the US President had convened a crisis meeting of world leaders to discuss the disaster in the Antarctic, and teams of the planet's best scientists and military engineers had gathered together and were desperately trying to come up with a plan to reverse the motion of the giant iceberg and send it back into the gap it had come from. Everyone was pulling together to try to contain the situation before the sheer mass of the iceberg tipped the world off balance.

Back on the ice sheet, having restored the remote camp to some form of habitable state and managing to salvage and repair some of the equipment including a skidoo, Chuck and Julie were awaiting rescue or the arrival of the rest of the IVSO team, whichever happened first. In the meantime, they were using their time productively to visit some of the other sink holes. They had dropped probes and taken core samples and other readings in the holes where they could get close enough to the edge without falling in.

At this particularly deep sink hole, their lifelines were anchored well back to allow for any edges crumbling, and Chuck lowered himself down on an electric winch that was attached to the skidoo. He communicated over the VHF radio with Julie who was controlling his descent, and he told her to stop when he came to a ledge half way down. He tested the ice for strength and stood up, taking his weight on his legs.

He leant out over the abyss and dropped a sampling kit down into the waters below. Once the samples were hauled back up and safely stowed in his shoulder bag, he pressed the transmit button on the radio. "You should see this Jules," he said, "it's awesome."

"I'd love to Chuck, but I don't think the harness will take my weight as well as yours, and we'd have no-one to operate the winch to get us both back to the surface either."

"Good point, but a shame nevertheless. It's like a great white cathedral down here, with columns of ice rising up from the bottom and holding up the roof. I don't think this roof will stay up for very much longer, I think it'll collapse quite soon so I'd better get out of here. Can you haul me up please Jules?"

Julie activated the winch again and Chuck rose back up to the surface with his samples tucked into his tote bag. The lifeline pulled him up and over the edge, and he cradled the bag as he got back to his feet and made his way back to the skidoo and Julie.

"Here's a few more samples for the archives," he said, placing them in a cooler box ready to transport back to the camp.

Back at camp in their tent with a hot drink and some food inside them, they catalogued the samples and did some preliminary examinations of the cores that Chuck had drilled. "Hmm, that's interesting," he said.

"What is?"

"Well, the spectrophotometer shows that there's a very high concentration of methane hydrates in this ice core."

"What does that mean?"

"It means that this is probably the reason that the sonic blasting has been going on. It's widely recognised as being a huge source of natural gas if safe extraction methods can be found. Methane hydrate is a cage-like lattice of ice which traps molecules of methane inside. If it is warmed or depressurised it will revert to water and natural gas. You only have to bring one cubic metre of gas hydrate back to the surface and it will release over one hundred and fifty times that much of natural gas - the energy content of methane occurring in hydrate form is immense, possibly exceeding the combined energy of all other known fossil fuels. This could be *huge* Julie, an enormous coup for the first organisation to develop the tools and technologies to allow environmentally safe methane production from polar hydrates. I bet that's what they have been trying to perfect under the radar; and if they had managed it ahead of the competition, they would be quids in. If these samples are anything to go by, there's a veritable fortune to be had down here."

"Well, that *would* explain the risk taking and all of the cover up activities that Global Energy have used. And why there is so much at stake that they would even try to kill us on that helicopter," said Julie.

"Now we know what they are up to, and they must know we know, we really are going to have to be careful out here. I don't think they have stopped trying to silence us, and if they know where we are, we could be in big trouble. I think we need to have a contingency plan in place in case they find us out in the middle of nowhere."

"What do you suggest?"

"I've been racking my brain to think about that Julie, but to be perfectly honest, I'm at a loss," was Chuck's dispirited reply. "If they do come out and find us alone and unarmed, it's not looking too good. The best we can do is maybe leave this as a decoy camp to distract them into thinking we have perished in the quake and set up one tent some distance away for our own use until we're rescued. If the skidoo is fuelled and packed with provisions, we can try to outrun them if they head our way. We've got a better knowledge of the ice surface in the immediate vicinity and we'll need to use that to our advantage. It's not much of a plan but the best I can come up with right now."

"It sounds good to me," said Julie, squeezing his arm. "What would I do without you?"

The pair of them set about taking down one of the tents and gathering together the supplies they thought they would need and then, climbing onto the skidoo, they travelled ten miles north of the camp, just far enough not to be seen on the horizon and close to the start of the sink holes.

The timing of their evacuation was just in time. Early the next morning the tracked vehicle lumbered over the horizon with Ian Smith at the wheel – they'd driven overnight accepting the risk of night-time driving in their urgency to get there. Their ruse of being the rescue party had worked like a dream and the two remaining vehicles had continued their journey to McMurdo: None of the other drivers wanted to head back out to WAIS over such unknown and unstable terrain anyway. It had been a long and tortuous journey with both men taking turns at the wheel and only a couple of short stops for food and rest. Conversation between them had been restricted to the minimum, merely discussing the outline of a plan for when they arrived at the camp.

Throughout the journey Ian Smith had been silently worrying about what he seemed to have signed up for. Tampering with the helicopter was one thing but killing innocent people right in front of him was something else indeed as he'd discovered in McMurdo. He was having severe doubts.

"Maybe I should back out and just face the music for the financial fraud and the attack on Julie Grant in the warehouse," he thought. "No-one can actually prove anything about the helicopter given it's at the bottom of a crevasse." But the thought of prison and not seeing his children weighed heavily on his mind.

Pulling up alongside the camp, Ian and Lance surveyed the tangle of tents and equipment. "You think they can have survived this?" asked Lance.

"Looking at this I think it's very unlikely, don't you?"

Lance was a cautious man, that's how he'd survived unscathed and uncaptured in his chosen field for so many years. "I think we should scout around and see if we can find any bodies," he directed. "Get the skidoos off the back of the truck so we can travel out a few miles, just in case they were off field testing when the quake hit."

"But it struck in the middle of the night. They're not going to have been out field testing in the dark," was Ian's logical comeback.

"If they were back here sleeping, we should be able to find their bodies then, shouldn't we? Just get those skidoos ready and we'll travel out in a grid pattern if they're not here."

Ian did as he was bid as Lance looked around the remains of the camp. Finding nothing, both men mounted a skidoo.

"Okay, we'll cover the northern quadrants first. You head due east for five miles, then turn north for five, then west for five and finally south for five to bring you back here, scanning to your left and right all the way. I'll cover the north-western quadrant and then we can do the same in the two southern quadrants later," Lance directed. With a glance over his shoulder to ensure Ian understood, he headed off west.

Ian was heading west on the third side of first quadrant, but just before turning south to head back to the camp, he saw Lance suddenly peel off his agreed course and head north-east at speed. "What the hell is he doing?" he wondered, and then he saw it: A small speck on the horizon, maybe five miles away. "I'd better follow on," he thought, and turned to follow Lance.

Julie and Chuck were scanning the horizon with binoculars when they saw first one, then two skidoos moving quickly towards them. "Julie, there's someone heading our way!" he yelled. "Quick, get on the skidoo, we need to get out of here."

Julie clambered aboard behind Chuck and wrapped her arms tightly around his waist. "Hang on tight, I'm probably going to have to take some evasive action," he directed.

In a matter of minutes Lance and Ian had reached the isolated tent and could see a skidoo heading away from them a couple of miles away. "We've got them!" yelled Lance over the sound of the skidoos idling engines. "We'll approach them in a pincer movement, try to surround them and drive them towards a crevasse. No guns unless necessary, we don't want to catch each other in any crossfire. Let's go."

Julie's heart was hammering in her chest as she looked over her shoulder to see what was happening.

"They've separated and are approaching us on both of our flanks," she told Chuck, who was concentrating hard on steering. "If ever there was a time to put our knowledge of the ice surface to use, then this is it."

Seeing a sink hole ahead, Chuck turned their skidoo to sit on the edge of it facing their challengers. "What the hell have you stopped for?" demanded Julie. "They're nearly on top of us."

"It's time for a game of dare Julie," came Chuck's response. "They can't ram us into the hole without following us to an icy death themselves. It's a sort of stalemate, and it's the best I can think of."

The same thought was going through Ian's mind but obviously not through Lance's. He gunned his skidoo and aimed directly for Chuck and Julie.

"Oh my God! Oh my God!" screamed Julie, as Ian's skidoo suddenly leapt forward too.

Chuck revved their engine and the three skidoos all charged forward, Lance aiming straight at them, and Chuck trying to drive between the two advancing vehicles. Suddenly Ian's direction of travel registered in Julie's brain.

"Chuck, Ian Smith isn't heading for us, he's aiming for the other guy!" she yelled. "Maybe he's on our side."

Thinking quickly Chuck turned sharply to his left to skirt the rim of the sinkhole. Lance was bearing down on them, totally focused on his quarry and seemingly unaware of Ian Smith's approach, when suddenly he felt the back end of his skidoo slew sideways as Ian rammed him from behind. Struggling to regain control of his swerving vehicle, Lance clipped the back of

Chuck and Julie's skidoo causing them to lurch away from the hole as he careered directly towards it before jumping clear, as his skidoo disappeared over the edge into the icy depths.

"Get the hell out of here!" Ian Smith yelled across to them. "He's got a gun."

That was all Chuck needed to hear, he shot forward away from Lance as the man struggled to regain his feet and get his gun out of his jacket pocket. Taking aim, Lance prepared to fire at Julie's retreating back, but Ian was quicker off the mark. Two shots rang out. One bullet flew across the gap between the two men hitting Lance in the chest, and the other hit him in the throat. With a look of shock on his face, he fell to his knees and toppled backward into the abyss.

"Goodbye to bad rubbish," Ian thought as he accelerated away to follow Julie and Chuck back to the camp.

Julie and Chuck made it back two minutes ahead of Ian Smith and jumped straight into the cab of the tracked vehicle, firing up the engine. How could they know Ian wasn't coming back to kill them too? He had just killed his cohort - maybe so there would be no witnesses. But weirdly, he had called a warning to them. What was he after?

"This is all very confusing Chuck," said Julie, "do you think he's a good guy or a bad guy? He saved us back there and now he's approaching fast. What do we do? We can't just leave him out here to die on his own if the man saved our lives."

"I don't know Julie, but we know he's got a gun and I'm not taking any chances," said Chuck as the vehicle lurched into motion. "He will either shoot at us or he will come alongside us on the skidoo which I guess may be the best indication we'll get."

"For what it's worth, I think he's fundamentally a good guy. It might just be a gut feeling, but it's never let me down before."

Ian pulled alongside the moving tracked vehicle, gesticulating wildly for them to stop. He didn't shoot at them, in fact he threw his gun away as a gesture of alliance. "Stop! I'm on your side," he shouted repeatedly.

Cocooned in the cab of the vehicle, Julie and Chuck couldn't hear what he was saying over the noise of the engine but the simple act of jettisoning his gun was enough for Julie.

"Stop the truck Chuck," she said, "we need to hear what this guy has to say for himself."

Chuck slowed down and stopped, leaving the engine idling, and cautiously lowered the driver's window a fraction.

"You've got two minutes to convince us that you're above board before we head out of here and leave you behind to freeze," Chuck called through the window.

"Thanks for stopping. I'll keep it brief. I know you've got no reason to trust me after the attempts on your lives, but I need to tell you that I was being blackmailed to take the actions I did."

"Who by?" shouted Julie.

"Ray Bergman. He got me to take some money from him during my divorce which I didn't declare to the courts or my ex-wife. He threatened to tell the courts and that I would be imprisoned and not see my boys again if I didn't do what he told me."

Turning to Chuck Julie said, "I believe him, but I'm still worried he might have another change of heart and try to attack us again. There's a rope in the back of the cab so even though he appears to be on our side, what about if we ask him to tie his legs together with it and then lie face down on the seat of his skidoo? I could sit on him while you tie his hands behind his back? You could put one of those sailing knots Skip must have taught you to good use."

Chuck could think of no better plan, so he relayed to Ian what they wanted him to do and threw out the rope. Ian was swift to comply: He didn't want to be left out in this frozen wilderness to die and knew he hadn't got anywhere near enough fuel to get back to McMurdo on the skidoo. Lying face down on the seat with his legs securely fastened, he offered his hands behind him. Chuck tied them tightly and then, releasing Ian's feet, frog-marched him back to the truck.

"Sit there in the back," he instructed Ian. "I'm going to fasten your hands and feet to the roll bar. You'll be as comfortable as I can make you but unable to reach into the front of the cab."

"I'd do exactly the same if the positions were reversed," said Ian. "I don't blame you for being wary, but I swear on my children's lives that I mean you no harm."

---- 51 ----

Wednesday 25th October
London

Headlines in newspapers all over the world were screaming about the massive new iceberg, but only one newspaper knew the likely cause of it, if not the potential for a global disaster. Mary Roberts was sitting in her office re-reading Julie Grant's article. The legal department had cleared it for publication and Mary planned on running it in tomorrow's paper, warts and all, as a sub-story to the Ross Ice Shelf disaster. She wanted a quote from Ray Bergman to include in the article and picked up the phone to call him.

"Could I speak to Ray Bergman please," she asked Jayne Grey.

"Who's calling please, and in relation to what, may I ask?" came the response. Even though Jayne was unaware of the cause of things in Antarctica, she did know Ray was very stressed about something. Out of loyalty to him, misplaced or otherwise, she considered it her duty to act as a buffer, maybe to buy him a bit of time.

"It's Mary Roberts from *The Telegraph*. He'll know what it is I want to speak to him about."

Jayne put Mary on hold and buzzed through to Ray. "Ray I've got a Mary Roberts, the Editor from *The Telegraph* wanting to talk to you. Do you want me to say you're in a meeting?"

Ray knew he was trapped: Mary Roberts, like her journalist Julie Grant, would not be fobbed off. He needed to confront her heads on. "No, put her through please Jayne."

"Ah, good morning Mr Bergman. This is Mary Roberts from *The Telegraph* newspaper. I wanted to do you the courtesy of letting you know we are running a story tomorrow directly linking Global Energy to the events in Antarctica and wanted to give you the opportunity to comment," she said pleasantly.

"Good morning Ms Roberts. No comment."

"But you don't even know what we're going to print?"

"Whatever I say will no doubt be distorted."

"*The Telegraph* isn't a gossip-mongering rag Mr Bergman. We are serious journalists reporting real news. Now, don't you want to hear what it is we have to say? Maybe give your own press department time to prepare a response?" probed Mary.

"Why would you want to give us time?"

"Ah, so he does know what we're talking about," thought Mary, Julie's correct in her assumption. Instead she replied, "As I say, we are serious journalists who want to provide our readers with a balanced viewpoint."

"First time I've heard of that," muttered Ray under his breath. "Okay, fill me in."

Mary spent the next few minutes outlining the gist of the article to Ray. He half-listened, noting no mention of the attacks on Julie Grant he'd sanctioned, nor of any link to the Ross Ice Shelf's 'Rossberg', but clear evidence of their illegal sonic blasting activities, while carefully formulating his response. If he was going to be quoted word for word in the press this might be the one opportunity he would have to salvage both Global Energy's, and his own, reputation.

"The oil industry is a tricky business Ms Roberts, as I'm sure you can appreciate. As oil reserves start to run out, it's dog eat dog, survival of the fittest. Everyone in this field is having to look to the future, securing their shareholder's interests. That necessarily involves research, Ms Roberts, and trialling of new techniques. I hold up my hand to the fact that Global Energy is at the forefront of those new techniques but assure you that everything we do has the future of the planet and its inhabitants as one of the primary concerns."

"That's just typical PR speak Mr Bergman," Mary fired back, "what about your activities down in Antarctica?" she pushed.

"As it happens I convened a board meeting yesterday to ask that very question. Our Development Director was investigating some new types of exploratory testing, and may even have formulated a hypothetical implementation schedule, but I can assure you that nothing would have gone ahead without the say-so of the board, and the full agreement of the countries party to the Antarctic Agreement," Ray said, knowing he had to acknowledge the existence of the blasting schedule but denying that it had been put into operation. "I can assure you that no such agreement was given by the board." Again, this wasn't a lie. Ray had never put the secret sonic blasting before the board for a formal decision.

"So, you're denying any responsibility for the events on the Ross Ice Shelf and WAIS?" Mary exclaimed. "Despite the fact that we have evidence of the planned sonic blasting schedule and corresponding spikes in seismic activity?" she asked, astounded.

"My dear Ms Roberts, Antarctica is a very unstable area. There are earth tremors virtually every day. I can assure you that any theoretical synergy between recordings and our testing schedule is just that, theoretical."

"So, what are you saying exactly, just so I can quote you directly?"

"I am saying that Global Energy considered alternative extraction techniques and sources of energy in Antarctica but are yet to act on any of them and that is all. Goodbye," and with that, Ray hung up the phone.

---- 52 ----

Wednesday 25th October
Antarctica

The journey back to McMurdo passed uneventfully, give or take avoiding the odd sink hole and crevasse or two, but fortunately for Chuck the tracks from Ian's outward journey were still just visible, making their return trip that much easier. Ian Smith had been the model prisoner, never once complaining or trying to escape, and indeed had proved to be a genuine and nice guy. He'd related his experience to them from the calving of the giant Ross iceberg and explained that the McMurdo station had very nearly been destroyed.

They'd done a lot of talking about Global Energy and its involvement in the disaster too; and Chuck and Julie now fully understood the hold Ray Bergman had over Ian. In fact, both Chuck and Julie felt rather sorry for him being fellow victims of the unscrupulous Ray Bergman, and they had untied his feet so that he could sit more comfortably.

"That man has got to be brought to justice," announced Julie. "He can't be allowed to get away with blackmail, arranging murders, and damaging the planet," she stormed.

"I agree," replied Ian. "Maybe if we act together we've got enough to bring him down."

"You'd do that, despite incriminating yourself?" asked Chuck.

"He doesn't need to incriminate himself in all of it really," said Julie thoughtfully. "A lot could be attributed to Lance and he's not around to dispute it. Ian, in return for us leaving you out of some things, would you be prepared to give a full statement to the police to back up the attacks on me and my property in London and the aborted attempt to kill us on WAIS?"

"Why would we want to do that Julie? This guy might have been being blackmailed, but he still tried to finish us both off, and you more than once," challenged Chuck.

"I know what you're saying, Chuck, but I do believe he was caught between a rock and a hard place, and his testimony would be the final nail in the coffin for Ray Bergman. Ian's still going to end up being prosecuted for withholding information with the intent to defraud his ex-wife and may end up with a custodial sentence, but he did save our lives out on WAIS and his statement would completely back up our stories."

Chuck still wasn't happy with Ian getting off scot-free. It was one thing not to mention him tampering with the helicopter, but the guy had also assaulted Julie at McMurdo. He was in an emotional turmoil, but in the end, he agreed with Julie's point of view, rationalising it and commenting, "Well I guess in the scheme of things we can let it go. After all, if this giant iceberg drifts too far north it may well be curtains for us anyway."

"What are you talking about?" asked Ian.

"Oh, something we learnt from a chap at IVSO, an expert in the field of seismology and related science. He reckons that if a large enough iceberg drifts far enough north, it will create an imbalance that will topple the world off its current axis, or words to that effect," paraphrased Chuck.

"How big an iceberg are we talking? And how far north would it need to drift?"

"I don't really know the answer to that Ian. It's something for the experts to work out, but from what you said to us earlier about how far north you had to travel along the Queen Elizabeth mountains before being able to turn away west to head across the remaining shelf, then it's a big bastard."

Ian looked at them both for a few seconds. "I'm willing to do what Julie asks, even if there's no real future for any of us because of this damn iceberg," he said quietly.

The three travelling companions were silent for a while, each pondering their own version of a disaster scenario and what it would mean for them and their loved ones. Chuck hoped Skip and Dom might survive if they were still aboard *Aztec* and be able to ride out any shift on the high seas.

Julie was thinking about Ian's reply. She had made up her mind that Ian was genuinely contrite and willing to help their cause in bringing down Ray Bergman, even at the potential cost of his own freedom, and she was going to give him a chance.

"Chuck, we wouldn't be here if it wasn't for Ian."

"I know, don't get me wrong, I am grateful to him, it's just … I don't want any harm to come to you Jules. But if you're sure, then I'll defer to your instinct."

Julie gave him a big hug and a kiss. "I hoped you'd see it my way. Shall I let him loose then?"

"OK."

Julie got up from her seat, moved across to Ian, and said, "I'm trusting you Ian, please don't let me down."

"You can trust me Julie," replied Ian looking her in the eye. Julie untied his hands and he rubbed his wrists

347

to get the circulation back into his hands. Chuck's knots were very good and very tight. There would have been no wriggling out of them any other way. He settled back into his seat and relaxed a bit.

"So, what happens next?" he asked Chuck and Julie.

"The Global Energy plane is still at McMurdo isn't it?" asked Chuck.

"Yes, why?"

"I think we'll take it back to England, after all, the pilots will be expecting you to return to London sometime soon, won't they? And you'll be able to bring along an employee and a reporter without raising any eyebrows."

"That could work. I can let Bergman know that my task is complete here without giving any details away and let him assume what he wants: No doubt with all the other problems he has on the table right now, he won't have much time or inclination to ask any questions."

"We can prepare a statement for the police on the way, which will mean that we can keep the pressure on him as soon as we get back. He has got to go down for this," said Julie.

"Agreed," said Ian. "I want to be rid of him and have my old job back. Sod the money, he can have it all back. I don't want it. I never did really, but I was at

348

such a low point over the financial hearing for my divorce I would have done anything. Well, I kind of did. I'm sorry about that. Sincerely. I regret everything I've done, except killing that murderous worm Lance. He really was a nasty piece of work."

"How are we going to explain his absence away to the plane's crew?" asked Julie.

"An accident out on the shelf. I saw him go off on his own looking to find you both when you weren't at the camp when we came to rescue you. He went off on a skidoo, and he must have driven accidentally into one of the sink holes in the twilight, I should expect. I looked for him but there was no trace," replied Ian.

Chuck nodded his head. "That's the story then. We never saw anything of him, and so we can only assume the worst. OK with that Jules?"

"Fine with me."

The remaining journey back to McMurdo passed pleasantly after that, and the conversation flowed easily between the three of them. Ian regaled them with the story of his divorce, how he had been prevented by his wife's solicitors from buying a new place of his own and had to rent a bed-sit instead, the fact that she had taken everything apart from the clothes he stood up in, and the fact that he now had a crippling court order against him for maintenance until she remarried or cohabited. On top of that he was expected to pay for school fees and incidentals such as holidays as well.

"I'm surprised you can afford it on a Global Energy salary," said Chuck.

"Well, it doesn't look as though I'm going to have to pay out for very long does it with prison on the horizon?"

"Maybe not, but that's the worst-case scenario. Let's look on the positive side. Does she have anyone else in her life?" he asked.

"I don't think anyone else is stupid enough to take her on," he mumbled. "Looks like I will be poor for a long while yet, although maybe if I do spend a spell in prison it would do her some good. She's a qualified chartered surveyor, so she will just have to get off her ass and go back to work to support herself and the kids. Right now, I'm just the meal ticket as far as she's concerned, and she is really going for the jugular, encouraged by her money-grabbing solicitors. If I am going to be incarcerated, it might not be so bad after all!" he said, perking up a bit.

As dusk fell, the station at McMurdo finally hove into view.

---- 53 ----

Monday 30th October
Washington DC

The team of scientists pulled together by the President had done their calculations, and they estimated the size of the 'Rossberg' to be 125 miles wide by 370 miles long, a staggering 46,250 square miles of ice several hundred metres thick, almost four times bigger than the largest recorded iceberg in history.

The 'Rossberg' was now being pushed along by the strong Antarctic winds and the current within the Ross Sea. It was moving steadily northwards by up to twenty miles a day, and at this rate, the lumbering giant would reach the Southern Ocean within a matter of weeks. Once in that notorious ocean, the currents, flowing steadily north eastwards, would proceed to push the berg in a reverse 'S', passing to the south of South Africa and the Cape of Good Hope. From there it would either continue north-eastwards towards the western extremes of Australia, or, due east towards the southern tip of New Zealand. But regardless of the direction it might take, with an iceberg of this size, the primary fear was that it would drift far enough north to disrupt the earth's equilibrium and cause the world to shift on its axis. It only had to travel two and a half thousand miles north, to a latitude of 45 degrees south, and the probability of a global disaster was extremely high.

Keith Mortimer had been given the chairmanship of the committee as it was he who had brought the issue to the attention of the President. He was sitting at his desk reading the latest estimates and calculations from his team of experts, when his phone rang.

"Dr Keith Mortimer," he said as he put the handset to his ear.

"Keith, hi, it's Julie Grant here. Chuck and I are back in the UK."

"Oh Julie, thank God you survived the collapse down in Antarctica. I was really worried about you. Are you okay?"

"Yes, thanks Keith, we're both doing fine. Sorry we couldn't contact you before now but the SatPhone you gave us got destroyed in the earthquake when a heavy container fell on it. We certainly did have a couple of hairy moments down there, but we've both come through relatively unscathed. Listen Keith, the real reason for this call is to tell you that we have more valuable information on the WAIS issue that you need to know about."

"Really? Go on Julie, tell me everything but I also have news for you: That wasn't a naturally occurring earthquake, rather an earth tremor caused by the collapse of a large section of the ice sheet. I rather suspect it was a continuation of the after-effects of the original disaster caused by Global Energy's sonic blasting activities."

"My God, we didn't realise that but now I think back Chuck did mention the potential for a surface collapse when he was taking samples from one of the holes. He described it rather like being inside a giant ice cathedral with vaulted ceilings hundreds of feet high supported by narrow columns. I guess if the columns gave way and the massive ceiling fell, it *would* feel like an earthquake. Something else we can lay at the feet of Global then."

"Yes, it very much looks that way Julie. Anyway, what was it you wanted to tell me?" Keith enquired.

"Well as I said, we, or rather, Chuck managed to lower himself into, and take some core samples, from some of the sinkholes on the icecap, and, well, Chuck did some analysis on them and found that there was a very high concentration of methane hydrates trapped in the ice. We think, no actually we are pretty sure, that this is what Global are trying to perfect their extraction process for, using the sonic blasting to bring them to the surface, before any of their competition develops their own extraction techniques."

"Hmm. An interesting viewpoint. Yes, that would make sense, given what we know already and the existence of huge reserves of methane hydrates under the seabed and in polar regions. If it is the case, then Global Energy can kiss goodbye to any future in the Antarctic. They'll be off the continent before they can blink."

"We agree with you Keith. Chuck and I are putting together my final report to submit to my editor at *The Telegraph,* and it is going to be both hard hitting and damning. I'm giving you fair notice so that you can prime anyone you see fit to inform before we go to press."

"Well, your first article has already caused a great commotion in the scientific world, and by all accounts, this one will probably create a major outrage in several countries, if not the entire world. The greed of one corporation effectively jeopardising the planet as we know it today. Are you aware of what is happening with the iceberg that the earthquake created?"

"Not really, can you update us?"

354

"It's not looking good at all. Our projections are that the 'Rossberg' will move steadily eastwards and northwards until it disrupts the equilibrium of the earth's spinning axis, and the planet will shift by several degrees, our latest estimate is that it might be as high as twenty degrees."

"That sounds a lot Keith, what will it mean in real terms?"

"It will put each hemisphere into a two-season, six-month cycle; one facing more towards the sun in permanent daylight with temperatures terribly hot, more like that of the equator today, but even more intense as there is no night to cool the earth down at all. The other hemisphere, by contrast, would be in total darkness, never seeing sunlight at all and would be frozen. The four seasons as we know them would no longer apply. It would be either very hot and daylight or extremely cold and dark. It would be a disaster."

"So, you're saying that there would be no temperate zones? What would we do about food? Aren't most fruit and vegetables currently grown in those areas?"

"That's right Julie. There would be a world shortage of grown produce unless new agricultural techniques could be found and implemented quickly. But it's not only what we grow that we need to be concerned about. Livestock, and especially wildlife, would

355

struggle to adapt to the new situation; global transportation would be affected by the frozen conditions; geostationary satellites used for GPS and navigation systems would no longer function; centres of population would not be equipped with any infrastructure that could handle the new conditions. The list is endless. Excuse the pun, but what we've just talked about is only the tip of the iceberg."

"So, is it likely to be an extinction of life event Keith?"

"Not quite, but it will make living on this planet a very different experience, and millions, perhaps billions would perish."

"What's being done to stop it happening? Surely in today's modern world there's a way of diverting this 'Rossberg' to keep it in the higher latitudes?" Julie asked.

"That's what the best brains we have are working on around the clock, to make our best prediction of the path 'Rossberg' will take, and to try to come up with some means of reversing its direction of travel. Ideally, we need to send it back from whence it came. Our biggest problem is that we're dealing with something that weighs many trillions of tonnes Julie, there's no man-made machine that can influence something that big."

"Does that mean there is no hope for us? We can't stop trying. If there's nothing man-made that can aid us, what about another force of nature?" Julie said, casting about wildly for a solution to this terrible dilemma. "I know! We could trigger another earthquake in Tierra del Fuego or somewhere at the bottom of South America to generate a tsunami to wash it back to Antarctica," she exclaimed. "You know all about volcanoes Keith, can't you cause one to erupt?"

"I wish we could, Julie. But if we could trigger an earthquake or volcanic eruption, and it is *if*, we can't control the outcome. A tsunami could travel in any direction; the ash cloud from a volcanic eruption will drift with the wind; tremors from one earthquake could trigger another more violent earthquake under the earth's mantle. There really is no way we can use nature against nature I'm afraid."

"Well what are we going to do? We can't just sit back and do nothing."

"Rest assured we're not. We'll continue to look for a solution while ever there's time to do so. And there is a chance the berg might just decide to stay in the Southern Ocean and reconnect itself naturally to the Antarctic land mass. Don't give up hope just yet," Keith said, in a vain attempt to reassure her.

"I'll try not to Keith, but I will discuss it with Chuck. He's also a scientist and might have some ideas that could help."

"By all means do so Julie, and please let me know of any ideas you get between you, no matter how trivial and silly they might seem."

"I will do Keith. Please also keep us updated on your progress too." And with that, Julie broke the connection and went off to find Chuck. They had some work to do.

---- 54 ----

Tuesday 31st October
London

The article that had been printed in *The Telegraph* on the previous Thursday had put Global Energy's share price into freefall. Every day since then, something else had been dug up and published to put Global Energy and its CEO further in a bad light. Ray Bergman didn't know which way to turn: He was truly damned. The board had turned on him under the leadership of Jeff Ramsey for undertaking the illegal sonic blasting, and they had passed a vote of no confidence in his leadership, but with a temporary stay of execution as no one else wanted to deal with the shit storm Global Energy had found themselves in the middle of.

"I really had no idea that the sonic blasting would trigger such a catastrophic chain of events," Ray tried to justify himself to Jeff Ramsey. "You know I only ever have Global Energy's success at heart."

"That's as maybe Ray, but on this occasion, it's backfired spectacularly. I can't see any clear way out of this predicament now: I'm truly at a loss."

"Yeah, that makes two of us," admitted Ray. "But we can't roll over and play puppy, we've got to fight back somehow, maybe come up with a means to help the situation."

"Oh? Do you have anything in mind?"

"Not at the moment but give me some time to think about it."

Julie had fully briefed Chuck on her conversation with Keith and had told him about the imminent disaster facing the world.

"It's like a ticking timebomb Chuck. We've got to try to come up with something that might help."

"I agree Jules, I've only just started to get to know you and it seems as though any future we might have looked forward to together is being ripped out from under our feet. I'll certainly put my thinking cap on: Nothing immediately springs to mind though, I must confess. We also need to move forwards by giving statements to the Police about the attack on us down in Antarctica on WAIS, not to mention those others that happened to you in London. Obviously, as we agreed, we can't mention the helicopter incident as Lance wasn't in McMurdo when that happened, and we've promised not to implicate Ian."

"Well, shall we get the statement giving over and done with, and then we can apply ourselves fully to the 'Rossberg' problem?" suggested Julie. "I'll call the Detective who dealt with the case over the London attacks on me and arrange for us both to go to see him."

"Fine by me. We're both clear on what to say, we're telling the truth after all, just omitting Ian's attack on you in McMurdo and the helicopter crash. Set it up." Julie made the call.

Detective Inspector David Jones was very interested to hear from Julie, especially when she said she believed she knew who had attacked her and who had been behind it: The Police had not managed to uncover any leads at all on the London attacks. She arranged to meet him that afternoon and to take Chuck along with her. On their arrival at the police station, DI Jones showed them into an interview room, offering them tea or coffee, switched on the recorder, and then sat down across the table from them to hear what they had to say.

Julie opened the discussion with, "Have you seen the recent article published in *The Telegraph* about Global Energy and its link to all the events in

Antarctica?" DI Jones nodded his assent. "Well," she continued, "I don't know if you noticed, but that article had my name on it. I've been investigating the link since early September and have reason to believe it was the Global Energy CEO, Ray Bergman, who was behind the London attacks in a bid to silence me, maybe scare me off reporting the facts I had researched and the conclusions I have arrived at."

"You have reason to believe, or do you have any evidence?" queried DI Jones.

"Both I guess, but before I outline what exactly I have got, I'd like to complete the story and paint the full picture for you. As part of my research into the initial 'supposed' earthquake on the Western Antarctic Ice Sheet, I managed to uncover the name of the Global Energy scientist who had to be rescued by helicopter. Let me introduce the scientist to you - Charlie Fallon. Charlie, or rather Chuck, was given an unexpected month's leave of absence following his rescue and during that time he also did a lot of analysis concerning the earthquake incident and its probable cause. Over to you Chuck."

"Yes, I'd got copies of the seismology readings on my laptop and when I looked at them after the event I realised the patterns were unlike any other earth tremor I'd seen before: Too regularly timed, so to speak. It triggered alarm bells in my head which I intended to follow up on once I was back in the UK after my month's leave, but Julie managed to track me down and contacted me before I returned. With what she had found out, and the data I had on my laptop, we realised something untoward had been going on down on the WAIS and undertook to investigate it."

"That was just before the attack on me in London, Detective Inspector Jones," Julie added to help the detective with the time line. "Because of these three attacks on the same day, I got well out of the city and went down to Falmouth to meet up with Chuck."

"You live in Falmouth, Mr Fallon?" queried DI Jones.

"No, near Sherborne in Dorset, but I spent my leave of absence sailing back across the Atlantic from New York with my sister and her husband. Falmouth was to be our first landfall," Chuck explained.

"This is quite some tale," said the detective somewhat speculatively. "Please do carry on."

"Well, knowing a bit about Julie's events in London, we thought that she would be followed down to the west country, so we decided to meet up in Fowey instead, just along the coast from Falmouth and a less obvious place for us to arrive back into the UK in case of prying eyes. We then planned a strategy to obtain the evidence that Global Energy was behind the disaster on WAIS, and I returned to Antarctica to collect that evidence, so we could prove it. Julie made her own way down, and we met up again at the new remote research station I had just commissioned."

"Yes," agreed Julie, "and that's when we discovered that the ice sheet had been pockmarked with giant sink holes. Chuck and I returned to Global Energy's satellite research station to collect the missing data and discovered all these holes." She smoothly avoided mentioning the attack on her by Ian Smith at McMurdo.

"So, what did you do next?" prompted DI Jones.

"Chuck quit his job and we flew to the US via New Zealand to meet Dr Keith Mortimer of IVSO, that's the International Volcanology and Seismology Organisation, to try to get a better understanding of what had happened to the ice sheet. Dr Mortimer had an opinion but needed samples and readings to be certain, so we returned to WAIS yet again to set up a temporary camp ahead of the arrival of a team of IVSO scientists."

"Quite a bit of travelling," commented DI Jones.

"Yes, we travelled through so many time zones that we didn't know our arses from our elbows," commented Chuck, "but we travelled back out onto the

364

ice sheet and set up camp. That's where we were when the next disaster occurred, that's when the 'Rossberg' calved off the Ross Ice Sheet. We're lucky to be alive."

"We lost communications and had no means of returning to McMurdo without transportation so had no option other than to sit it out in the wilderness. Either the IVSO team would arrive as planned or we would be rescued: We knew Keith Mortimer wouldn't leave us out there to die," explained Julie.

"There was a third option we considered," said Chuck, "and that was that Ray Bergman might send out hired killers to finish us off."

"Why on earth would you imagine that?" asked DI Jones. "It's a big leap from a mugging in London to contract killers in Antarctica," he said, raising a sardonic eyebrow.

"Christ," thought Chuck, trying to think on his feet, "what do I say now?"

Julie instantly came to his rescue. "It was my opinion, Detective Inspector Jones. I'd sensed I'd been watched and followed ever since I left London and it just seemed the logical conclusion. If someone wanted to silence me, what better place than to have me simply disappear in a frozen wasteland where my body would never be discovered. Chuck would have just been collateral damage."

"Hmmm," muttered DI Jones, clearly not convinced by this explanation. "Let's get to the end of this tale and see what we've got."

"Well, as a precaution, we left the temporary camp we'd established and set up another, much smaller one, some distance away. Rightly or wrongly we concluded that anyone with ill intent would not settle until they'd found us, or our bodies, and would search until they did," said Julie.

"Wouldn't a rescue party do the same?" queried the detective.

"Probably," said Julie, "but we didn't think of that at the time." She realised that their story wasn't stacking up without telling the detective of the attack on her at McMurdo and the near fatal helicopter crash, but she ploughed on, hoping to convince the detective with the final part of their story.

"If I can just finish the story then you'll see my fears weren't unfounded," she continued. "Two men on skidoos *did* appear, approaching our new camp at speed. We just knew they were not a rescue party and fled on our own skidoo, out onto the ice sheet towards the sinkholes. Our skidoo couldn't travel as fast as those of our pursuers as we had two people on it, so we really thought we were lost. But then a miracle happened and one of our pursuers saved our lives: He

366

deliberately crashed his skidoo into that of his compatriot's allowing us to escape. His fellow assassin lost control of his skidoo and careered into one of the sink holes, lost for ever." Julie paused at this point, trying to read DI Jones' face for clues of whether he believed their story. The detective's face was a closed book, "No clues there," she thought, "I'd better keep going."

"So, to cut a long story short, Chuck and I raced back to the original camp and locked ourselves in the cab of the tracked vehicle the two men had used to come out from McMurdo to find us. We knew our remaining pursuer wouldn't risk damaging the vehicle as it was his only means of escape too, but we reasoned he could still have shot at us through the cab windows if he was intent on killing us. He didn't, and that, combined with him apparently saving our lives near the sink hole, convinced us he might be on our side. Close-up, Chuck recognised him as Global Energy's Head of Security, Ian Smith. Anyway, we took a bit of a gamble and got him to truss himself up before we exited the cab and allowed him to climb aboard," she explained.

"And on the long drive back to McMurdo, that's when we discovered that Ian had been blackmailed by Ray Bergman to assist the hired killer in finishing us off," Chuck summarised, "but he didn't, he saved our lives instead."

"And is this Ian Smith willing to corroborate your story? Give a full statement to the police?" asked DI Jones.

"Oh yes," Julie assured him. "He's very willing to do just that. He wants to rid himself of the threat of blackmail, no matter what the consequences."

Detective Inspector Jones finally seemed to believe them, and Chuck and Julie leaned back in their chairs in relief.

"Okay, moving forwards, we'll need full statements from the two of you, and of course from Ian Smith, before we can take any further action against Ray Bergman, but rest assured if it all stacks up, and the CPS feel we have enough evidence for a prosecution, we will move very quickly to bring Mr Bergman to justice."

Leaving the police station two hours later, having given their statements and provided DI Jones with Ian's contact details, Chuck and Julie felt oddly deflated. They'd done all they could to put Ray Bergman and Global Energy firmly in the frame for the disaster in Antarctica and pointed the finger at Ray for trying to silence them forever.

Over the next two days, Detective Inspector Jones called on Ian Smith and brought him into the police station for interview. Ian, true to his word, gave a full disclosure of the events brought on by Ray Bergman, emphasising that he was being coerced into working for Ray under threat of blackmail, but omitting the fact that he had sabotaged the helicopter before its flight to Mario Zucchelli Airport and assaulted Julie at McMurdo as well.

He made his official statement under caution, he had been formally arrested and charged with assault for the attack on Julie and Chuck on WAIS, accepting a bribe from Ray Bergman, and contempt of court for misappropriating funds and not declaring them. As there was no evidence that he was directly responsible for the death of Lance, and with no body to examine, there were no further charges to make. He was put into a holding cell pending the next Magistrates Court session when he would be bound over for trial.

---- 55 ----

Friday 3rd November
London

DI Jones, armed with his sworn statements and back-up, went to the Global Energy HQ, showed his warrant card, and asked to see Ray Bergman. Being directed to the seventh floor by the receptionist, DI Jones strode down the corridor towards Ray's office. Jayne opened the door for him and he simply pushed past her, announced his name and declared that he had a warrant for Ray's arrest. He read Ray his rights and his assisting officer placed his handcuffs around Ray's wrists, his arms behind his back. Jayne stood stock still, horrified at the spectacle, unable to respond. Ray was incensed at the effrontery of the police officers, and he struggled against the restraining cuffs.

"I want my lawyer!" he shouted at Jayne, "get him out here now!"

"Yes sir, right away," she said as she hurried back out to her desk. She picked up the handset and dialled the number for the company lawyer.

Meanwhile, the police officers manhandled Ray, who was cursing them profoundly as he went, along the corridor and into the lift. The other directors had heard Ray's commotion and several heads popped out of doorways to see what was going on. The sight of Ray being hauled off by the police was a shock to all of them and they ducked back into the safety of their own workspaces to avoid witnessing the debacle.

As he was led out through the reception area to the waiting squad car, Ray had stopped shouting and cursing, and walked in silence, glowering with anger, outrage, and embarrassment. He was the head of a multi-national energy corporation for fucks sake! This could not be happening to him! How would he ever recover from the ignominy of it all? All staff heads turned and watched his passage in silent disbelief, but as soon as he was through the entrance doors, the office gossip started immediately, trying to find out what he had done. They would all discover the truth soon enough.

Sitting in an interview room, Ray declined to comment on anything before his lawyer arrived at the police station, and he stonewalled all questions thereafter. At the end of the interview he was formally charged with extortion and conspiring to commit murder and was remanded in custody pending trial:

Unbeknown to him, he was placed in the holding cell next to one of his accusers, Ian Smith.

Saturday 4th November
London

Chuck had temporarily moved into Julie's house to give her some comfort that there was help on hand in case anyone else tried to break in or attack her again. They didn't know whether Ray Bergman had made other arrangements to eliminate her for the stories she had published. He was obviously vindictive, and they had no idea whether he might try something again.

They were both having a coffee in the kitchen when DI Jones rang the doorbell. They poured him a cup and he joined them at the breakfast bar. He told them that he had called by to let them know what had transpired with the case since their formal interviews and statements, and to tell them that they both needed to be available at short notice as they would be called as witnesses when Ian and Ray's cases came to trial. Chuck and Julie agreed to be available.

After DI Jones had left they sat quietly at the breakfast bar together.

"So, what happens now?" asked Julie, "it can't all be over, can it?"

"It looks like we are beginning a new phase in our lives," said Chuck. "You've just been made a Business Editor - congratulations once again, well deserved - and I've lost my job with Global Energy, albeit with some gardening leave until the Ray Bergman situation is all done and dusted. I think life is going to be a bit unusual for a while. It's not every day you get the CEO of a multi-national energy company arrested for illegal activities is it? I'd better start looking for another position and this time, I'll look for something that is preferably located somewhere warm, just for a change."

"You'll find another job, Chuck."

Julie paused for a moment. "Can we talk about the 'Rossberg' issue?" she asked him. "What do you think will happen there?"

"That's for Keith and his team to work out. I think we have to leave it up to the experts now."

---- 57 ----

Monday 6th November
Washington DC

Keith Mortimer and his team were in a meeting at the IVSO headquarters, reviewing the passage that the 'Rossberg' had made over the previous two weeks and they were discussing their predictions as to where it was likely to be heading. Kevin Chu, one of the team's leading oceanographers, and an expert in ocean currents, was presenting his theory on where he expected the iceberg to go next. He had a PowerPoint presentation projected on the screen in the meeting room with a series of slides showing, day by day, the recorded position of the berg so far.

"The 'Rossberg' has been floating free for nearly three weeks since its calving from the ice shelf, and we calculate that it has travelled over three hundred and fifty miles with the Ross Sea Gyre from its original position. It is moving steadily across the Ross Sea and out towards the Southern Ocean, positioning it just here as of yesterday." Kevin indicated the position on the screen with his laser pointer. "Once it clears the tip of East Antarctica, it becomes prey to the myriad south polar currents."

He moved on to the next part of his presentation, which was his forecast for the days to come. He seemed somewhat excited, eager to share his views, and everyone in the room was paying close attention to what he had to say. He pushed his spectacles up to the bridge of his nose before continuing.

"I believe that the 'Rossberg' will initially head in an anti-clockwise direction with the East Wind Drift inside the Antarctic Divergence Zone." He paused for a moment to let that fact sink in around the table, then he continued. "Ladies and gentlemen, it appears that lady luck might actually be on our side," he said to the team. "From its current orientation, the iceberg has its long face on to the current, and so it is my opinion that, in all probability, the iceberg will continue on its current path for a few more days. Then it will curl around the northern edge of East Antarctica, and run into a small, uninhabited, ice-covered archipelago called the Balleny Islands, which are about a hundred miles off the mainland."

Pausing for breath he flipped to the next slide which showed the Balleny Islands in greater detail. He indicated with his laser pen where on his presentation slide the location of this small island chain was relative to Antarctica, checking that his audience were all on board. Heads nodded around the table, he had milked the moment enough, it was time for him to continue.

"As you can see from this slide, there are three main islands in the group," he pointed to each in turn with his laser, "the largest being Young Island here, and several other islets and rocks above sea level, all running in a northwest-southeast direction. Altogether, these islands and rocks provide almost 100 miles of an obstruction for the 'Rossberg'. If it moves as I forecast it to over the next ten days it should simply grind to a halt, trapped, in fact wedged, between the Ballenys and East Antarctica. I believe that the prevailing current will then continue to push it further and further into the gap, and so it should ultimately reconnect back to the land mass, effectively forming a bridge between the islands and the mainland," he concluded, a big smile on his face at being able to impart such a positive scenario. After several days of hard work and analysis, everyone on the team was exhausted, and desperately in need of a potential solution to the problem.

"That's the best news I've heard in over a week!" exclaimed Keith, rising from his seat and slapping Kevin on the back. "How certain are you that Young Island and its neighbours will stop it?" he queried.

"Well the island chain might only be a quarter of the length of the 'Rossberg' but they should do the trick, providing it maintains its longitudinal orientation to the coastline. If you think of the size of a door wedge in relation to a door in comparison, then you can see they should easily be able to bring it to a grinding halt," Kevin concluded.

"Excellent news indeed, and a very neat solution to a critical problem. Now, is everyone else around the table happy with Kevin's rationale?" Keith asked of the remaining team leaders, looking around at their faces one by one. Each head nodded their assent. "Are there any flaws you can see, or problems Kevin has overlooked or oversimplified?" he pushed.

"Quite the contrary," Andrew Brown, the team's leading meteorologist said. "As Kevin has forecast, the 'Rossberg' should be pushed along by the East Wind Drift from its current position and remain inside the Antarctic Divergence Zone. It will need to have moved several hundred miles offshore before the iceberg meets the West Wind Drift which will push against it. With these consistent polar easterly winds, there should be little or no deviation from the projected route as far as I can see."

No-one else had anything to add.

"Well, if we're all comfortable that nature may be providing us with a solution, I'll let the President know that things are looking more promising." With that Keith closed the meeting adding, "You should all take a couple of days break over the next week. I'll assign a skeleton team to monitor the 'Rossberg's' path. I'll get my secretary to co-ordinate it and let you know the roster. Thank you all for your hard work."

---- 58 ----

Tuesday 7th November
London

As he had promised to keep them in the loop, Keith Mortimer had relayed the news from his previous day's team meeting to Julie and Chuck, letting them know the team's projections. Julie made copious notes as he talked, making sure that she had the facts essential for the next article in *The Telegraph* which would keep all her readers interested and informed. She would type up the article after the phone call.

"Thanks for the update Keith," Chuck said. "It seems like the 'Rossberg' side of things appears to be as good as over, and I hope that this Kevin Chu is right, but in the worst-case scenario, if something goes wrong, there is still a need to do something else to avert a probable global disaster. What's your plan B?"

"To be honest, Chuck, right now, there isn't one," said Keith. "Given the sheer size of this problem, we think we really have to rely on nature to take care of it. It's simply too big for us mere mortals to try and divert it by any other means. Unless you have any other suggestions?"

"Well, since you ask Keith, I have been trying to think about what could be done to try to turn the tide against the 'Rossberg', so to speak, and drive it back to Antarctica, and, well … I have had an idea. It's early days yet, and I don't want to say too much at this stage as I need to develop my initial thoughts. I need some time to run a few calculations and potential scenarios, but I believe it may just work."

Julie looked up at him sharply from her laptop. He hadn't mentioned any of this to her over the past few days. What was he up to?

Chuck continued with the phone call. "In the meantime, Keith, let's see if the iceberg does do what you predict. It might all be academic in the end."

"I agree," said Keith, "but please do develop your idea, and let me know as soon as you have something concrete. We might just need something radical if it all goes belly-up."

---- 59 ----

Friday 10th November
London

Chuck had been closeted away on his own in the office at Julie's home for a few days developing his idea and weighing up the odds of it being a possible Plan B solution to the 'Rossberg' problem. Julie had returned to *The Telegraph* office to take up her new role as Business Editor, and she had been calling him periodically every day, wanting to know what he had in mind and pushing to be involved, but he had stalled her, wanting the time to himself to focus on his idea with a clear head. Finally, after three days of models, projections and theories, he was ready to run it by her and was waiting for her to come home after work.

"Oh, so now you're ready to talk to me about your solution, are you?" was Julie's opening remark as she stepped through her front door to find Chuck waiting for her in the hallway. She had been disappointed, and a bit miffed to be excluded, but soon recovered her good humour as he kissed her on the cheek and gave her a big hug. "Come on then, fill me in on all your deliberations."

Leading the way into her home office, Chuck sat back down at her desk indicating that Julie should sit in her office chair in front of the laptop. "OK Jules, I want to run my big idea by you and see how you react," he opened. "It's rather ironic really that the whole basis of my thinking revolves around the very thing that caused the problem in the first place."

"What, you mean sonic blasting?"

"That's exactly right. I've been researching the topic over the last few days and think there may be a chance that we could use the same technique to control the direction of 'Rossberg'."

"How?"

"Well, my thinking is that a number of suitably placed charges deep down in the base of the berg could create enough impact to fractionally alter the direction of the monolith. If we can insert enough charges in the right places, we can hopefully dictate its path."

"What, so we use sonic blasting for ever and a day to keep 'Rossberg' in the Southern Ocean?" Julie queried.

"No, not exactly. It's not tenable to continue blasting over the longer term. The chances are it would weaken the integrity of the berg and it would shatter into smaller pieces. We would then have to try to manage an ever-growing fleet of bergs which, depending on where they drifted, could be a real hazard to shipping in places like the Drake Passage off the tip of South America. No, what I'm thinking, is that we use the charges sparingly, just enough to drive 'Rossberg' to a final resting place, out of harm's way. My initial thought was to send it back to where it came from, but that would be against the winds and currents, and would make it nigh-on impossible to achieve," he continued. "We need to use the winds and currents as much as possible, so I'm thinking we drive 'Rossberg' somewhere it can safely run aground and stay there."

"Such as the Ballenys?" said Julie, "Rossberg is already heading their way so we could prod it in the right direction to ensure it hits."

"I doubt there's enough time to help with that trajectory Julie: It's only a few days off reaching the Ballenys so we'll just have to let nature takes its course there. No, I'm thinking of identifying another safe haven, as part of the Plan B I discussed with Keith."

"Sounds good Chuck. Where do you have in mind to send it then?" Julie asked, warming to his idea. "And who will have sufficient knowledge of sonic blasting to make this work ......? Oh!" Julie trailed off, realising the primary candidate would be Global

Energy. She could now understand the irony Chuck had alluded to.

"I haven't got as far as the where, but I can see you've worked out who I'm thinking of for providing the expertise," Chuck said.

"Christ, Chuck, can you see Ray Bergman or Global Energy wanting to help us? We've just got the guy arrested for conspiracy to commit murder, not to mention the London assaults."

"Well that's where I disagree with you Jules. I think Ray will see it as an opportunity, not to clear his name, but at least a way to reduce any sentence heading in his direction."

Julie paused, pondering this notion. "So, who's going to ask him to help? You, the disgraced employee? Or me, the hated newspaper journalist? Not an easy choice."

"I actually think we should get it as a directive from the President of the USA. Ray Bergman is an American citizen after all, even though he's currently living in London. But before we take things any further, if you think my idea is plausible, shouldn't we run it by Keith Mortimer?"

"I think we've got nothing to lose, Chuck. Let's call him, he'll still be at work."

Keith was pleased to hear from Julie and Chuck. He was in particularly good spirits, given that 'Rossberg' was continuing along its forecast trajectory and he was thinking very positively.

"Good evening you two. How are things in good old England?"

"You're sounding very upbeat," Julie replied, "we're both very well thanks."

"I'm actually feeling very relieved. The 'Rossberg' is still moving along Kevin's forecast trajectory. It looks like the problem really could be solved!"

"That's wonderful news Keith, and a big relief. To some extent it may negate the reason for our call though …. you remember Chuck mentioned he had an idea about a possible Plan B in case 'Rossberg' deviates from the projection?" she continued. "Well he's spent the last few days developing it and we would like to run it by you, just in case it's ever needed, so to speak."

"Really? Tell me your theory"

Chuck relayed the details of his idea of directing 'Rossberg' to a safe-haven in the event that nature's solution should fail. He explained the principles of sonic blasting that he had investigated on the internet, related them to his experience on WAIS, and said that to calculate the best places to site the detonations, he would have to do some blasting simulations and check the results. Keith listened with great interest.

"To be able to perform these simulations, I would need an accurate 3D scale model of the berg Keith, ice thickness, surface area, height above and below the water, the works," Chuck outlined. "Presumably Kevin Chu has one that he has been using for his projections?"

"I believe so but how detailed it is I don't know. I'll check with him and get one to you as soon as possible," replied Keith. "The new satellite over the Antarctic is equipped with special equipment that can detect the depth and/or thickness of any object. We have been using it since the collapse to chart the remaining thickness of the ice on the polar cap. I'll arrange to reposition the satellite and set it to work on the 'Rossberg' and let you have the details shortly."

"Great, thanks Keith," said Chuck. "If 'Rossberg' misses the Ballenys and is carried further in an anticlockwise direction into the Southern Ocean, then we're going to have to consider other underwater obstructions as well as land masses to bring it to a halt. To that end I'm going to need a map of the ocean floor to identify any suitable mountain ranges once we know the depth of the ice, as well as details of ocean currents and wind patterns."

Keith was silent for several seconds. "I've got a team of the top brains in the world working for me on this Chuck, and no-one has suggested an underwater obstruction as a possibility to stop this thing. I don't know whether I should be grateful to you or annoyed with them, but on the surface of things it sounds as though you may be onto something. I'll get the information you need sent over as soon as possible."

"Thanks once again," said Chuck. "Being on gardening leave I've got time on my hands now, and I hate sitting around doing nothing."

"It's a waste of great talent," replied Keith. "What will you do going forwards?"

"Oh, I don't really know. I'm looking around on the market for something else to move on to," said Chuck.

Keith paused for a few moments. "Well, I'm sure something will turn up for you."

Ending the call, Keith thought about their discussion. IVSO could use talent like Chuck Fallon's, he seemed to have his head screwed on, and he didn't have to try to come up with a solution for the 'Rossberg', yet he had done so. That showed initiative. He would investigate the possibility of an opportunity for him within IVSO.

---- 60 ----

Sunday 12th November

Two days later Keith was able to send Chuck the 3D model of the 'Rossberg'. The model showed that the ice in the berg was actually much thicker than anyone had previously expected, and he had ensured that this new information was relayed back to Kevin Chu so that he could revisit his projections on the path the 'Rossberg' would take. Keith had realised that any ridges in the seabed could potentially disrupt the berg's passage by rotating it as it went on its way, and he wasn't convinced that this was a parameter Kevin had considered.

Having received the 3D model from Keith, Chuck immediately loaded it into the program data file he would run his analysis software on. He also fed in the latest information regarding the wind speed and direction, and the set and rate of the ocean currents, so that he could generate a more accurate computation of where any charges would need to be placed. Finally, he uploaded the seabed topography maps, then set his program to work. "Fingers crossed all this information comes up with something sensible," he mused. He knew it would take his program around two hours to slice and dice the data in all directions. "Time for a quick cuppa," he thought.

Over in Washington the news wasn't good: Kevin Chu hadn't factored in the sea bed in his trajectory calculations and he was horrified to see an underwater ridge running perpendicularly from the foot of the Balleny chain which could potentially deflect 'Rossberg' from its course. Taking a deep breath, he picked up the phone to call Keith Mortimer.

"Keith, it's Kevin Chu. I've re-run my forecasts and fear I may have bad news for you. There's a chance that 'Rossberg' may be deflected by underwater seamounts and deviate from my predicted course."

"You'd better get up to my office and fill me in," Keith instructed before he put the phone back on its cradle. He had a bad feeling that things had just taken a turn for the worse. "I guess I shouldn't have expected everything to work out so smoothly," he thought putting his head into his hands. "How the hell am I going to face the President with this news?"

Kevin was in his office within minutes, armed with charts and calculations. Once he had spread them all out on the meeting table, Keith moved over to join him.

"Look, just here," Kevin indicated on the chart, "there's an underwater ridge that runs off the shallower southern end of the archipelago. It rises over four hundred metres off the sea bed and, if our data on the depth of 'Rossberg' is correct, it could impact around the centre of the face of the berg within two days. If it does, we're looking at one of two scenarios depending on where exactly it hits.

"I'm with you so far," said Keith.

"Well, I now believe that the point of impact will act as a fulcrum and the berg will pivot on this point. If the point of impact is east of the centre, it will deflect 'Rossberg' inland of the Ballenys and drive it to wedge against the mainland, very much what we are hoping will happen. If, however, it impacts west of the centre, then 'Rossberg' will be rotate in the opposite direction and will be driven further out into the Southern Ocean, missing the Ballenys altogether, and will then be prey to the ocean currents," Kevin explained. "If that's the case, we're back to square one with no means of controlling this monolith."

"And do you have a sense of which side of the mid-point the berg is likely to impact the ridge? What probability are we looking at of it being set adrift?"

Kevin hesitated before meeting Keith's eyes. "It's hanging in the balance Keith. Realistically, we've got a less than forty-sixty chance of it getting trapped in between the Ballenys and the Antarctic coastline. That is the best I can say."

Keith was furious, wondering how this oversight could have happened, but he bit down on his anger realising that his energies would be better channelled into directing the team towards helping to develop Chuck's Plan B, and praying that it would work.

"Okay, Kevin," he sighed. "That's not what I hoped to hear from you at all. You'd better recall the full team so that we can brainstorm this new situation we're facing. This afternoon, 2pm in the boardroom, for everyone that can get back in time."

As soon as Kevin left his office, Keith picked up the phone to call Chuck at Julie's house. The future of the world could now rest on Chuck's Plan B.

---- 61 ----

Monday 13th November
London

Chuck had been running his simulations for approaching thirty-six hours, frequently studying the output and making fine adjustments to the parameters and logic before running them again. He was exhausted but following the phone call the previous afternoon from Keith, he knew he had to keep going. Julie had stayed up with him all night, offering moral support and bringing regular cups of coffee to keep him awake. He was finally happy with the results and reasonably confident that he had identified the correct number and locations for the sonic blasts that would be needed to redirect the massive iceberg. Leaning back in his chair to stretch his aching back and neck muscles, he called Julie over.

"Okay, I think I'm there ... well at least as 'there' as I'll ever be."

"That's fantastic news, do you think it's going to work?"

"Well it certainly looks promising on paper. Given the size of the beast we're dealing with and the risk of fracturing it into a flotilla of 'mini-Rossbergs', together with the wind and currents in and local topography of that area, my simulations have indicated that we can only deflect 'Rossberg' by a matter of a few degrees either way with the number of blasts it's safe to expose it to. As I explained before, we need to utilise the currents in the Southern Ocean to assist us in the deflection, and to a lesser extent the winds. From what I can see, there are several underwater mountain ranges in the area, which is good news, but not many of them meet the criteria we are looking for. With the berg being only three hundred metres deep and Southern Ocean water depths of over seven thousand metres in places, we need a very high undersea mountain range in relatively shallow water given that abyssal oceans typically only have four thousand metres tall sea mountains. And we also need one formed into an arc that effectively provides an underwater harbour into which we can drive 'Rossberg' if we are to stand any chance of permanently stopping it," he explained. "I guess we need an undersea caldera surrounded by mountain peaks as our safe-haven."

"So, does such a thing exist? Have you identified a suitable range?"

"I have one suggestion," came Chuck's cautious reply. There is an underwater range buried beneath the Drake Passage off the tip of South America which could do the trick, but it's on a major shipping route and an iceberg the size of 'Rossberg' situated slap bang in the middle of it would be hazardous. It's touch and go whether or not we can deflect 'Rossberg' sufficiently to get it there, even with the ocean currents helping us. Ideally, we need to stop its progress *before* it reaches Drake's Passage, so we really need to identify somewhere else instead."

"Well at least you have a Plan B which is more than Keith's team have come up with. I think it's time we called him and run it by him."

Chuck picked up the phone and dialled Keith's office number. He answered straight away.

"Hi Keith, it's Chuck. I have run my simulations now and I believe that I have something to run by you."

"Great Chuck, your timing is perfect: We will find out later tonight whether or not 'Rossberg' will be stopped by the Ballenys. What have you got for me?"

Chuck outlined his findings from the simulation programme and Keith listened intently.

"Let me get this right Chuck, you think you can divert the iceberg by up to five degrees in either direction by using the sonic blasting process? That might just allow us to select a resting place for it and keep the world from toppling. Can you come over to Washington right away and bring your simulation data with you? I want the team here to be able to sense check your calculations, and I want you to present this to the President personally."

Chuck nearly fell off his chair with shock. "You want me to present my idea to the President?"

"Yes, I do. It's your idea, and you deserve the credit for it. I'll get my secretary to book your flight and accommodation, and have a car pick you up to take you to the airport. Pack your bags."

Chuck replaced the telephone handset and sat motionless for a few seconds, letting the situation sink in. Julie was thrilled for him. With a 'whoop' she threw her arms around his neck and kissed him.

Chuck called DI Jones and cleared his trip to the US with him in case the hearings for Ian Smith and Ray Bergman required his presence. DI Jones said that it wouldn't be a problem, but to pass on his US contact details as soon as he had them.

Chuck flew through Julie's house picking up his gear and packing his clothes ready for the car to take him to the airport. Julie felt a bit left out that she wasn't to go with him, but she had to focus on her next articles for publication. She would prepare a report outlining the approach to tackling the iceberg and hold off on submitting it until Chuck's calculations had been ratified. As the car pulled up outside, she kissed Chuck goodbye and wished him luck. "Keep me posted on progress," she said, "and make sure someone takes a photo of you with the President!"

Hours later, Chuck had arrived at Washington's Dulles Airport. He quickly cleared customs and immigration compliments of his fast-track status, and after collecting his bags, he was whisked away in a limo to join Keith and his team at IVSO. The team were on tenterhooks as 'Rossberg' neared the underwater ridge, praying that it would cause a deflection to the west, effectively halting the massive berg.

"Welcome Chuck," Keith said, shaking his hand. "I'm afraid you've arrived at a critical point: We've just received the latest satellite images of 'Rossberg' and are comparing them to those from the last few days to determine the orientation of the iceberg. It's reached the pivotal point and these last images will prove with certainty which way it's heading."

Chuck could sense the tension in the room as worried eyes all focused on Kevin Chu as he made his calculations. Silence reigned as the numbers were crunched, checked and re-checked. Kevin's face dropped as he prepared to announce his findings: 'Rossberg' had pivoted badly and would miss the Ballenys.

Everyone around the table was in shock. So much had been riding on this solution and the odds had simply gone against them. With his head in his hands Keith spoke quietly, "Okay Chuck, it looks like we're going to be needing your Plan B after all. What do you need from us given what's just happened?"

"I'm going to need an updated forecast trajectory to enter into my simulation model Keith, together with the latest meteorological data. How soon can you have it ready for me? I'd like to be able to re-run my model overnight if possible."

"We'll work on them straightaway, you should have them in a couple of hours. Go and grab a bite to eat and then come back afterwards. We've all got a lot of work to do tonight and I need to brief the President."

62

Tuesday 14th November
Washington DC

By early morning, Chuck had reworked his figures and was ready to present the results. He joined Keith and several of the core team members, all keen to see how his simulation would pan out now that the planet's future was once again in jeopardy. Chuck handed over his laptop to a technician who connected it to the presentation projector. Chuck set the simulation display running and stepped back to let it do its thing.

After a couple of runs through, he stepped to the front of the conference table and explained the various parameters behind the workings of his simulation – the size and thickness of the ice; the prevailing currents with their set and rate; the various calculations he had made; the other variables that were considered and included, and so on. At the end of his explanation he opened the floor for questions. The team responded instantly, asking very probing questions, challenging his thought processes, and wanting to get their hands on his algorithms.

Keith had given Chuck total freedom to explain his model and was impressed by the way he kept his head in such difficult circumstances, even under quick-fire questioning by the team. "We really could use someone with his talents," he thought.

Chuck passed copies of his files to the team members who disappeared back to the labs to cross-check and ratify the data he had provided. It would take them some time to pull together their results, but time well spent in such a critical situation. In the meantime, he was required to speak to the President and explain how his solution might work. His knees were quaking at the thought of it, but he was equally thrilled at the prospect of spending time in the company of the most powerful man on earth. His life had certainly turned around in the past few weeks!

Keith had arranged a meeting at the White House for 2pm. They arrived fifteen minutes early and were shown through to one of the conference rooms near the Oval Office. Chuck had his laptop with him, and once again, he had the presentation set up ready to roll when the President arrived. His throat suddenly went dry and he asked for some water. Keith smiled: He had been in a similar situation before now and he understood Chuck's trepidation.

"How do I address the President, Keith?"

"Mr President, then sir."

"OK, thanks," replied Chuck, mopping his brow with a tissue.

Right on 2pm, the President entered the room followed by his entourage. He shook Keith's hand and extended his arm towards Chuck. "You must be Chuck Fallon," he said shaking Chuck's hand firmly. "Thank you for your efforts in this issue. We all need to pull together to come up with a solution to our 'Rossberg' problem, and Keith tells me that you have something that might just save the planet."

"Thank you, Mr President, I certainly hope so."

"OK son let's hear it," replied the President as he sat down in one of the chairs.

Chuck went through his presentation showing his simulation that revealed where the sonic blasting charges should be placed, and the possible effect that the blasting would have on the direction of travel of the iceberg. The President listened with interest and at the end of the simulation display he turned to his advisors. "Well guys, what do you think? Can we use this?"

"Mr President, how can we be sure that this sonic blasting will be able to turn the iceberg?" asked one of them.

"I can answer that sir," said Chuck.

He went on to describe the process of sonic blasting and showed the audience how the resonance set up by the blasting activity sent shockwaves through the ice without destroying its structure, pulsing against the harder ocean floor and causing ripples that would build up into an effective wavelength which, in turn, would bounce back at the correct angle to 'push' the ice in a given direction. His calculations had shown that at most he would only be able to change the direction of a monolith of such gargantuan size by a maximum of five degrees, but that might be enough to move it where they wanted.

Clearly impressed by the material presented to him the President asked Chuck to commit himself to the project for as long as necessary and promised that he would be paid handsomely for his services. Chuck acknowledged the President's request and instantly agreed. Keith was more than happy at this: It would give him plenty of ammunition to get a job offer on the table for Chuck to join IVSO. Hell, he even had the President as a sponsor.

When the meeting at the White House was over, Keith and Chuck returned to IVSO where the team were finalising their examination of Chuck's model. They reconvened shortly afterwards, and Kevin Chu took the lead in the meeting discussion. He said that first and foremost, the team hadn't found anything wrong with Chuck's approach. Chuck smiled inwardly, pleased with that outcome.

The team *had* found a couple of additional variables that they would like included in the model, and Chuck agreed to add them into the equation. The rework required to achieve this would take him the rest of the evening, and so the team agreed to meet first thing to re-run the simulation. Chuck went to work on it.

Later that evening he called Julie at home.

"Hi Jules, it's me."

"Chuck! It's lovely to hear your voice. How's it going over there?"

"Well, I think I impressed the President at least – he asked me to join the team for as long as it takes, and he will pay me as well."

"Chuck, that's great! Well done you. I'm proud of you. What is happening now?"

"I don't know if you've heard Jules, but the 'Rossberg' failed to be trapped by the Ballenys last night and is now heading towards the open ocean? All

403

the team members' hopes were shattered, and my Plan B is now the only plan on the table. I've just finished making some fine-tuning amendments to my model to cater for a couple of extra variables that I had overlooked, and now it's running again to see what difference they make to the outcome. On the whole, I think that it's pretty accurate and might be the answer we so desperately need, that's assuming we can identify a suitable resting place for the iceberg of course."

"Well fingers crossed, Chuck, if anyone can pull a rabbit out of the hat it's you. Do you have any idea how long you will be out there? I'm kind of missing my new best mate."

"No idea Jules. I'm missing you too, by the way. I guess I'll be here for a couple of weeks at least, but I'll keep you up to date and feed you all the information you need for your next article."

"Thanks Chuck, I appreciate it."

63

Wednesday 15th November
Washington DC

Chuck had his reworked figures available by the time the team had reassembled in Keith's office at 8:30am. Standing at the front of the room, he waited for everyone to settle down with their coffee and pastries before beginning. Keith sat at the head of the table and observed the proceedings. He really rated Chuck and wanted him to shine. Chuck ran through the simulation again, pointing out the subtle differences between his original model and the reworked one, indicating the new locations for the sonic blast sites. The audience concurred with his results.

"How do we progress from here?" asked Keith. "Who do we know that has the skills to undertake such a task? Anyone got any ideas?"

Chuck put up his hand. "I do Keith, but it's somewhat unorthodox."

"I don't care about unorthodox," said Keith. "Who are you thinking of?"

"Global Energy."

A rumble of discontent rolled around the table. Everyone had heard that it was the underhand blasting activities undertaken by Global Energy that had caused the problem in the first place. No-one was happy with Chuck's choice.

"Hear me out folks, please," Chuck countered. The noise around the table slowly died down allowing him to continue. "I agree with you all wholeheartedly. Believe me, I have a greater reason not to want to have anything to do with Global Energy than anyone, but let's face it: They have got experience and some expertise in sonic blasting techniques. They have been doing it far longer than anyone else in the market. Maybe it's their chance to balance the scales and do some good." The murmuring continued in the room.

"OK team, it looks as though beggars can't be choosers, and right now, we are all beggars," said Keith. "None of us like the idea, but it is the best one we have. We might need the President to bring pressure to bear on Global Energy to get this done, but I have every confidence that they will be persuaded. Let's bring this meeting to a close. Chuck, I'd like you to accompany me to the White House again, we have some more explaining to do to the President. Let's get this thing moving."

An hour later they were sitting in the Oval Office at the White House with the President and his two closest advisors. Chuck relayed his idea to use Global Energy's sonic blasting team to try to alter the trajectory of the giant 'Rossberg'. The President went quiet for a moment.

"Hell, it looks like we don't have a choice here, but I'm damned sure that Global Energy will lose their mining rights in Antarctica, and anywhere else I can bring any influence to bear. They're finished as far as I'm concerned, and we'll take care of their CEO too. Dave," he said turning to his aide, "sort out a meeting with the heads of the CIA and FBI. We need to extradite this guy from Britain and bring him home to face the music."

"Yes sir, Mr President," said his aide as he rose from his seat and headed through the Oval Office door.

The President turned his attention back to Keith. "Keith, we need to find out where there are undersea obstructions big and tall enough, and in the right position around Antarctica to be able to stop this thing. Have you got any suggestions yet?"

"We thought we had something we could use, but this was discounted because of other seamounts in the way that will deflect the 'Rossberg' northwards. So, the answer is not yet sir, but the team are working on it as we speak. I'm confident that they will have an answer for that question by the time we get back to IVSO. It's their top priority, and we have the best brains on the job."

"OK, keep me posted as soon as you have anything concrete. Chuck, I need you to let me have an exact inventory of the equipment you need, and the names of the people to operate the sonic blasters. We will get them moved onto the 'Rossberg' straight away to set up and be ready in good time."

"Yes, Mr President. You'll have the details as soon as I collect them. I will need to contact Global Energy to be able to get some of the information you are looking for, and in that respect, it would help immensely if you could 'pave the way' for me so that I don't meet with any resistance."

"Consider it done. Now, gentlemen, let's get to work."

Keith and Chuck returned to Keith's office in IVSO to find Kevin Chu waiting for them. He had a roll of ocean charts in his hand and he proceeded to lay them out on the conference table. "I'd like you to look at this chart," he said eagerly, "we are pretty sure that we have identified some new underwater seamounts that are tall enough to stop the 'Rossberg', these ones here, well away from shipping lanes," he added placing his finger on the chart.

Keith looked at the chart where Kevin's hand was. There were indeed several seamounts in the area that rose high enough from the seabed to cause the 'Rossberg' to impale itself on them and halt its progress.

"Given the forecast path of 'Rossberg' Kevin, how far from these new seamounts will it be?"

"The iceberg should pass a few degrees to the north of them."

"In what timeframe?"

"I estimate that if it maintains its current speed, 'Rossberg' will pass them in two weeks' time."

Turning to Chuck, Keith asked, "Roughly how long do you need to set up the blasting sites Chuck?"

"If we start straight away, we might just be in time."

"Then you'd better start making your phone calls to Global Energy."

---- 64 ----

Thursday 16th November
London

The Global Energy board had reconvened to expedite the requirements of the US President to provide resources immediately for the sonic blasting mission in the Antarctic ocean. The President had demanded Jeff Ramsey accept that Chuck Fallon was now in charge of the programme, and that he should be given the company's full support and access to as many resources as required. Jeff had capitulated immediately, somewhat amazed that he would even be speaking with the President.

Chuck Fallon had called him shortly after his conversation with the President, and he had asked for help too. Jeff had expected Chuck to be somewhat overbearing, given his elevated position in all of this, but he wasn't. He simply stated the facts of the matter and asked Jeff to enable the rescue mission to proceed by providing all the equipment and personnel from the

'PROJECT UNDERMINE' blasting programme. Now he needed to get the rest of the board onside.

"Good morning everyone, thank you for attending at short notice," he addressed the directors. "The reason I have convened this extraordinary meeting is that our help has been directly requisitioned by none other than the President of the United States." He paused to let this fact sink in, then continued. "Believe it or not, Chuck Fallon, yes, Chuck Fallon has been given control of this mission, which is trying to save the earth from disaster by redirecting the portion of the Ross Ice Shelf that calved from the mainland. They call it 'Rossberg'. They want to use our sonic blasting technology to make this happen, and they want us, Global Energy, to provide all the equipment and manpower."

"How the hell did Chuck Fallon get into this position?" asked an indignant Digger. He was affronted that he hadn't been asked to do more. To his mind he had far more mining expertise in his little finger than Chuck Fallon did in his entire body.

"Never mind that Digger. We have the opportunity here to try to salvage at least some of our reputation in the energy market by trying to save the planet. Apparently, if it is left unchecked, this iceberg carries enough weight to tip the world off its axis and plunge us all into nuclear winter for six months every year. We don't want that."

"What do we have to do Jeff?" asked Terry Smart.

"We vote here and now to support this initiative and commit all our resources to make it happen. All those in favour?"

Hands rose all round the table in response.

"Motion carried. Thank you all," he said closing the meeting.

Jeff made several phone calls to McMurdo and set the ball rolling, having all the sonic team gather up their equipment and spares, and be ready for immediate departure. He then called Chuck as soon as he thought he would have arrived in the office at IVSO to relay the news.

Chuck had already been allocated military transportation by the President, and he despatched the planes to McMurdo to collect the sonic blasting team and their equipment. The army pilots were used to landing on sheets of ice and would put the planes down on the flatter parts of the 'Rossberg'.

Time was running out, and it would take days to set up the blasting pattern to be able to turn the giant iceberg. Drawing some survival gear from the IVSO stores, Chuck made his way to the Fort McNair airbase where another plane was waiting to transport him and essential supplies for the mission. As he strapped himself into his seat, the enormous responsibility he had just been given started to hit home and he began to panic. What if it didn't work? What then? Time would tell.

---- 65 ----

Friday 17th November
On the 'Rossberg'

By the time Chuck had arrived in the Antarctic, the camp had already been set up on the 'Rossberg', and a runway marked out for them to land on. Sliding to a halt next to the other aircraft, the ramp was lowered at the rear of the aircraft for Chuck to step down on to the iceberg. "This is a first," he thought to himself. "We're floating round the ocean on a massive lump of ice. I hope to God this works."

His first task was to take an inventory of the equipment the team had available, and to assign roles to the members of the sonic blasting team from Global Energy. Each member was to be accompanied by a team of military personnel who had been trained in Arctic survival, to ensure their safety, and who would also undertake the physically demanding drilling activity.

These new teams were all given their individual positions for the blast sites which would be continually updated by satellite, and they each carried the necessary core drilling equipment to be able to place the sonic charges at the right depths for the blasting to be most effective. It would take one or two days for them to get to their respective sites and then two more to drill their cores to the correct depths. Once that was complete, then all the charges needed to be linked and synchronised. That would take another day, possibly two. It was going to be incredibly tight.

The drilling teams departed for their sites, and Chuck continued to refine his simulation model, checking and re-checking every parameter and every variable. It had to be right. He would only get one chance at this before the iceberg was pushed away to the north to wreak havoc.

---- **66** ----

Tuesday 21st November
On the 'Rossberg'

Progress had run according to plan: All the charges had been laid and linked, despite a fault on one of the controls for synchronising the blasting, which the team had managed to fix in the time allowed. All the physical equipment was now in place and ready for when the go ahead was given. Chuck was apprehensive as so much rested on his solution, yet he was also in very high spirits. Keith had called him late the previous evening to offer him a job as a Senior Vice President of Scientific Research in IVSO with a very good benefits package. Things were certainly looking up for him – all he had to do now was pull off this rescue mission.

The control team had gathered in the main operations tent. A monitor on its stand showed the iceberg, and the position of all the blasting sites with an indicator for each showing its status. All sites were primed and ready, it just needed one button to trigger the whole process.

Chuck and the team were waiting for Kevin Chu's final prediction on the route the iceberg would take, and to know by how much it needed to be deflected. The prediction arrived fifteen minutes later, and Chuck reviewed the data.

"OK folks, we're up – predictions are good, and we are all set. Is there anything anyone has in mind that we haven't considered?" he asked, scanning the anxious faces around him. "No? Good. I'll call the President."

He rang through to the Oval Office where Keith was sitting with the President. "Sir, it's Chuck Fallon here, we're good to go on your approval."

"Push the button Chuck, and God help us all."

Chuck pressed the firing button and the sonic blasters started to set up their levels of resonance. It would take a while for the soundwaves to synchronise and pulse together, bouncing off the seabed and forcing the water below to push the underside of the iceberg. It would be a day or so before any significant benefit of the thrust could be measured, and Chuck and his team would continually monitor the sonic pulses to make sure that everything continued as expected. The blasting needed to move the iceberg a full four degrees to the south to achieve what they wanted, to slam it into the seamounts running in a line and stop it in its tracks.

---- **67** ----

Thursday 23rd November
On the 'Rossberg'

Chuck had had little sleep over the past few days, and the strain was beginning to tell on him. He was irritable with his team members, and very listless. His team understood the pressure he was under and tried to cut him a little slack, but they were also feeling the same pressure and occasionally tempers flared.

The team were waiting for the latest satellite readings on the progress of the 'Rossberg'. Today was the day that it should ground on the first of the seamounts and they should notice a change in the rate of movement as the seamount bit deep into the underbelly of the iceberg. If it slowed after one contact, then with the following seamounts coming into play, the berg should grind to a halt.

Receiving the latest readings, they entered the coordinates into Chuck's model and waited anxiously for the results. Incredibly it did appear to be slowing down! Everyone cheered and slapped each other on the back, celebrating the good news. Chuck was heartily congratulated and praised for his idea that had saved the world, and suddenly the stress seemed to be lifting from his shoulders.

"We shouldn't be counting our chickens yet guys," he said with a word of caution. "Let's see what tomorrow brings before we get too overjoyed about it. We're still at a critical stage."

Nevertheless, he picked up the phone to let the President know the latest. The President was delighted and offered his congratulations too. It was a step in the right direction, and even though they weren't out of the woods yet, it was certainly more hopeful. Keith endorsed that opinion and he was also delighted when Chuck accepted the position at IVSO. "That's great news Chuck, welcome to the team."

Chuck then called Julie to let her know the good news.

"Fantastic news, Jules: It looks as though my plan is working! 'Rossberg' has noticeably slowed down on impact with the first seamount. If all our calculations are correct, we should be able to stop it dead in its tracks."

"That's marvellous Chuck. I knew you'd do it!"

"And that's not all. I've been offered, and accepted, a job in Washington with IVSO as a Senior Vice

President of Scientific Research. What do you think about that?" he exclaimed excitedly.

She was both thrilled for him yet somewhat disappointed that it would mean they wouldn't be in the same country and be able to see each other as often as she would like. But she suppressed her disappointment and focused on his success. "That's great news. Well done, it's a marvellous opportunity for you and a chance to make a new start," she said while inwardly reflecting that they could work out the details of their relationship potential in the days ahead.

---- 68 ----

Friday 24th November

The team waited anxiously once again for the latest report from Kevin Chu. They had retrieved the coordinates from the receptors on the iceberg and had fed them into Chuck's model. The results showed that the iceberg's movements had all but stopped. Kevin's report would now indicate the influence that the ocean currents were having on the iceberg and whether it would drive itself further onto the remaining seamounts in its path and become well and truly stuck.

Things were looking very promising and when Kevin predicted that on its present trajectory, with the current driving it onwards, the iceberg would fix itself on the fourth and fifth seamounts in the chain as well, the team had a real cause to celebrate and everyone broke out into loud cheers and congratulations. Chuck breathed a sigh of relief and immediately called the President to give him the good news.

"Congratulations Chuck, you and your team have worked a miracle down there. Please pass on my thanks to everyone concerned. We will have a big party in Washington when you get back."

"Thank you, sir, we'll all look forward to that!"

He called Keith next to relay the news, then Julie. "Hi Jules, it's me. How are you?"

"Chuck! It's great to hear your voice."

"We did it Jules! We've stopped the 'Rossberg'!"

"Wow! Congratulations Chuck. *You* did it! *You've* saved the world. My hero! We should celebrate: I'll come over to Washington and be there when you get back. When do you think you'll arrive?"

It'll take a couple of days to wind things up here and leave sensors in place to monitor the iceberg, but I'll be there on Monday."

"I'll see you in the hotel, can't wait!"

---- 69 ----

Monday 27th November

Chuck had sent the sonic blasting team back to McMurdo where they would remain until the Global Energy drilling licence was withdrawn by the members of the Antarctic Treaty. After that, they would all probably be looking for new jobs, but that wasn't his problem. He had had enough of Global Energy to last him a lifetime and he was glad to be out of their employ.

Arriving back in Washington, he was driven from the Fort McNair airbase and had had a joyful reunion with Julie. They spent the morning together catching up on everything: Her job as an Editor; the latest articles on the 'Rossberg' and how she was going to write the final one; and his new job at IVSO. In recognition for what he had done for the world the President had granted him his green card, enabling him to work and live in the US permanently and he was looking forward to the next chapter in his life, with one reservation. They finally addressed the elephant in the room and moved onto whether they would be able to maintain a long-distance relationship from either side of the Atlantic.

"Do you think we can pull it off?" she asked him.

"We can certainly try. If it becomes too much, then we do have choices," he replied.

"Well, I could always become the US correspondent for *The Telegraph* I suppose …." said Julie smiling.

"Let's see how we go!"

Epilogue

9th May

The 'Rossberg' had grounded onto four of the five massive seamounts and shuddered to a halt several months earlier. Everyone believed that it was firmly fixed and would remain there until the ice sheet expanded across the narrow strip of sea that separated it from the mainland and joined it all back together again during the next winter freeze.

In reality, the combined force of the winds that continually drove against the iceberg's sheer sides, and the current that enveloped it from below and continued pushing on its underwater face, had enough force between them to drive the ice onwards to flow *around* the obstructions that were holding it.

The 'Rossberg' had started to inch forwards again, the underwater ice gradually flowing around each seamount in turn, until finally it pivoted around the fifth and last obstruction and moved back into deeper waters, free of any hindrance. It was now being propelled northwards and eastwards by the Antarctic

Circumpolar Current, the only current that flows completely around the world, driven by the constant winds. It was truly in grip of the Southern Ocean, heading around the northern tip of East Antarctica. Its next stop would be landfall … but the question was, where?

Printed in Poland
by Amazon Fulfillment
Poland Sp. z o.o., Wrocław